HOW TO RUIN A DUKE

A NOVELLA DUET

GRACE BURROWES
THERESA ROMAIN

RHAPSODY FOR TWO BY THERESA ROMAIN

ACKNOWLEDGMENTS

Writing a novella doesn't always take a village, but this one did! Thanks to Rose Lerner for the brainstorming session, Joyce Lamb for the impeccable copyedit, and Sarah Rosenbarker for the proofread.

As always, thanks to my husband, my greatest support and first reader, and to my daughter, even though she wanted the heroine to be named Lauren. (Sorry, honey, but she just wasn't a Lauren.) And thank you to Amanda, especially for the perspective of a string player.

Above all, thanks to Grace Burrowes, writing partner extraordinaire! I'm so glad we could work together again. Your characters inspired me to be better. Thanks for the loan of Edith and Emory in my story.

AUTHOR'S NOTE

The term "luthier" for one who builds and repairs stringed instruments didn't come into common usage until the late 1800s. In the absence of another word that serves the purpose as well, I've lent it to Rowena for use in 1819.

CHAPTER ONE

―――――――――――――

"The Duke of Amorous had many pleasures. He was equally delighted by cards as carriages, equally seduced by paramours as piquet, equally charmed by eau de vie as filles de joie."
From *How to Ruin a Duke* by Anonymous

MAY 1819

Bond Street, London

Rowena Fairweather had many pleasures. She was as equally delighted by piecing together a damaged violin as she was at bringing an instrument into tune. She was seduced by records of income from her luthier's shop when profits exceeded the inevitable long columns of household expenditures.

And on days like this one, when her accounts bled red ink and the rent on the shop building was soon to increase beyond a prayer of paying it, she was charmed into forgetfulness for a few brief moments by a book.

At last, her turn had come for a copy of *How to Ruin a Duke*, the titillating novel that had all of London Society buzzing that it was no fiction at all. Rumor had it that the book was a thinly veiled revelation about the handsome Duke of Emory's private life—much like the novel *Glenarvon* that had skewered Lord Byron three years before.

The author of *Glenarvon*, Lady Caroline Lamb, had been ostracized for writing such a livid satire of Society. Wisely, the author of *How to Ruin a Duke* hid under the cloak of anonymity. Which meant London's elite had the pleasure of gossiping not only about the Duke of Emory, but also about who could have written the book.

As a shopkeeper, Rowena was hardly a member of London's elite. But she entered their homes to tune their pianofortes; she repaired their violins and restrung their harps. It was good business for her to know their fortunes and pedigrees...along with the latest gossip.

And so it was for business, she told herself—and not entirely for curiosity's sake—that she had put her name down for a copy of *How to Ruin a Duke*. Her subscription to a circulating library—an expense shared with her friend Lady Edith Charbonneau—allowed her to devour every Gothic novel published. But today, on this misty spring day, the Duke of Amorous was more fascinating even than an insane monk or a mysterious skeleton in a castle tower.

Elbows propped on her worktable, she turned the pages of the volume with growing wonder. How much gin could a duke drink without dying of it? Why would he race from London to Brighton in a curricle by the light of the moon? In what manner could a man wager against himself in the White's betting book?

As her right hand weighted down the pages, she gasped at one particularly scandalous anecdote. "He hid a *note* inside a *violin?*"

Lifting her head, she regarded the tools of her trade. The long worktable with the great magnifying lens in an articulated frame. Tools for carving and clamping, for applying glues and varnishes. Neat racks along the wall for scraps and planks of boxwood, rosewood, spruce, maple, ebony. Strings of pale catgut in neat loops. Instruments in all stages of repair, from the restored violin ready to be returned to Lady Davidson, to the just-arrived violoncello with a broken neck, its scrolled top and pegbox dangling sadly from the strings.

And the Duke of Amorous, and perhaps Emory, had shoved a note inside one of these lovely instruments as if it were a mail coach. Rowena shook her head. "What a monster."

From a cushion on the workshop floor, all the better to chase and eat beetles, Rowena's hedgehog Cotton lifted her spiny head and twitched her little black nose as if in agreement.

Had the Duke of Emory really inspired every action of his fictional near-namesake? Rowena would ask Edith. Edie had worked in Emory's household for two years as the companion of the present duke's mother, leaving her post only five months before. She'd know how true to life the portrayal of Emory was.

But Edith would have to wait her turn to read this book, as she had taken both *Nightmare Abbey* and *Frankenstein* before Rowena. Rowena had had to wait for endless-seeming days to read them herself, while Edith had hinted winkingly at every twist in the plots. Not that Edith would *really* spoil the secrets of a good novel. Unlike the Duke of Amorous, she wasn't a monster.

As Rowena turned the page, the bell over the shop's front door jingled.

"Hullo?" called a male voice from the other side of the velvet curtain that separated the workshop from the small public office.

Rowena sighed. How badly she had wanted to forget her worries for a while, to sink instead into the latest popular work of delicious scandal.

Never mind. Customers, clients, patrons came first. She left the book on her worktable, then smoothed her black hair and ducked around the heavy curtain into the office where she welcomed clients and carried out simple jobs. She arranged her hands behind her back and prepared her polite, public smile.

Welcome to Fairweather's, Luthier to the Crown, was what she ought to have said to the prospective customer. Two issues halted her tongue before it could utter the familiar script, so that only an "Oh!" of surprise burst from her lips.

First, the man who entered was neither a liveried footman nor a tonnish papa. Those two sorts of male shoppers, both representing a pampered and wealthy young lady of a musical inclination, were Rowena's bread and butter during the London Season.

But this man was too young to be the father of a Society maiden, too plainly dressed to be a footman. He looked about thirty, only a few years older than Rowena's twenty-six years, and was garbed in well-cut but simple clothing.

Second, he was holding a horn. Not a violin, a viola, or even a violoncello. A horn, with nary a string in sight. On the floor, an open instrument case splayed.

For a moment, Rowena fumbled for words. At last, she said, "Welcome to Fairweather's, sir. This is a luthier's shop. Is all well with your horn? It's not the sort of instrument I usually work on."

"You are the Fairweather of the shop name, then?" The man raised puckish dark brows. "I expected someone older and—"

"Male, no doubt," Rowena interrupted smoothly. "Before my father passed on a year ago, you'd have got both age and masculinity. But I represent Fairweather's now, and I've had more than two decades of experience building and repairing stringed instruments."

"Very well. This ought to be easy as winking for you." He heaved his horn onto the sleek counter between them.

Rowena's gaze flicked from the brass instrument to the dark eyes of the customer. They were warm and red-brown like heart of rosewood, uncommon for use in violins but a lovely surprise when it appeared. The good cheer in this man's expression was also uncommon but, in its way, lovely as well.

She tried not to smile. "I assume you are aware that a horn is not a stringed instrument."

"I am," he granted. "I'm also aware that something is blocking the flow of sound, which caused me to be sacked by the family that hired me to give lessons to their son. I've only just time to get to a rehearsal at Vauxhall Gardens, and I'd prefer my horn to emit notes so that I won't lose two jobs in one day."

"A reasonable wish."

"I knew you'd understand. And when I passed your shop, I thought, well, a luthier is better than no one."

Now she did allow herself an amused quirk of the lips. "Surely you meant to say 'a luthier is better than almost anyone.'"

The man's eyes crinkled at the corners. "Did I misspeak? That's exactly what I meant to say. A luthier will know how to fix my horn, because luthiers are excellent and wonderful."

"Wise man. Very well, I'll look it over. If need be, I'll take it into my workshop, but I might be able to help you here."

A horn didn't have a terrible lot of parts. Either the structure was damaged—and the shining surface looked all right—or there was something caught inside. Crouching, she peered into the bell but saw nothing.

"I played at a musicale last night and the horn sounded fine," explained the man. "I must have used all my crooks for changing keys at one point or another, so the problem's not with one of them."

"Hmm." She needed something fine to fish about for an obstruction. Rowena considered the tools behind the workroom curtain, then instead plucked a pin from her heavy twists of hair. Stretching the curved bit of metal into a straight wire, she fashioned a little hook at one end, then plunged it into the depths of the horn. She wiggled the pin about, easing it into the innards of the horn to feel for anything that wasn't as it ought to be.

"Ah. There we have it. There's something in here." With her makeshift tool, she tugged at the obstruction.

"Let me help you with that," the man blurted. "I can do that for you."

Oh. She'd used her right hand to fashion the hook. Damn. She hated this sort of response, when courtesy turned into condescension.

Rowena wasn't ashamed of her right hand, exactly, but she didn't like it being stared at. Save for the thumb, the fingers on that hand were truncated and twisted, the nails little chips. She'd been born that way; she was accustomed to it, even if the world wasn't. Though her fingers sometimes pained her, she prided herself on being as dexterous as anyone with a perfectly matched pair of hands.

So she shot her customer a Withering Look—so withering that only capital letters would do to describe it. "You came to me for help, sir. Allow me to oblige."

He hesitated, but instead of protesting, he said, "I'm sorry. Of course. You're right. Carry on."

A ready apology was impossible to argue with, especially when the person apologizing was reduced to speaking in two-word fragments. So she only nodded, then returned to her work.

She'd never been fishing—one wouldn't want to eat whatever was pulled from the Thames—but she imagined she was angling for some elusive prey now. Just a little twist of her wire hook, and she'd have it...

"Aha! I've captured the Great Horned Blockage. A rare species, I hope." Rowena fished out a wad of paper and set it on the counter.

Her customer poked at it cautiously. "*That* was in my horn? Good Lord, it's half the size of an egg."

Rowena recalled the troubling passage from *How to Ruin a Duke*, currently reposed on her worktable. "I think someone's been clever and passed you a secret note."

"A note. In my horn." The customer gave the folded paper a dark look. "A *note*. It's because of that cursed book, isn't it? *How to Ruin a Duke*. Have you read it? I haven't yet, but I know the duke puts a note in a violin. My fellow horn player at Vauxhall has been inspired to exchange notes with every woman in London."

"Every woman? He's prolific. But I've missed receiving mine. How sad for me."

"If you'd met Botts, you'd know it wasn't a tragedy. He's an incorrigible flirt."

"And you are...?"

He extended a hand. "Simon Thorn. Not an incorrigible flirt, I hope, but newly a great admirer of luthiers."

He shook hands with her as if they were old friends. As if her right hand was perfectly normal, perfectly worth shaking. *Thorn.* The customer's surname suited him, a simple and crisp sound to match his appearance.

"Rowena Fairweather," she replied. His hand felt good on hers, warm and weighty and broad. But she pulled back after a moment, for she wasn't in the profession of groping strange men's hands. She was in the profession of repairing instruments.

A realization struck her. "Notes! Hidden notes! *That's* what happened to—well, I'd better not say whose violin, but a certain customer of mine. The sound post has been knocked out of position four times this past week. She said it was due to vigorous playing—"

Simon Thorn choked.

"—but I'd wager she was fumbling for a note."

"You could be right. At least you got to collect four fees for your pains."

"And at a higher rate than usual for providing emergency service." Rowena grinned. "Do you want to read your note?"

"Yes, all right. You've earned the right to have your curiosity satisfied, Miss Luthier Who Can Fix Anything." He unfolded the paper and read out, "'Mr. Amorous—you cannot be ruined except by your own folly, and what an entertaining spectacle that is!'"

His brow creased. "That's not even my name. What is this rubbish? Is it a threat?"

"Mr. Thorn," Rowena tried out the name delicately. "Someone is flirting with you. That text comes from *How to Ruin a Duke.* May I?"

She extended a hand—her right, boldly—and took hold of the paper. "'Have many pleasures.' 'Essential qualities.' 'Cards and curricles.' Yes, those are from *How to Ruin a Duke* too. It's full of alliteration. 'Meet me at...' Ahem." She thrust the paper back at Mr. Thorn, her cheeks growing hot. "If that last bit is from the book, I, ah, haven't got to that part yet."

"Clearly, I should read it. It must be a most intriguing book." With a sigh, he crumpled the note. "So, someone wants to foster a flirtation with me, but without putting any thought into it."

"Now you're being alliterative too. Maybe you wrote this note to yourself."

He scoffed, but before he could reply, a whisper of movement at the curtain had Rowena turning away. It was no person, but a spiny little mammal wandering in from the workroom.

Thorn craned his neck to regard the new arrival. "Who's this?"

"The younger Miss Fairweather by far." Rowena scooped up the animal, cradling the familiar protective ball that Cotton made of herself. "This is my hedgehog, Cotton. She gobbles down all the insects that would otherwise eat my woods and resins and glues."

"A useful partner, then." Thorn extended a hand toward the animal, then halted. "May I pet her?"

Rowena liked that he wanted to, liked even more that he'd halted himself and asked permission. "Of course you may."

She set Cotton on the counter, where the hedgehog nosed at the shining brass horn with her little quivering snout. Thorn was gentle as he stroked her prickly back, so gentle that Cotton didn't even roll up again.

Rowena liked that, too, the care he took with her pet.

Once Cotton had determined that the horn wasn't food, she regarded Rowena with reproachful black button eyes. *No treats?* Then she picked her way gently along the counter, pausing every step or two to sniff the air as if something new and delicious might have entered the shop.

Perhaps it had. Rowena regarded Mr. Thorn from the crown of his hat to the toes of his boots, and she couldn't fault the sender of the hidden note for its seductive tone.

So she asked, "Who could have stuffed a note into your horn?" Curiosity might have killed a cat, but it had never been known to harm a person or hedgehog.

"The mother of the young fellow I was meant to be tutoring?

Wife of the man who dismissed me? I can't imagine who else." Thorn frowned. "Maybe that's why he dismissed me, if he saw his wife shoving a note into my horn."

"Dear me, yes. Flirting with a married woman? How scandalous."

"In this instance, it was one-sided. I can't help what someone writes to me in a note." He sounded frustrated as he began to pack his horn back into its case. "If *How to Ruin a Duke* is to cost me clients, I ought to bill the author."

"Fortunately for him or her, the author is anonymous."

"Ah. Bad luck for me." He shook it off, flashing a grin. "Or not so bad, since it brought me here."

"I thought you weren't an incorrigible flirt, Mr. Thorn."

"Well. Not incorrigible." Those brown eyes were warm on hers, or maybe it was Rowena who was warm. And why not? It was a fine spring day, and the light slanting through the shop windows was bright and clear.

"As we're indulging each other's curiosity, Miss Fairweather, will you tell me how you came to run this shop?"

"Because I'm a Fairweather," Rowena said simply. "It's in my blood."

Though she wished she had as much fortune as she did pedigree.

Fairweather's was a shop to be proud of, nestled in the heart of London at an elegant address. On Bond Street, there was foot traffic at all hours, with a jeweler and a music seller and a china warehouse and a cutler almost at hand. Her great-great-grandfather had chosen the spot well, fashionable and fast-paced, and taken a ninety-nine-year lease.

Unfortunately, that lease was now up for renewal, and the landlord offered the building at a dramatically higher rate. The old rent of one hundred pounds a year was a scramble and scrimp now that Rowena was doing the work of two on her own. To pay one hundred fifty guineas? She might as well have been asked to fetch St. Edward's Crown from the Tower of London.

"The shop is secure and in good hands," she added, as much for her own benefit as for Thorn's. "I build upon generations of good reputation."

"And this good reputation persists under the management of a young woman?" Thorn appeared curious rather than skeptical, so she gave him an honest reply.

"It does to anyone who's honest about the matter. Even before my father's death a year ago, I was doing much of the repair work. He had developed arthritis, so mine were the hands and his the mind, until he'd taught me all he could."

In truth, though Rowena maintained the same quality of work, Fairweather's wasn't quite the same anymore. Her father had been chatty and personable, making a friend of everyone whose instrument he took on for repair. Customers seemed to miss him as much as Rowena did—and upstairs, in the family quarters, she felt her solitude even more.

Once upon a time, she'd been told, the large building bustled both upstairs and down. In past generations there had been Fairweather brothers and sisters and their offspring, sisters-in-law and elderly grandparents and even a spinster aunt or two. A true family workshop, like the Amatis in Italy in an earlier century.

But Rowena's father had married late, and her parents had had her still later. Her mother had died in childbed, and the spinster aunts and grandparents, too, had all moved along to the other side of life.

Rowena couldn't miss what she'd never had, but she could miss the idea of it.

Now it was just her, a cook who came three times a week, a maid-of-all-work, her old nanny, and her hedgehog Cotton. It all felt rather threadbare, regardless of the thickness of the velvet curtain. There was a carewornness that came from the spirit, not from the eye.

But perhaps Rowena was the only one who perceived it. Simon Thorn appeared to be enjoying the conversation, as though he thought all was well with both Fairweather's and its proprietress.

"Do you like the work of a luthier?" He leaned forward, elbows on the counter, and fixed those curious dark eyes on hers. "I've had many occupations, but never yours."

Did she like her work? She'd never thought about it. She had taken it for granted since she'd first stretched a catgut string that this was the work she would do.

Alongside her father, she'd more than liked the work, once. She'd loved it. But there was less to enjoy about running a family establishment alone.

Save the shop, her father had told her with his dying breath. *Run it as I've taught you, and all will be well. I'm relying on you. We all are.*

She'd thought at the time that he meant Nanny and Cook and the maid, Alice. But she wondered now whether he had meant the century of Fairweathers who had done business at this spot. All the previous generations whose expectations now stacked upon her, burdening her.

She took up the ruined hairpin and tried to bend it back into shape. "It's difficult work, but it is satisfying. I like bringing music back to instruments that have lost it."

"As you did to mine." He smiled. "What do I owe you for your intervention, Miss Fairweather?"

All of a sudden, she didn't want to turn this chance meeting into a transaction. "Oh, nothing. There's no fee." She snapped up the still-wandering Cotton before the animal could stumble over the edge of the counter.

"But you made my instrument playable again. That's worth something." He straightened up from his slouch, pulling a purse from his pocket.

"A favor for a fellow musician. I'm only out a hairpin."

He hesitated, then put away his purse again. "I'm in your debt, then."

"You're not. You're really not." She knelt, depositing Cotton on the floor to wander in search of delicious insects. When Rowena stood to face Thorn again, she added, "Bring me a new hairpin sometime if you wish. Or if you have the time now, play me something pretty."

"Now that's an irresistible request. Why not both?" He smiled at her, his expression open and sunny as he unfastened the case holding his horn.

As he took up the instrument, she noticed every detail. The easy comfort with which he hefted it. The softness of his gaze as he rummaged through memory for a tune. His left hand gripped the golden scribble of tubing and lifted the instrument, and his right hand hid within the bell. Rowena glanced at her own right hand and thought—not for the first time—that she'd have liked to try playing the horn.

Then his lips shaped, a tight press against the mouthpiece like a kiss with purpose, and a tune so old and familiar issued from the horn that Rowena had to laugh and sing along.

"Lavender's blue, diddle diddle,
Lavender's green,
When you are king, diddle diddle,
I shall be queen.
Lavender's green, diddle diddle,
Lavender's blue,
You must—"

She cut off the song in the middle of the line. *You must love me, diddle, diddle,*

'cause I love you. And then came the next verse, about lying together, and her cheeks burned at the thought.

How could she have forgotten how forward this song was? How hopeful and needy? It was embarrassing to sing those words as if they were her own.

Thorn halted his playing when she stopped singing, lowering the horn. "Didn't you like it?"

"Of course. Your playing is lovely. I just don't remember any more of the words," she lied.

"Ah, I can't help you there. I can remember a melody if I hear it even once, but I can never recall the words."

She bit her lips. "Why did you choose that tune?"

He shrugged. "It's called 'Lavender's Blue.' I was trying to think of a song, and you're wearing blue."

Indeed she was, a blue day dress she'd chosen because it matched her eyes.

His reply was matter-of-fact rather than flirtatious, which she liked. *Please, let him not be an incorrigible flirt.* If he were, he teased every woman, and his smiles meant nothing.

For the second time, Thorn packed his horn away. "Thanks again for your help. I'll bring you that hairpin soon, all right?"

She waved this off. "I was only teasing. Don't worry about it."

"I don't worry about hairpins, Miss Fairweather. But I'd welcome the chance to see you again."

That grin, cheeky and sweet at once. *Was* he flirting with her?

Maybe she should have charged him a fee after all and sent him on his way.

Or maybe she should have sung more of "Lavender's Blue" with him.

"Oh," she said, just as when he'd entered the shop.

This incoherence seemed to please him, for the grin persisted even as his hand drifted from hers, as he left the building. The little bell over the door jingled its farewell to him, and then Rowena was alone.

Except for a wandering hedgehog underfoot, old Nanny upstairs, a sometime cook in the basement kitchen, and a maid dusting the few chambers that weren't shut up.

They were relying on her. They all were.

She really should have charged Mr. Thorn a fee. But if she had, he wouldn't come back again—and with the obligation of a hairpin hanging over him, he just might.

Not that it mattered if he did. She was a luthier, not a...a...horn-note-puller. A folk-song-singer. A hairpin-provider.

She pushed aside the velvet curtain and returned to her work-room. *How to Ruin a Duke* tempted her from the table. The violon-cello with the broken neck beckoned her from its resting place against the wall.

"Work first," she decided.

Oh, she knew her financial problems couldn't be solved one instrument at a time. They couldn't be solved before the lease ended, not by anything less than a miracle. But miracles happened occasion-ally—and she wouldn't find that miracle in the pages of a book, no matter how salacious. The Duke of Amorous's problems vanished in the face of his infinite resources, but he wasn't going to stop by to fix hers. She had to face them herself.

The thought was usually discouraging. But at the moment, as she loosened the tuning pegs of the wounded violoncello, then uncoiled the strings to free the broken piece of the instrument's neck, she found herself humming.

A brisk young man, diddle diddle,
Met with a maid,
And laid her down, diddle diddle
Under the shade...

CHAPTER TWO

———————————

"Do not take a duke to partner! He will draw you astray and then run
off with the spoils while you are trying to discover where he has
led you."
From *How to Ruin a Duke* by Anonymous

By night, Simon Thorn saw Vauxhall as it was intended to appear: a
wonderland of glowing lights and whirling music and secret whis-
pers. But during the day, he couldn't help but notice the flaking gilt
and pasteboard that made up London's favorite pleasure garden.

The orchestra pavilion where the musicians practiced and played
was a half hexagon of white scrollwork at the center of the park's
Grand Walk. The pavilion was boosted above the ground and
festooned with lamps, lit at night to make it look like a jeweled crown.
The effect was probably striking, but at all hours, the musicians were
left cramped and crammed. Their stage had them elbow to elbow,
and the red wool jackets they wore while performing were as hot as
fur blankets.

Still, it was steady work. And with the loss of Lord Farleigh's son
as a student, this was the only source of income left to Simon. He'd

have to find other employment, and soon. The vicar from Market Thistleton—his sole source of news on the people Simon had left behind—had broken the silence Simon had requested on Elias Howard to mention that Howard was having trouble with his hand again. This time he was contemplating the desperate move of an amputation, the poor devil.

And it was all Simon's fault. He'd been a fool of a boy, more eager than careful as a tinworker's younger apprentice, and he'd caused the accident that left the older, wiser, better Howard—a much more skilled apprentice—injured and ruined.

For thirteen years, he'd sent whatever money he could, but dribs and drabs of coin were no better than a droplet of laudanum on a grueling pain. It didn't fix the problem; it didn't soothe the ache. Only a grand dose, a grand investment, would do that. And playing a horn didn't pay Simon enough, just as training horses hadn't, working as a law clerk hadn't, selling vials of gin labeled as cures for baldness hadn't. And a dozen other jobs he had tried over the years, always moving toward London, always away from the place he'd once called home.

Rehearsal stretched on under the watery afternoon sun. Simon settled his horn in his lap and picked at the peeling paint of the railing surrounding the orchestra pavilion, waiting for the conductor to finish squawking at the fiddles. One of them—Hawkins, as usual— was horribly out of tune. Just as usual, Hawkins was blaming the fiddler next to him.

"Hawkins wouldn't have this job for a minute if he wasn't married to the conductor's daughter," muttered Botts, the other horn player in the Vauxhall orchestra.

"Right you are," Simon agreed. "I met a luthier today who could set Hawkins straight."

"Wish he'd come by and do it," Botts replied. "Then we'd get through our rehearsal and I could get home for a bit of sleep before tonight's performance."

Simon decided not to correct the pronoun Botts had applied to the luthier. It wasn't as if Miss Fairweather was his personal discovery, but somehow he didn't like the idea of Botts making light of her. Or worse, pursuing her with one of his tawdry notes.

Like Simon, Alfred Botts was a bachelor; unlike Simon, he had no other financial obligations. Playing at Vauxhall paid the bills during the Season. Botts confided that when Vauxhall closed for the year, he planned to try his luck with a few orchestras on the Continent.

"Might as well learn what French women are like," Botts gloated. "Or Italian women, or Austrian women. M'time's my own."

"Your time," Simon reminded him, "is also Violetta's, and Frances's, and Mariah's, and Bertha's, and…who else have you sent love notes to in the last few weeks?"

"All right, so I'll leave a few fluttering hearts behind me." Botts winked. "None of 'em have to know about the other ladies, do they?"

"Horns! Quiet!" The conductor, a well-padded man named Clarke, slapped a flat palm onto the music stand before him, sending his papers into a disorderly shuffle.

Botts lifted his hands in a gesture of apology. Simon picked another fleck of white paint from the railing. Since he wasn't giving lessons to Lord Farleigh's son anymore, maybe he could get work repainting some of the faded buildings at Vauxhall.

As Clarke grumbled and rearranged his music, a messenger hared across the quadrangle of the Great Walk. The youth tramped up the pavilion steps and thrust the paper at the conductor. "His lordship said I wasn't to wait for a reply, but that you'd best obey."

When Clarke unfolded the message, his thundercloud expression turned yet grimmer. He darted a look at the horns. "Very well. Thank you."

And Simon developed a bad feeling about what was written in that note.

The messenger left the way he'd come. Crumpling the message, Clarke said, "We'll end rehearsal now. You're all dismissed. Be back half an hour before the park opens tonight."

Amidst the chaos of people rising, of instruments being stowed in tight quarters, the conductor's voice floated above: "Thorn. A word, please."

And Simon's feeling went from bad to worse.

He didn't inhabit lofty circles of Society. So if a "his lordship" was involved in the note, and obedience, and Simon too, there was a non-zero chance that Lord Farleigh was involved.

Damnation. After packing his horn as slowly as possible, letting the other musicians drift away, he strolled through the lessening crush to stand at the conductor's side.

"Sir? You wish to speak to me?"

Clarke took too long squaring his music sheets, then slipping them into his satchel. As tall as he was broad, he finally looked up and caught Simon's eye. "It's about the note brought by that messenger."

And Simon knew his bad feeling was justified. "From Lord Farleigh," he guessed, and Clarke nodded.

"I don't know what you did to him," said the older man, "but he's displeased with you. Says you've a bad character and he'll blackball Vauxhall throughout the ton if you're kept on in the orchestra."

Simon cursed.

"Exactly," agreed Clarke. "He's influential enough to do it. The Barrett brothers are trying to cut costs, to keep Vauxhall profitable. They've asked me to reduce the size of the orchestra, but I've been fighting them on that. If there's a chance you could lose them business in the beau monde, though...well, I'm sorry. I've got to go along with this. You understand."

He hadn't said the words *You're out of a job*, or *You're the one being blackballed*. But the meaning was clear enough.

"Oh, yes. I understand very well." The crumpled letter Miss Fairweather had pulled from the horn was rubbish in Simon's pocket.

He understood that Lady Farleigh had wanted to live a bit of *How to Ruin a Duke*, and he'd been conveniently at hand. The flirtatious missive had been a scandal of opportunity; he didn't fool himself to the contrary.

Unfortunately, her husband hadn't seen the matter that way. And in one day, Simon had lost both his jobs.

His horn was heavy in its case, the handle digging into his hand as he trudged down the steps of the pavilion for the last time. Thinking, thinking.

He had done many jobs besides playing a horn. The question was, which would he seize upon next? He needed money for Howard, and quickly. And with one lesson at a time, one rehearsal and performance at a time, he'd never earn enough. Not while his employment and pay depended on the whims of those with more power than he.

Miss Fairweather, now, she had it a bit better. She took the tasks she wished to and turned down the ones she didn't. She was her own mistress. It was a striking autonomy.

He wondered whether she might know of anyone who needed music lessons. He wondered whether he ought to be dreaming bigger than lessons and what form that dream ought to take. He had to dream for Howard first, before he dared think of himself. A man owed his old friend that much, at least, if he ruined that old friend's life and then ran out on him.

After returning to his lodging with his horn, he was no closer to a decision about what to do next. So he settled on the one action he'd promised: He bought a packet of hairpins.

It was early evening before he returned to Fairweather's, a proud, square-shouldered building on the still-bustling length of Bond Street. At this hour, the door of the luthier's shop was locked to customers. Unexpected disappointment flooded Simon when he tried the handle. He peered through the glass inset at eye level and caught a glimpse of movement inside—and before he thought better of the impulse, he knocked.

After a moment, a maid came to the door, with Miss Fairweather a step behind.

"Mr. Thorn." He heard Miss Fairweather's voice, muffled through the door, and was gratified that she recalled his name.

He held up the packet of hairpins to show her the reason for his visit. "Sorry about the time," he said, hoping she could hear him well enough through the door. "I didn't realize you'd be closed. I'll come back tomorrow."

He'd wanted to see her, but now he felt slightly foolish to have drawn attention to his presence.

Miss Fairweather bit her lip, hesitating. "That's all right. You can come in for a bit." He saw her turn away, say something to the maid, who curtseyed and hung about, dusting idly at a counter that didn't need dusting while her mistress undid the locks and opened the door to Simon.

"Good evening, ladies." He touched his hat to them both, then removed it. "Miss Fairweather, I came by with a bribe and a question."

"A bribe?" She was still in the blue gown from earlier, the one that matched her uncommonly clear and clever eyes.

He handed over the packet of hairpins, enjoying her laugh. "And a question."

Miss Fairweather turned to the maid. "Alice, you may take your supper in here. Get it from Cook."

The young maid nodded, and Simon understood: They were to be chaperoned.

Or not quite, for Miss Fairweather said, "Come into the work-shop. I'm at a tricky stage and can't leave my work."

He had coveted a look behind the curtain, where the heart of the business clearly lay. Now Miss Fairweather tugged it aside and allowed him to enter.

The shop held the smell that had wrapped around him so thoroughly the last time he'd been here: fresh wood, newly planed; something astringent like varnish or glue; and materials sweetly musky from age, like degraded old tapestry cushions and crumbling leather instrument cases. A light well spilled the dusty blue evening sun, the powdery color just before the day resigned itself to sunset.

"Time to light a few lamps," said Miss Fairweather, and she did just that, settling them at the corners of the large worktable. The golden flames highlighted instruments and bows around the room, some in pieces and some whole, while on the worktable lay a damaged violoncello.

It was this latter on which she was clearly working. He didn't know all the names for the parts of the instrument, only that a long ebony-looking board with a scrolled top usually held the strings. But this was beheaded, its strings removed and neatly coiled to one side.

Miss Fairweather resumed a task she'd been in the middle of, working with a flat brush and a sliver-thin file. She dipped the brush into an open-mouthed flask, then brushed along the seam of the broken board as she slowly worked the file alongside. That odd right hand of hers, with its short fingers, was as sure and certain as the left, and for a moment he simply admired the steadiness of her progress as she did...whatever she was doing.

"May I ask about your work, or would it ruin your concentration?"

"If it would, you'd have already done it." She looked up with a smile, so Simon didn't feel chastised. "I'm using mineral spirits to dissolve the glue so I can remove the fingerboard from this instrument. You see someone broke its fingerboard and neck, and I'll have to replace the one and repair the other."

"How do you repair the neck of a violoncello?"

Brush, brush, brush. Pry, pry, pry. "I'll drill into the sides and place dowels. Sometimes it holds, sometimes it doesn't. But it's best to try that first before giving up on the existing part."

He wondered at the amount of effort. "Is it worth it? Attempting such an extensive repair instead of replacing the instrument?"

"It's worth it to the owner," she said simply. "So it's worth it to me. I always do like to save an instrument instead of giving it up for lost."

"You like to bring music back to it," he recalled, pleased when she smiled at him again.

"Exactly. But removing a fingerboard is slow work," she added, "so I'm glad for the company. Cotton's deep asleep, so she's no help."

With a jerk of her head, she indicated a cushion on the floor that Simon hadn't noticed. The hedgehog slept atop it, curled into a prickly ball and making little snuffling noises as she slept.

"Is she usually a good conversationalist?" Simon teased.

"She's a good listener, and I'm a good conversationalist. I can carry on a conversation entirely by myself." Miss Fairweather looked sheepish. "The maid, Alice, doesn't tidy in here. I do. So I spend quite a bit of time in the shop even once it closes. Sometimes Nanny —that's Mrs. Kitt, but she's lived with the family since long before I was born—comes down here to read to me, but the stairs are difficult for her."

Simon noticed a book at one side of the worktable. "*How to Ruin a Duke,*" he read from the spine. He had the sudden urge to fling it out the window.

"If you're thinking about flinging it out the window," Miss Fairweather said with uncanny insight, "don't. It belongs to a subscription library. And I really ought to finish it today, because I promised it to my friend. We share a subscription to a library, and I've the first turn with *How to Ruin a Duke.*"

"Why that book?"

"Because it's entertaining." She worked the slim file more deeply into the seam between fingerboard and neck, creating the first small gap. "Don't you ever want to set aside your troubles for a few minutes? To read about someone else's woes?"

"Not really. I'd rather not think about woes at all." Much luck he ever had with that.

She gestured with the brush, flicking drops of white spirits onto the worktable. "That's the magic of this book. The Duke of Amorous's woes are nothing like real ruin. I can read it, enjoying

knowing the wagers and races and pranks and inebriation will cause
no real harm."

"They've caused harm enough to me." He recalled his original
purpose. "Look, I did say I had a question."

"Ah, yes. To go with the bribe."

"The problem is, I've been targeted by Lord—I'll just say the
husband of the woman who stuffed a note in my horn. As you know,
I've lost my post giving lessons to his son. Well, he also had me sacked
from the Vauxhall orchestra."

Miss Fairweather's brows knit. "That's horrible. How terribly
unfair to you. He should sack his wife instead."

Simon felt too tired for wrath. "It was a foolish action inspired by
a foolish note. I hope there won't be any consequences for her. But I
did wonder if you know of anyone who might need horn lessons. Or
anything of the sort."

She capped her flask, setting aside her brush to dry, and shook her
head slowly. "Sorry, no. I don't know many people in the brass
community. If you could tune pianofortes, I could give you all the
work you could handle. *Can* you tune pianofortes?"

"I could learn."

She laughed, a bit hollowly. "Not quickly enough to help me.
You'd have to tune a hundred instruments before you had a knack
for it."

"You need help?"

"I suppose I do." From the neat racks along the far wall, she
retrieved a tool with a broad, flat blade and worked it into the violoncello's fingerboard seam alongside the file-looking tool. "This building's lease is up at the end of the month, and the landlord has
informed me he'll be raising the rates. Far beyond my ability to pay,
but I can't lose the shop. Fairweather's has been a London establishment for a century."

A wonderful idea began to form from the misty half plans at the
back of Simon's brain. "Then let's work together. I'll help you and
we'll settle things for you."

She bit her lip. "Why should you help me?"

"Because you have too much to do and not enough money."

Rocking the flat-bladed tool back and forth, she opened a gap between neck and fingerboard and moved down the length of the violoncello, doing the same. "That's the case for everyone in London except the Duke of Amorous or Emory, if this book is to be believed."

"Not quite. As of today, I have not *enough* to do and not enough money." He nodded at her hand. "And there's the matter of your right hand."

She halted her work at once as if blasted by frost, and he knew he'd said the wrong thing. "I just mean..." He wasn't used to fumbling for words, but it was very important to put this correctly. "I have a friend with an injured right hand. I wish I could help him more."

I wish it wasn't my fault. I wish it never happened. I'll never be able to help him enough.

He was still saying everything wrong. Too much, too little at once. For a long moment, she regarded him, and he felt as if she were a judge about to render a verdict. "I was born like this," she said. "It is not an injury, and I don't need extra help because of it."

"I understand. I put that badly."

"Indeed you did."

"But you do need help," he pressed. "You just said everyone in London does. I certainly do. So maybe we can help each other."

She popped free the long strip of ebony from the neck of the violoncello. "I don't have money to pay an assistant, Mr. Thorn."

"Call me Simon," he offered. "If you like. And I wouldn't ask for any pay until you've exceeded what you need for your lease. I've a random assortment of possibly useful skills, so I'll handle everything for your shop but the repairs. You might try a new marketing strategy, perhaps: How to Ruin a Violin."

A surprised laugh burst from her lips. "Fairweather's is the luthier to the Crown! Such publicity would be undignified."

"Perfect. The Crown is undignified at present." An understatement. The Prince Regent was notorious for his profligacy and scandals.

"True. And the Crown has not paid the shop for some years." Miss Fairweather took up a piece of fine-grained sandpaper. "There's too much work for me already. How can I keep up if your methods succeed?"

Simon thought about this, then ticked off three possibilities. "You could charge more. Be more exclusive. Or you could move the shop elsewhere."

"No. I can't move the shop." With the sandpaper, she rubbed at the roughened wood face exposed by the missing fingerboard. "For more than a century, people have found Fairweather's here. Without the building, there's no shop. Without the address, there's no Fairweather's."

"All right, then you'll have to charge more. That's the best way to appear more exclusive while actually being less exclusive."

"I would be excluding anyone who can't pay an exorbitant price."

"And why should you not? This is a business and your livelihood. You've the endorsement of the Crown, so why chase further blue bloods? You should be basing your decisions on money, not rank."

"That's a fair idea," Miss Fairweather mused. "The *ton* is the worst at paying their bills."

"Ah! Maybe you need a skull-cracker to dun your clients who don't pay."

She choked. "Is that one of your random assortment of possibly useful skills?"

"Not so far, but I'm keen to try it out." He shrugged. "I'll do whatever's needed to help you. What do you have to lose?"

"My home, my business, the reputation laboriously built by my forebears. But I suppose that's the case whether you help or not."

Drawing a lamp closer to the instrument, she eyed its sanded surface. Her every action indicated expertise, experience, a certainty that she was doing what she ought. It was lovely to watch, and he realized that he envied her. Not only her skill, but her place in the world.

For years, Simon had avoided having a place in the world. Or a home or a business. His reputation in Market Thistleton? Best not to think of that—which was why he had left, moved on, tried new employment, moved on again.

Miss Fairweather spoke up. "What do you want out of this partnership, if I agree? Are you keen to become a skull-cracker, or do you just need a way to make money?"

"My wishes are purely mercenary," he admitted. "I need to send money home, and teaching one horn lesson at a time would never be enough. I need something steadier. Right now, I'm not busy enough for my own liking."

She looked curious. "Does something drastic happen if you're not busy?"

He tried to sound glib. He desperately wanted her to count on him, or to think he was the sort of fellow worth her time. "Too much thinking. We've all got things we want to forget, and it's easier to forget things if I'm busy.

"Anyway, I'll work hard for you. And once I've...oh, maybe twenty pounds in my pocket, I'll be on my way."

Naming a figure, planning to leave—there, that was familiar. He immediately felt more at ease.

Of course, two hundred pounds would be better than twenty. Two hundred would be enough for an annuity, so Simon would never have to scramble for Howard again. But twenty was a start, more than a start. It might even be an ending to some of the ongoing burden he'd lived with for more than a decade.

"Twenty pounds is a significant amount of money," said Miss Fairweather.

"I have a significant purpose in mind for it," countered Simon. "And remember, your lease gets paid before I earn a penny."

"Should I be worried about these things you want to forget? One scandal and I'm done for. Generations of work are done for."

Simon eyed *How to Ruin a Duke*. "Not if the social trespass is of your choosing. Haven't you learned anything from that blasted book?"

She blinked. "Not that particular lesson."

"Think about it." Ideas were beginning to shuffle and take form in Simon's head. Oh, this could be fun. "You're not part of Society. You work for Society. I know, because I work for them too—or did until earlier today. You need to be proper, but you don't have to meet the same standards as one of their unmarried daughters on the marriage mart. You're not competing. You're...yourself. There ought to be no one to compare to you."

He studied her: frank blue eyes, freckled nose, tidy black hair from which lamplight plucked chestnut and mahogany. "There *is* no one."

"All the easier to dismiss, then."

"Or all the easier to remember. We just have to sort out how to make people think of stringed instruments all the time."

"We?" She arched a brow.

"Do you prefer going it alone?"

She sighed. "No, I don't. All right. Would you like some tea? I would like some tea." She crossed to the curtain and drew it aside, saying, "Alice?"

The young maid presented herself in the doorway. More tidy of dress than of manner, she was young and coltish, with a cheerful, generously freckled face and dark red hair peeking from under her starched cap.

"Alice," said Miss Fairweather, "bring us a pot of tea. Very strong." She looked toward Simon. "Sugar? Lemon? Milk? What sort of trappings do you prefer?"

"Whatever you're having is fine." Tea wasn't always easy to come by. He'd never bothered to develop much of a preference.

"Nonsense. No one is *fine* with tea in any old way. Alice, bring them all, since our guest is shy."

Once the maid had bobbed her head and tromped off the way she'd come, Miss Fairweather returned her attention to Simon.

"Miss Fairweather, I really don't need tea."

"Rowena," she corrected, then boosted herself up onto the worktable. "And I *do*, and you're keeping me company. Come, sit beside me and let me hear all your brilliant ideas for saving my shop. I'll try to be as good a listener as Cotton."

More clumsily than she, he clambered atop the table, careful to avoid instruments, lamps, and the damned copy of *How to Ruin a Duke*. "You'll allow me to work with you, then? We're partners?"

"Yes, until my lease is renewed."

"Partners, then. Rowena." Her name was a tune on his lips.

She extended her right hand. Simon shook it, that unique hand that didn't look like any other hand he'd seen and that could carry out dexterous tasks he'd never attempted.

"Partners," Rowena echoed and grinned at him.

It spread through him, as bright and playful as a horn dancing up a musical scale. And he knew he'd do anything to help this woman, to make her need him—even if it could be for only a short while.

CHAPTER THREE

"A duke takes to vice like a duck to water. One might think a duke sunk in sin is a square peg in the round hole of Society—but trust this author! The Duke of Amorous's peg is his greatest preoccupation."
From *How to Ruin a Duke* by Anonymous

The damaged violoncello still lay atop the worktable the following morning, but Rowena decided to begin the day with a smaller task: by trimming a new tuning peg for a Rugeri violin. A beautiful instrument with a spruce belly and a back of flame maple, it was owned by a young matron who hadn't played a note since her wedding day.

"I'd like to begin again," Mrs. Beckett had confided to Rowena when she entrusted the violin to her the day before.

I'd like to begin again, too, Rowena thought. She craved a fresh start, with no red in her ledger.

Fabricating a tuning peg was a fairly simple task, and simple was what Rowena wanted right now so her thoughts could roam. Not only over how the new peg would fit, but also what she'd agreed to the evening before.

Time with Simon Thorn. A partnership. The hope of saving the shop.

And a pair of mischievous brown eyes, a hand on hers, and a packet of hairpins he hadn't needed to bring.

He would return this morning, before she opened the shop, and they would discuss further plans for drawing new business. Effective immediately, she had agreed the evening before, she would double her rates for all new jobs—except for tuning pianofortes, a task most luthiers didn't accept. Those jobs were tedious enough that she'd charge triple.

It seemed presumptuous to charge more than her father had after all his decades of experience. But then, as Simon had pointed out, if her father had charged the same rate for all of Rowena's years of memory, he had likely undervalued his work. Which led to Rowena undervaluing her own.

"And it's not as if meat and bread cost what they did twenty-eight years ago, when I was born," he had added. "Or rent, as you know."

She couldn't argue with that.

So, he was two years older than Rowena. She had squirreled away that fact about him, as she did every other tidbit of gleaned information: that he needed money for someone back home, wherever that was. That he'd speak frankly about many things, but not that.

Anyway. For all her proud talk of luthiery when she met Simon Thorn, she'd never thought to consider her value separate from her father's. He'd set a precedent she had always followed—and it had taken the arrival of an attractive stranger with a horn to make her wonder why.

Hmm.

She eased one of her carving tools over the nearly completed peg, shaving away tiny bits of dense boxwood. It turned easily in her hand, all silent potential. Silence was part of sound and sometimes quite the loveliest part when it allowed one scope for meandering thoughts.

One more shaving, then she tried the peg in its intended spot.

No, it wasn't a perfect fit yet. She needed her magnifying lens to check the surface of the boxwood peg for rough spots. Gazing about the cluttered but organized work space—a place for every board, supply, tool—she saw at once that it was missing from its spot at the end of the worktable.

"Nanny," she grumbled.

Nanny had got Alice, the maid, to pilfer it again. Rowena would bet on it. Nanny had grown shortsighted over the years, and she'd been impatient to read *How to Ruin a Duke*—just as she was to read every other one of the Gothic novels Rowena and her friend Edith passed back and forth. Rowena's magnifying lens went missing several times a week, and it was always to be found beside Nanny, held over the pages of their latest book.

Rowena set down the tuning peg, then gathered up Cotton—snuffling about on the floor—to keep the hedgehog from the paste jar. Cotton loved to eat paste almost as much as she loved crunching on beetles. More than once, Rowena had found the hedgehog's little snout daubed with the concoction of flour and water and alum.

Hedgehog bundled in her arms, she marched upstairs to the living quarters. The building stacked up three floors above the shop, but the household rarely used any of the rooms on the top two stories.

Alice squeaked when she saw Rowena turn the bend in the stairs. Duster in hand, she fled into a room off the corridor.

"I know you took my lens, Alice," Rowena called after her. "It's all right, but I need it back."

Alice poked her head forth. "Nanny has it. She's in the parlor."

The parlor. An awfully grand name for a room in which they rarely welcomed guests. Nanny had her old friend Mrs. Newland over for tea now and again, but the days of card parties and chattering blue bloods had gone with Rowena's grandparents.

Alice was right: Here was Nanny in the parlor, a tidy room with cheerful paper on the walls and a worn but still-lovely carpet on the floor. The old woman sat in her favorite seat, a short sofa with a wooden frame and a hard tapestry-covered back. She'd softened the furniture with cushions over the years, each beautifully embroidered. Her swollen feet, cradled in soft slippers, rested on a low footstool.

Nanny had indeed taken Rowena's lens, setting it on the end table beside her sofa. The magnifier was a big, beautiful half orb of transparent glass set into an articulated frame on a stand. It was unwieldy, almost the size of the book Nanny was reading. Not for the first time, Rowena thought she should get a sliding tabletop magnifier for the household. Just a fat lens that one slid along the page.

But right now, every penny counted. By all rights, Rowena shouldn't even be subscribing to a library anymore, though a life without Gothic novels and romantic Society tales would be sorely lacking in savor.

If one had no romance or scandal in one's life—and really, the only good sort of scandal was the sort that came with romance attached—then one needed to find it on the page. And romance had been sadly absent from Rowena's life for several years, since the abrupt departure of the awkward lover she'd once thought to wed.

It was because of the in-between social class she occupied, perhaps. She wasn't high-bred enough for the nobles, and she terrified the young men of the merchant and working classes by running her own shop.

For a little while longer, at least.

Nanny looked up from *How to Ruin a Duke*. She had a face like a pumpkin, round and well-creased, with a smile of infinite kindness and merry gray eyes. Though they were hidden behind thick spectacles, she still required the lens. "This is an excellent book. We should buy a copy of our own."

"When the shop is doing a bit better," Rowena said gently. "A gentleman named Mr. Thorn is going to help me with that."

"Oh? Is he a luthier too?" Nanny peered over her spectacles, all curiosity.

This expression always made Rowena want to fidget and blush. "No. He's a bit of everything else, though, so he says. He wants me to increase my rates and to market the shop with new sorts of advertisements."

"Good suggestions. I like them." Nanny closed the book, holding her place with one crabbed finger. "And you're paying him...how?"

Rowena explained the strange terms of their deal: the new lease to be arranged first, then twenty pounds for Mr. Thorn to send home. "And then he'll be off, and you and I can carry on just as we have."

Rowena couldn't imagine life without Nanny in it. She'd been Rowena's father's governess before Rowena's, Thus she had never had any qualms about confronting Mr. Fairweather. When Rowena had been born with thready membranes constricting the fingers of her right hand, her father had wanted her to receive extra help.

Nanny had harangued him for coddling his daughter, for asking Nanny to cut Rowena's food and help her eat and brush her hair and any other little task.

"She can do it herself," Nanny had insisted. "She's a Fairweather. You should teach her everything you know. It might take her longer to learn, but she can do it."

And Rowena did, sometimes crying with frustration, or from the pain in her restricted fingers. But over the years, she'd schooled her mind and body not to give up. Maybe she couldn't do things exactly like everyone else, but she could still do them. Her way.

Even so, her father had become reconciled to her hands only when she picked up a violin for the first time. He showed her how to hold it, pressing the bow into her right hand, then brightened. *Thank God it's your right hand with the damage,* he'd said. In any other profession, the left would be the more expendable, but a string player needed her left for the fingering and the right only for the bow.

Her father had made a luthier of her, as long ago as she could remember.

And Nanny? Nanny had made her a capable human.

She owed the old woman everything, so Nanny's look of disappointment just now wrung her heart.

"Must we?" Nanny sighed. "Carry on just as we have?"

"Why, what's wrong?"

"Oh, Mrs. Newland is having a difficult time with the stairs too. I wanted her to come to tea today. I even bribed her by offering to read to her from *How to Ruin a Duke*! But she said she needed to rest on her day off." Nanny's longtime friend was a housekeeper for a well-to-do family in Mayfair.

"Painful knees are painful knees, despite the promise of reading about the Duke of Amorous," Rowena replied. "I'm sorry. Should we send Alice over to her with a package of treats?"

Nanny waved this off. "Her mistress'll take care of her all right. I just get lonely for my friend."

"I understand," Rowena said. "I've got to take the lens back down with me now, but I'll leave Cotton with you. And I'll come check on you every hour—how is that? I can read you bits of *How to Ruin a Duke*."

"No need for that. I know you need to work." Nanny stretched out her hands for Cotton, settling the hedgehog on one of her innumerable embroidered cushions. "But when that Mr. Thorn of yours arrives, send him upstairs to meet me. That'll do just fine."

Rowen considered protesting *that Mr. Thorn of yours*, then decided that Nanny would enjoy that far too much. Besides, she rather liked the sound of it. So she only took up the magnifier—leaving the book with Nanny, with instructions to Alice to read to the old woman as Alice's time permitted—and returned to the workshop.

With the magnifier back in its place on the worktable, Rowena tilted the lens and peered through it at the boxwood peg. Ah! There was the problem: a spot that lacked the satin-smooth finish of the rest. It was the work of a minute to fix it. Once sanded, the peg fit into its spot as neatly as if it had been carved by Rugeri himself.

Someday, perhaps, people would speak of Fairweather violins as they did of Rugeris, or Amatis, or instruments by Stradivari or Klotz or Guarneri. Rowena had never constructed a finished violin from raw wood, but...someday. Someday she would. Over the years, she had surely learned every step needed; she'd surely worked on every piece and part.

Mrs. Beckett's Rugeri violin was a wondrous concoction of woods: a neck and sides of maple, a top of spruce, tuning pegs of boxwood, a tailpiece of rosewood, and a fingerboard of ebony. It took a forest to make a violin, and this was a beautiful one. Refitting the tuning pegs was a small task, but one that gave Rowena great pleasure. She could never afford such a fine instrument for herself—but now that she had repaired this one, she ought to make certain her work was satisfactory by playing it.

It was only responsible to do so.

She rubbed each gut string with a little olive oil, then knotted them to fasten them in the tailpiece before stretching them over the bridge, up the neck, and secure about the tuning pegs.

Then she put her own bow to the strings and drew it across. Lightly, smoothly, like a nobleman's valet might rub a silk handkerchief over a polished boot. Notes vibrated in the quiet morning shop like raindrops in a puddle, like marbles cascading to the floor. A spill of clear sound, its ripples persisting when the note itself was gone.

Perfect.

Oh, not the playing. The playing was horribly out of tune. But the peg was a perfect fit. Rowena bowed again, giving a practiced twist to each tuning peg as she drew the bow across the strings. Playing two at a time, creating perfect fifths of sound, she brought the violin's strings into harmony with each other just as she'd brought shape to a formless piece of wood.

It was immensely satisfying, though her bowing fingers cramped and ached by the time she was done. Only then did she recall that the day had hardly begun, that her work lay scattered all around her, and that none of it would be enough to pay Mr. Lifford, the landlord, for the continued lease of Fairweather's.

The lovely spring day suddenly seemed gray.

And then, from the other side of the velvet curtain, there sounded

a knock at the door. Rowena peeked around the edge of the curtain—
and the day became sunny after all, the clouds brightening.

Simon Thorn was here.

SIMON ARRIVED at Fairweather's embarrassingly early in the day,
yet he couldn't manage to feel embarrassed. It was too good, too
rewarding, to see Rowena Fairweather's spring-sunny smile as she
unlocked the door of the shop to him.

"I'd not have thought you an early riser," she said. "Most musicians aren't, since they have to play so late at parties and balls."

"Maybe I'd have had a harder time getting up if I'd played at
Vauxhall last night, but as I didn't, I'm terrifyingly full of energy."

"Terrifyingly?" She arched a brow. "I'm not easily terrified."

"I should have guessed that. If I'm very lucky, maybe I can keep
up with you." He smiled. How could he not? Today she wore a rust-
brown gown, and her eyes looked very blue. She was autumn leaves
and spring sky.

"I did promise to come early," he added, "so that I could catch
you before you open the shop for the day. Can you take a few
minutes to walk down Bond Street with me? I want to show you
something."

She looked back into the shop, called a few words to someone
upstairs—the maid, perhaps?—and without further delay stepped
through the doorway and joined Simon on the pavement. "Let's
go, then."

Simon blinked. "I admire promptness, but are you sure you're
ready? Don't you want a...hat or bonnet or whatnot?"

"Will a hat or bonnet or whatnot help me understand what you
wish to show me?"

"No, of course not."

"Then let's be off." She grinned at him. "I'm behind on my work, but I'm ready for a break. Behold an escapee from Fairweather's. Have you had a brilliant idea that will help me?"

He offered her his arm. "Not brilliant, perhaps, but adequate at the very least."

When she took his arm and said, "Lead on," he changed his mind: He was damned brilliant, after all.

It was brilliant, damned brilliant, to be outside on a cool May morning. The day had not yet decided whether it wanted to become hot or pour down buckets, and in this undecided state, it was full of possibility. A bakery exhaled glorious scents, and a costermonger's wagon clopped by laden with every growing thing from aubergines to apricots, bright like a tangle of beads in a jewel box. Maids in neat uniforms and starched caps darted into early-open shops. Later in the day, the tonnish would yawn and stretch and promenade down the fashionable street, idly shopping—but for now, Bond Street belonged to those who worked. Those with purpose.

Simon's idea, he explained to Rowena as they progressed down the street, was to turn the front window of her shop into an ever-changing display. "People overlook the familiar, but they notice when something is different. See the way this print shop's window always has something new in it? We cannot pass by without taking a look."

They halted before just such an example, which today featured a satirical caricature of—who else? The Duke of Amorous, who bore the dark hair and aristocratic appearance of the Duke of Emory. Unfortunately, the nobleman's dignified appearance was undermined by his pose: clothing askew, nose red from drink, bleating "God Save the King" outside of Almack's.

The sort of person who cared about Almack's would care very much that the duke had bespoiled it by singing outside of it—and now an impulsive, possibly drunken wager of a moment was immortalized *in* print and *as* a print. Poor fellow. Simon would almost feel sorry for the duke, if he hadn't been born into immense wealth and privilege. Emory had never had to take on an apprenticeship for which he'd been ill-suited, and at which he'd been an utter, ruinous failure.

Well. Maybe. Simon supposed that just because someone was born to become a duke didn't mean he was well-suited to the role.

But then there was Rowena Fairweather: born to be a luthier, and so deliciously capable that he could not imagine her as anything else. Though he *could* imagine her as anything she put her mind to.

"At the moment," Simon pointed out, "your shop's window contains only a sign, with a curtain blocking a view of the workshop. What if you drew that aside, so people could watch you work?"

"I wouldn't like that." She clenched her right hand, tucking it under her left arm. "I'd be too distracted if people were watching me work."

That was fair. "A second option, then. 'Visit Fairweather's! Watch an instrument be built!' Have you a violin you could take apart, piece by piece, and then put back together? Every day, you could make a change and the next step would be on display."

Rowena turned away from the caricature, thinking. "Now that idea, I do like. I've been wanting to build instruments of my own, and this could inspire me to begin. But to start at once, yes—I've a few instruments that don't play well anymore. They were never well made to begin with, poor things, and over the years they've been treated roughly. But they could still be used to teach."

"You talk about them as if they're alive. Now I feel I've suggested vivisection."

Rowena laughed. "An autopsy, maybe, to understand what went wrong in a body. That ought to intrigue the curious if we put up a sign. 'Violins dissected daily.'"

"I was thinking you *could* add another sign in the window. Something more to draw the eye than the instrument itself. For the time being, do as this print shop does: tie your messages into *How to Ruin a Duke.*"

"Be ruthlessly fashionable, you mean?" A shining carriage trundled along the cobbles. Rowena followed it with her face, eyes. "Fairweather's has been changeless for a century, but I suppose I can't sustain the old ways alone. You think I should have cards printed for the window? Little messages or stories?"

"I can hand-letter nicely," Simon replied. "I worked as a clerk for a time. If you're changing out the cards often, no need to go to the expense of a printer."

"A clerk and a musician." Rowena looked up at him curiously. "What else have you done with yourself?"

His heart beat more quickly. "Many things, but never mind that. What do you think of a little tale called 'How to Ruin a Violin'? I can imagine it now:

"'Loosing the strings, the Duke of Music plunged his hand into the forbidden hollow to pluck at the treasure hidden within. He thus displaced the sound peg, and he never could get his instrument back in tune. He brought it to Fairweather's, where the proprietress fixed the old sinner's peg.'"

"It's sound *post*, not peg," Rowena chortled. "And your little tale sounds as if I provide a scandalous personal service. Best not *quite* word it like that."

He thought that was part of the appeal, himself, but she was in charge. "Something more classical, then? 'If music be the food of love, play on. Come dine on passion at Fairweather's.'"

She breathed in deeply. "If you're going to talk about food while the bakery is putting forth that marvelous scent of cinnamon, I'll need cake." Then she snapped her fingers. "Cake! Everyone loves being presented with unexpected treats. Perhaps free pastries with every purchase?"

"And constant pastries for the proprietress?" When Rowena shrugged innocently, Simon laughed. "Let's see what I can do with duke-ruining before you start throwing cakes at people. Not that it's not a good idea, but I'd like to keep you from going to extra expense."

So, she liked sweets. He'd remember that.

And he'd keep mentioning expense: saving her money, saving her trouble. He would wind himself into her life so that she would not want to be without him. Already, he did not want to be without her.

The realization was startling. He stumbled, the pavement suddenly unsteady beneath his feet, and the irregularity of his step pulled Rowena close against his side. "Sorry," he mumbled. He wasn't sorry, for lithe and sweet-scented Rowena beside him, but he should be. He shouldn't try to pull her close in any way. He should help her and collect his money for Howard, and then exit Rowena's life—but oh, his heart was parched and lonely, and her blue eyes were spring water and her clever mind was a wonderland.

He couldn't drink from that spring; he couldn't explore that wonderland. He could help, collect money for Howard, and move along. That was all.

He had to keep reminding himself.

"You might consider an apprentice someday." His voice sounded stuffy and falsely cheerful. "You might find many eager souls in Bloomsbury, or among the ranks of my fellow musicians."

She waved this off, nudging at a pebble with the shiny toe of her boot. "I don't have time to train an apprentice. Foolish though it might sound, I'm too busy to get help."

"Except from me," he blurted.

"Ah, well. You jumped into my life and started helping. I didn't have to train you."

"Taking a little time now to train an apprentice would help you in the long term." Why was he trying to help her dispense with him?

Because it would help her. Full stop. It was for her good, and the good of Fairweather's. What a selfless fellow he was.

She looked interested. "You seem keen on the idea. Would you care to be an apprentice yourself?"

I tried that once. It was a disaster. "No." The word came out sudden and harsh. He tried to temper it, to sound merrier. "I'm not suited to that sort of work. I'm a come-and-go sort of fellow. Though I do like knowing I'm doing some good before I go."

"But you hardly know me," Rowena said. "Why should you care what good you do for me?"

He looked at her, hatless and freckled in the morning sun, and wondered how he could *not* care. How anyone could not.

"I don't know what you dream about while you're asleep," he said. "Or your favorite flavor of ice, or why you named your hedgehog Cotton. But I know what you dream about when you're awake. There's something familiar about you."

He permitted himself to look at her deeply, a long drink of sensation. "Besides, our fortunes are connected now."

"Because you connected them," she reminded him. His face must have fallen, for she added swiftly, "Not that I mind. I am grateful for new ideas. I am very glad you came into the shop. And—and my favorite flavor of ice is pineapple."

This was hardly a profession of love, but it made Simon feel marvelous all the same. "I like pineapple too. And maybe I'm not as come-and-go of a fellow as I thought."

She smiled. "Come and go once more, if you don't mind. Come back to the shop, and take a look at the window before you go."

As they retraced their short path to the luthiery, she admitted that there was a sort of security in knowing that her life had always been decided. "It's allowed me to be more than if I'd been born into a different family. As a Fairweather, I've learned a trade—really, an art. I've become part of a tradition." As Simon opened the front door for her, the little bell jingling a greeting, she added, "I'm not only...me."

"There is nothing *only* about you," he said.

She greeted the maid who had kept watch over the shop—the girl's name was Alice, Simon recalled—then led Simon into the workshop to poke about the space.

"Do keep the curtain drawn," she requested. "My hands aren't very pretty. That's part of why I didn't want the shop window to show me at work. I hide my hands when I can, since they're unfeminine."

Simon shook his head. "They're attached to your body, so they must be feminine."

She laughed, replacing a violin bow in a rack along the wall. "Please don't think I'm not proud of what I can do. But I recognize it's not within the scope of the ordinary."

"That is why you shall triumph." Simon stepped closer to her, and before he could restrain himself, he took up her hands in his. "Your hands repair musical instruments, so they are talented. Your hands care for an old woman and a household and a hedgehog, so they are caring. And your hands belong to you, so they are beautiful."

She blushed. "You say exactly what people want to hear."

Did he? Maybe he did think about what would suit his audience. A man who sold his labor—be it metalworking, copying documents, playing a horn, or training a horse—needed to win over the people who might hire him. He needed to convince potential employers he was capable, even when he knew himself to be nothing of the sort.

But with Rowena, he'd come to her in a state of incompetence. Twice! First with an unplayable horn, then without a job. And somehow, both times, she'd chosen to work with him.

To accept his presence in her life.

"I say what I mean," he told her, because behind every heartfelt desire to persuade was simply desire. To find security. A chance. To find...hope.

Still holding her hands, he lifted them to his lips. Brushed his lips over them both, each in turn, then released them. He didn't mean it as a seductive gesture; it was just something he couldn't stop himself from doing.

Rowena was looking at him with flushed cheeks; with wide eyes and lips parted in surprise.

He loved it. "I should say I'm sorry, but I won't because I wouldn't mean it."

"I'm not sorry." She sounded dazed. Delighted.

"Well." For a moment, they only blinked at each other, two souls surrounded by exotic woods and beautiful instruments. Simon had the urge to stay here, to beg to stay. To belong here as he never had before.

"Well," he said again. "I should go. But," he was unable to refrain from saying, "I'll be back tomorrow."

"You will?"

"With a sign for your shop window."

"Oh, right." Rowena still looked misty. "I will look forward to it."

To seeing him? At the very least, to accepting his help. Which meant that he could make her life a bit better.

It seemed a wonderful goal.

She spread out her hands before her as if they'd changed. Could she still feel his touch on her skin? The scent of her skin had captured him. The pressure of her fingers lingered within his.

Who was he trying to fool? The touch of her hands wasn't enough. He wanted a place in her life, in her wonderfully certain and solid life, and he wouldn't stop longing for more.

Even a come-and-go fellow wanted, sometimes, a place to stay.

CHAPTER FOUR

"It is too late, it is presumed, to enquire whether [the public] interests
are or are not injured by the description of desperate characters,
depraved conduct, and daring crimes?"
From *Glenarvon* by Lady Caroline Lamb

For the rest of the day, Rowena was conscious of her hands as she
worked.

Simon Thorn had kissed her hands, had made them—made *her*—
feel not only necessary and right, but beautiful.

No one had appreciated her hands before, not even herself, save
in the most impatient sort of way. She'd had admirers, even a lover
she'd expected to wed, but her imperfect right hand was in the end
too much for the man to overlook.

Well, not only her hand. Her honest speech. Her hard-won skill.
Her determination to run Fairweather's, at the time alongside her
father. So be it. She'd rather be alone than be expected to change who
she was.

But being admired exactly as she was? How heady. How lovely.

As she coaxed the strings from the tailpiece of the battered old violin that would become the shop-window display, she looked again at her hands. The left, with the long span of the fingers, with neat nails and calluses. The right hand, with its strong thumb and truncated fingers, its slivers of nails.

They weren't a matched set, but they were both capable. These were hands that could build. They were, indeed, beautiful. Simon Thorn reminded her to admire her own abilities by gently, sweetly, admiring her himself.

The whole gesture felt not like a seduction, but like an appreciation—and that was seductive indeed. There had not been enough air in the room when Rowena remembered to draw back her hands, lightheaded and buoyant.

Maybe Simon Thorn was seducing her, after all.

She wished he would. If he did, she'd allow it.

Maybe she'd even hurry the process along.

THE NEXT DAY was gray and mizzling, the sort that inspired Rowena to plunge deeply into work. The sort that brought the beetles out of their hiding places, delighting Cotton. The hedgehog was in an ecstasy of gluttony, padding around on her little clawed feet and nosing into tiny spaces to find and crunch down her favorite food.

"Better you than me," Rowena told her pet. "And thank you."

She spoke cheerfully, yet today seemed a bit lonely. Nanny's knees hurt her, and she didn't venture down to the workshop to keep company with Rowena. When Edith peeked into the workshop as morning drew on, Rowena could have hugged her friend in gratitude.

"Have you finished reading *How to Ruin a Duke*?" Edith said by way of greeting. "No one talks of anything else, and I'll perish of curiosity if I don't get my hands on our library copy."

Rowena laughed, and now she did allow herself a quick embrace before she directed Edith to her friend's usual perch on the end of the worktable. "I'll get a chair in here eventually," she promised, not for the first time.

Edith was in truth *Lady* Edith Charbonneau, an earl's daughter. Had her father not died deeply in debt and without an heir, Edith's life would have proceeded in a far loftier realm than Rowena's. But it hadn't. After being orphaned as a young adult, left to care for her teenage step-brother, Edith had taken a post as a lady's companion to the Duchess of Emory—the present duke's mother. Edith and Rowena had been permitted to occupy the same space between gentility and those who earned their bread, and therein they made friends.

After two years of seeming domestic tranquility, Edith had left her post abruptly some five months before. She told Rowena she was pleased to have more time to work on a manuscript of domestic advice, which once sold, would secure the financial future of both Edith and the step-brother, Foster, for whom she served as guardian.

This wasn't an explanation of why, or what had happened. But Edith didn't share explanations easily. She was a Gunter's ice in person: elegant, beautifully constructed, cool, sweet. She was also so very *much* that she sometimes made Rowena feel quite medium. She was very tall, very pretty, very well-mannered, very vigorous, very intelligent—and very independent. She'd been very fashionable as well, though in recent months, the threat of penury had led her to sell whatever could be sold. She now wore an unfashionable pink cloak over a gown stripped of all ornament—yet not even this could chip at her dignity.

She was also very kind, which made her a most excellent friend, and she understood how quickly fortunes could fall and privilege could be destroyed.

So Rowena wouldn't pry into her friend's reasons for leaving what seemed to be a good post. She could merely accept what Edith told her, offer a listening ear and a stack of novels, and carry on with her work.

"Working, working," Edith commiserated. "How busy you keep. Have you had any news from your landlord?"

"None that's good." Briefly, Rowena explained her plans with Simon Thorn to increase income and better advertise the shop. "I'll reap great rewards in a few months, maybe even a few weeks. But it might not be soon enough." She hated to think about that, so she hadn't been—but ignoring the problem over time had only made it more urgent.

Edith poured out a cup from the teapot Alice had left in the workshop that morning, adding milk and sugar to her tea. When she spooned in yet more sugar, Rowena wakened to the awareness of other problems beside her own. Had her friend eaten that day? Edith was looking thin, and it would be just like her to give her own breakfast to Foster.

So Rowena made up an excuse. "I'm hungry. Will you join me in a scone? Cook made some yesterday, and they'll be dense as rocks if we don't finish them today."

"You eat while you're working?"

Rowena set aside the tools she'd been using to pry apart the unfortunate violin for the shop window. "I can pause for a few minutes." She rang for Alice and ordered a tray.

As she spoke, she noticed that Edith drank deeply of her tea, wincing at the heat even as her eyes closed in relief. When Alice departed, Edith smiled. "Thoughtful of you, Rowena. I'll be delighted to share your prandial pleasures."

"Prandial pleasures," Rowena echoed with a laugh. "I'm hearing alliteration everywhere. This is what comes from reading *How to Ruin a Duke*."

"I wouldn't know, since you won't relinquish it," Edith said crisply.

"It's the greatest guessing game society's played in a long while. Every other customer in my shop is speculating about who the author might be. The butler in Emory's household? That poor woman the duke all but jilted last year? Everybody has a theory."

Edith looked thoughtful, cradling her teacup in slender hands. "I begin to wonder myself, Ro. Emory always seemed dignified to me. I know men can behave quite differently when ladies aren't around, but Emory..." She trailed off and stared into the teacup, as if fortunes might be read in the dregs.

"I thought you didn't care for him," Rowena said delicately. Edith had never said so directly, but her silences could be telling.

"I respected him, and his current situation would try the patience of a saint. I do not envy the author of this book when Emory discovers his or her identity. There's ruin, and then there's *ruin*."

Rowena suspected that Edith understood real ruin as well as she did. Real ruin was unforgivable disgrace, unpayable debt, unpardonable shame. *How to Ruin a Duke* was titillation, three hundred pages of gossip over which it was safe to giggle and whisper.

When the world saw real ruin, it looked away. Real ruin was to be feared as if it were contagious.

But when someone who cared began to suspect real ruin, that person came for a visit. Or offered a scone. Or read from a coveted book.

Or, Rowena thought, they helped a struggling business create a new plan to succeed.

And in return, if someone cared, they offered whatever that person asked—whether it was twenty pounds or the touch of a hand. Or more, much more.

And so Rowena turned the subject from the fraught *How to Ruin a Duke* to one she knew would interest and distract her friend. "Let me tell you about Simon Thorn," she told Edith. "And all our plans for this shop."

SIMON ENTERED Fairweather's with his hands full of papers and cakes, only to find Rowena entertaining a caller. This was clearly not a customer, for the visiting young woman had been permitted behind the velvet curtain, and she even sat on the worktable where Simon had perched on the first day of his acquaintance with Rowena.

"Hullo," he said by way of greeting. "Who'd like a cake?"

Rowena introduced Simon to her friend, Lady Edith Charbonneau, and admitted that they'd just devoured a plate of scones. "But what kind of cakes have you brought? No one is ever sorry to receive cakes."

"I thought the same. These are cream cakes." He placed the packet next to the blond woman, Lady Edith, who looked extremely interested and began to open the paper wrapping. "I've brought your signs for the front window too."

He'd had to borrow a quill and ink and buy blank cards from a print shop, but Rowena didn't need to know any of that. Nor was she to think of the trouble he'd gone to. She was only to look impressed when she saw the result—well, the sixth result, as he was out of practice with his fine and flowing clerk's script—of his first advertising card for the window of Fairweather's.

Rowena responded just as he'd hoped: with a lift of a brow, a quick flashing smile. "It's beautiful. What an elegant hand you write." She returned the card to him, brushing his fingers with hers as she held his gaze.

He felt as gawky and pleased as a boy, her touch firing his nerves. For too long, probably, he stood like a statue, only staring at Rowena. She was clad today in a rust-colored gown that made her look like a burnished musical instrument, and his mind flooded with all sorts of dreadful, hopeful puns about wanting to play her.

A throat cleared, snapping them from their mutual reverie. When Simon turned toward the source of the sound, it was to see Lady Edith sporting a knowing smile. "Excellent cakes," she said. "Thank you, Mr. Thorn. Will you show me this mesmerizing sign you've brought?"

He did so. As Edith scrutinized the scripted card, she said, "My brother, Foster, saw you at the Mallery Lane Theater, I think? You were slipping cartes de visite into all the violin players' cases."

"Oh, no," replied Simon. "Not the violins. *All* the string players. Well, most of them. I should have asked, Rowena, can you work on harps too?"

Rowena looked offended. "Of course I can work on harps. And lutes, and mandolins, and guitars. If it has strings, I can repair it."

"Kites?" he asked. "Tasseled rugs?"

Edith covered a smile, then handed back the card.

"I'm insulted by your doubt." Rowena adopted a tone of haughtiness over laughter.

"I can make a kite sing. Or I could, if I ever tried it."

"Good woman. I admire your confidence. And Lady Edith, should your brother attend Covent Garden tonight, he will find me haranguing the orchestra there. I've also enlisted my fellow horn player from Vauxhall, Botts, to send all the fiddles this way if they need work done."

Edith turned to her friend. "All repairs, Ro? You're not building any instruments?"

"I'm not even doing as many repairs as I'd like," Rowena replied. "Everyone seems to have bought a pianoforte in the last year, and they all went out of tune after winter cold and spring rain."

"I've taken three new bookings in the past hour," Edith told Simon. "I've been playing clerk while she works."

"Three new bookings at the higher rate?" When Edith nodded, Simon whistled. "Well done. That's the most lucrative task. But, Rowena, you don't look pleased."

She hesitated. "I'm never *pleased* to tune a pianoforte, though I'm grateful for the work. It's just—"

The shop door's bell jingled.

"I'll see to it." Edith slid from the worktable, casting a regretful glance at the remaining cream cakes, then strode into the small front room.

Rowena turned her attention to the violin she'd been delicately taking to bits, so Simon accepted her silence and went to work in the shop window. He was able to arrange a curtain in the window to afford the workshop its privacy while also displaying his "How to Ruin a Violin" sign—without the little story Rowena had laughingly protested.

Piece by piece, he placed in the parts of the violin Rowena handed him, then stood the neck on end and topped it with a second card. "How to Repair a Violin: Consult Fairweather's." He was aware of curious passersby peering at him as he worked. Good.

Simon clambered from the window area, careful not to disarrange the new display, just as Edith re-entered the room.

"This violin needs a new saddle, so says the man who deposited it into Fairweather's care." Edith brandished a small instrument with an uncommonly red varnish. "Did you know violins had saddles, Mr. Thorn? How equestrian."

Rowena indicated a place for her friend to set the instrument. "You booked the job at the higher rate? The new rate?"

"Of course." Edith winked. "Maybe even a bit more than you told me to charge. He was happy enough to agree, and he left half the fee in advance. You can get this done within a week, can't you?"

"Of course," Rowena echoed. She looked around the workshop, clearly counting up the tasks that lay before her. "That one's ready for varnish...that one needs a sound post...the Rugeri needs to be returned...the fingerboard there...oh, and now the three pianofortes. Yes. A week will be fine."

She didn't appear to be at ease, and Simon guessed at the end of the sentence she'd been about to utter when the shop bell interrupted. "But it's not enough."

Slowly, Rowena shook her head. "I can't do enough work, and quickly enough, to secure the lease. Not at one hundred fifty guineas per year."

This time when they looked at each other, there was no crystalline flirtation. This shared glance was knowing and heavy. Without a windfall, she wouldn't keep her shop—and he wouldn't gather money enough to help Howard.

No. That wasn't an option. "I'll think of something else," he promised. "Something that will help you in time."

"Is this experience, or arrogance?" asked Edith.

"Experience." He hoped. "I've always thought of something in the past, so there's every reason to assume I will again. Just as it's experience, not arrogance, for Miss Fairweather to say she can fix that violin within a week. She's done it before and knows what to do."

"People are not instruments," Edith pointed out.

"I could draw you a poetic comparison," Simon replied. "About how we all feel in harmony with certain parts of life, and some things set us to vibrating like a gut string. But I'll just offer you another cake."

"I take it back," said Edith. "People are instruments, and you know how to play them. I can be entirely won over by cakes."

"And you, Rowena?"

"I'm not won over by cakes," she replied.

"What are you won by?"

She looked at him with a touch of bleak amusement, and he knew his own answer. He was won by a pair of frank blue eyes. Had been won, maybe, the instant he entered the shop on a whim, hoping the luthier would have a tool that could swiftly unstop his horn.

"Well," Edith broke in. "I see that I must be getting on my way. Rowena, are you ready to relinquish *How to Ruin a Duke*?"

Rowena tapped her nose. "'Ready to relinquish'? Alliteration again. It's everywhere."

"Your attempt at distraction won't work. Hand it over, won't you? You've had it for a week already."

"Nanny keeps taking it! I'm not finished yet."

"I won't have time to read it before our turn is up," Edith protested.

"*Frankenstein*," Rowena reminded her. "*Nightmare Abbey*. Remember those? I had hardly any time with them."

Edith rolled her eyes. "I was nearer the circulating library. It only made sense for me to pick them up and read them first. But here, look what I have." She rummaged in her bag. Simon watched curiously as she pulled out two bound volumes.

Edith squinted at the spines. "*Glenarvon.* You've read that." She stuffed that volume back into the bag, then extended the other book to Rowena. "*Northanger Abbey.*"

Rowena folded her arms, rejecting the book. "I want *Nightmare Abbey.*"

"This one's also good," Edith wheedled. "It talks about all sorts of wonderfully horrid novels. Though it's not quite a real Gothic. The heroine imagines all sorts of horrors, but nothing bad ever comes to pass."

Rowena pulled a face. "What fun is that?"

Simon laughed. "Eat a cream cake, then explain to me why you like Gothic novels so much."

"If I must." Rowena plucked a pastry from its packaging—now Simon's thoughts were alliterating too—and considered as she bit into it. Simon tried not to become utterly spellbound by her expression as she savored sweet cream and delicate crumb, but such a look of bliss was difficult to ignore.

"I think," Rowena said once she'd eaten the cake, "Gothic novels are simply the best of all sorts of stories. In what other book could there be skeletons, brooding gentlemen, family secrets, and dark lightning-struck towers?"

"Sounds like Twelfth Night with the Prince Regent," muttered Simon, causing Rowena to splutter.

"But if you're wondering why I like all those sorts of things," Rowena added, "maybe it's because they have little to do with my ordinary life. Like *How to Ruin a Duke.* It's merely entertaining."

"And adventure?"

"And peril, and heroines solving it." She took up the rejected copy of *Northanger Abbey*, then flipped through it. "I dearly love the idea of sorting out one's particular type of peril."

He could certainly understand that. And yet. "It doesn't always work out well for the heroine," Simon pointed out. "Think of 'The

Vampyre'—published last month in *New Monthly Magazine*. It ends in the tragic death of Aubrey's sister, drained of blood on her wedding night."

Both women stared fiercely at Simon as if he'd just suggested juggling Cotton. "What? What's wrong?"

"We haven't read it yet!" Edith exclaimed.

"You are a *monster*." Rowena pointed at Simon. "You're worse than the Duke of Amorous. He puts notes inside violins, but *you*— you talk about the endings of books!"

This was befuddling. "But you love Gothics. I thought you'd have read it."

"No!" Rowena howled. "And now I know the heroine *dies*? What sort of story is *that*?"

"Quite a horrid one," Simon said tentatively. "Sorry. I just—I thought we were talking about books."

Edith jumped in, thank the Lord. "I would love to read more books of practical advice. Rather than *How to Ruin a Duke*, I'd like to know *How to Solve Anything. How to Answer any Question*."

Rowena relented, though her movements as she straightened tools were still choppy. "You're writing that book already. I'd like to know *How to Make Money Appear from the Ether*."

"Are we suggesting titles?" Simon asked. "*How to Get Two Ladies to Forget You Told Them the Ending to a Story*. That's the book I need."

Rowena waggled a metal file at him. "That'd be a short book. One can't get people to forget, but to forgive."

"Ah. *How to Gain Forgiveness*. That'd be a worthy title too."

If he had that book, he would read it every day. He'd have read it for thirteen years. And maybe, if it really existed and if its methods worked, someday Howard would forgive him.

"Indeed it would," said Edith, a hollow note in her voice. She bade the two of them good-bye, leaving the copy of *Northanger Abbey* behind on the worktable. "Thank you for the cakes, Mr. Thorn. I shall tell my brother to watch for your cards at the theater."

When she was gone in a whisper of velvet curtain and a jingle of silver door bell, Simon apologized to Rowena. "Not only about 'The Vampyre,' but...well, I wanted to help you make your fortune. I've a little skill at a lot of things, but not enough at any one of them to be any use."

"Good heavens! I forgive you for telling me about the poor woman's demise. It is only a story, after all. And you have a skill that I admire very much."

Admire? She admired something about him? He tried to drawl the question, "Oh? What is that?" rather than sounding eager as a pup.

He probably didn't succeed.

But Rowena didn't seem to mind. "You persist," she explained. "You don't give up. You try something, and then something else, until it all works out."

Did he? That sounded quite a bit better than being a come-and-go fellow who never settled to anything. "Why do you think so?"

"You tried to work with me, and then you tried a different way, and eventually I agreed. If you can win over a stubborn luthier, you can win over the people of London. So. What are we going to try next?"

What wouldn't they try next? He had many ideas, none of them related to the shop. Grandiose ideas, romantic ideas...steady and rooted ideas. Ideas about staying, about making a home. Trying to deserve it, with his whole heart.

Rowena was still awaiting his reply. He cleared his throat. "Well. I have a suggestion that isn't strictly business-related."

"All right." She picked up the violin that was missing a saddle.

"In fact, it's not at all business-related."

Her cheeks took on a faint color. She set the violin down at once. "You intrigue me."

"Oh, good. You see, I would like to kiss you. Would that be all right?"

Her smile was sweet and slow, spreading like sunrise over hills. "Yes, please. Finally."

And she took his face in her hands. Looked him in the eye. Caught up every stray bit of his soul that might be revealed, reflected it back, made it whole.

"You asked what I was won by," she told him. "It's this. I'm won over by this. Just you, and the questions you ask, and your trust in my reply."

This woman, this wonderful woman. He was drowning and he was saved.

She still didn't know who he'd once been, but she knew who he was now. Thank God, she would allow him to kiss her, because knowing her was a startling pleasure—but simply knowing her without touching her, tasting her, taking her in his arms, was nowhere close to closeness enough.

A simple kiss, a single kiss, was enough to fill his heart. The brush of lips on his, cake-sweet and laughing, held more pleasure and promise than any passionate interlude had before.

Now he was becoming alliterative again, which proved how deeply she'd wound herself into his mind. How long had he known her? Always, he thought. He'd just been waiting to meet her.

He knew, even as he held her in his arms, that it wouldn't be long before he'd have to go.

Yet already he knew he'd never want to leave her, and that one kiss would never satisfy.

CHAPTER FIVE

"The Duke of Amorous is a man of infinite resources and infinite leisure. Alas for him, he lacks the infinite charm of manner that would allow him to take the greatest pleasure in his good fortune!"
From *How to Ruin a Duke* by Anonymous

When Rowena drew near the town house of the Duke of Emory, she wondered whether she ought to go to the servants' entrance or the front door. She wasn't quite a lady, with her case of piano-tuning tools and the freedom to walk alone in public.

But she *had* been invited to the household, albeit for a task. Two days before, the duke's footman had brought piano-tuning request number four—and before the day was out, she'd added numbers five and six to her schedule for the week.

To the devil with it. She was a busy woman. Rowena marched up the marble steps and rapped at the front door.

When the elderly butler opened it to her, she announced, "I'm from Fairweather's, here to tune the duchess's pianoforte."

"Yes, Miss Fairweather," intoned the old servant, as stuffily as if he hadn't seen her take tea with Edith here in past years when Edith had served as the duchess's companion. "But Her Grace has always had the pianoforte tuned by *Mr.* Fairweather."

Rowena lifted her chin. "As Mr. Fairweather passed away nearly a year ago, I doubt Her Grace would find his skills adequate. And if my father was the last to tune the duchess's pianoforte, the instrument must be sadly jangled by this time. You will be fortunate if I do not raise my rates."

He eyed her gloved hands clasping the handle of her case of tools. "I doubt whether you will serve the purpose."

He began to shut the door.

Rowena's thoughts whirled. What would Simon Thorn do or say? He wouldn't give up. He'd press from a different angle.

So she shot out a foot, catching the door against the toe of her boot. "If you refer to my unmatched set of hands," she said crisply, "I assure you they are less relevant than my experience and skill. And if you again refer to my sex, well, Her Grace is no doubt aware how much better a woman has to be than a man to get even a fraction of the respect he's afforded."

She squared her shoulders. "Now, will you allow me to enter and complete the task Her Grace's emissary engaged me for? Or must I explain to the duchess that her pianoforte remains out of tune because you are too limited to respect female knowledge?"

The butler appeared extremely displeased, yet he drew aside and admitted Rowena to the foyer. "Wait here."

She was grateful for the reprieve, her heart pounding and cheeks hot, as if she'd just done battle. And she had, hadn't she? What the ducal butler had seen as weaknesses, she'd asserted as irrelevancies or strengths.

Drawing in a deep breath, she calmed herself, then inspected her surroundings. She'd been here before as Edith's guest, though not for some time. The Duke of Emory's London town house, where he lived with his widowed mother and younger brother, was an elegant but unusual building. The spacious octagonal foyer communicated ducal power in its every inch, from the mosaic of the family crest on the floor, to the sweeping grandeur of the central staircase that vined upward.

Rowena was surrounded by the scents of wealth, too, of lemony cleaning oil and the flinty smell of air trapped between marble floors and plastered ceilings. She preferred the familiar surroundings of her workshop: the fresh smell of cut wood; the sweet-scented, resinous copal and the astringent shellacs that she used to make her varnishes.

No matter. Tuning pianofortes paid the bills, and if she was *very* creative and persuasive, perhaps even the lease. She'd have to speak to Mr. Lifford, her landlord, about offering quarterly payments rather than one annual outlay. It was a possibility that had occurred to her recently.

"I'll show her to the music room." A rumbling masculine voice floated down the grand staircase.

"Yes, Your Grace," came the reply in the butler's vinegary tone.

So. The old butler had tattled on her to the duke, and the duke was allowing her in. She experienced a flash of triumph, then of curiosity when she realized she'd get another look at the man who inspired *How to Ruin a Duke*.

The Duke of Emory rounded the curve of the staircase with heavy footfalls. His Grace was a large man, a little too rough for male beauty, with a strong jaw and weary eyes.

Rowena curtseyed to him. He nodded a greeting. When he reached the foyer, he said, "My mother and brother are gallivanting around Town, while I find myself short of invitations. You will know why, I am sure."

The book, of course. *How to Ruin a Duke.* "Yes, I know why."

"Scandal is all right as long as we pretend not to know about it. That veil is gone."

Rowena understood. "Lady Caroline Lamb suffered for writing *Glenarvon* a few years ago, but without an author to blame for...that book...you bear the scandal."

"Indeed. If I could unmask the lady responsible for this libel—" He cut off the sentence, looking grim.

"I thought it was written by a man," Rowena said.

"No one knows." *It's all too much*, said his expression, and she understood him as she'd never understood an aristocrat before.

She couldn't reconcile this man with the flippant, frippery Duke of Amorous. But it wasn't her business to do so.

"This is not why you have called." The duke recalled himself. "I am told that you are the finest piano-tuner in England."

Right. *That* was her business. "Only England?" Rowena drawled. "Someone's insulted me."

The duke's haughty mouth curved. "The music room is upstairs. If you will accompany me?" As they ascended the stairs, Emory added, "I would pay you more to cut all the strings than to bring the instrument back into tune, but my mother thinks a lady ought to play the pianoforte regardless of her level of skill."

"I'm far too wise to step into a family feud," Rowena replied. "Show me to the instrument, and I'll have it in tune for you. Should you wish to cut the strings, Your Grace, and risk your mother's wrath, I can be found in Bond Street and will happily restring the pianoforte for you for an exorbitant fee."

"Fair enough. You will please not cut the strings at this time."

They had reached their destination, an airy chamber papered in a floral print and dotted here and there with chairs and smaller instruments: a harp, a violoncello. In the center of the room, a shining black-lacquer pianoforte held pride of place.

"When my footman made this appointment with you," the duke said, "you mentioned the possibility of keeping your shop on retainer. While my mother is hard on instruments, she is not so musically skilled that she notices the difference. I do apologize if the footman raised false hopes."

Rowena set her case of tools on the plush carpet beside the pianoforte. "Of course not. I thank you for entertaining the possibility at all."

Ah, well—it had been worth mentioning as a means of ensuring steady income for the shop. She was disappointed, but only in the same way she'd once been when her father refused to buy her a puppy. She had hoped, but she'd only ever expected the answer *no*.

"I'll leave you to your work, Miss Fairweather." With an inclination of his head, Emory departed the room, leaving her alone with the pianoforte and her tools.

Or so she thought. She opened and propped the instrument's lid, then the duke's voice sounded behind her from the doorway. "I am told you've had help at your shop recently."

"Edith?" Rowena's head jerked around. "Sorry. Lady Edith, do you mean?"

His lids fluttered, but he otherwise betrayed no emotion. "I do not refer to Lady Edith. I mean a young man named Simon Thorn. Lord Farleigh doesn't like it."

Lord Farleigh. The man whose wife had stuffed an amorous page into Simon's horn...how long ago? Not long, yet she could hardly remember not knowing Simon. But then, she'd been awake and working almost ever since.

Or awake and with him.

The duke paused, long enough for Rowena to wonder at the size of the figurative sword dangling over her head. Was this a threat? "Your Grace?" she prodded delicately.

"I do not like that Lord Farleigh has an opinion on the matter and have informed him so. He will not interfere with Mr. Thorn. Or with your shop."

Mystified, Rowena thanked him.

"Think nothing of it. I do not care for bluster and menace." And this time, he did depart, leaving her to work with her tuning hammer and her mutes of cotton felt.

Years of experience had her working with pianoforte strings as much by feel as by ear, leaving her free to ponder.

So. The Duke of Emory had exercised some of his privilege on her behalf. Or would it be more correct to say he'd protected Simon? Either way, Rowena was certain the credit lay with Edith. Rowena was known by the duke's household to be a friend of Edith. There was simply no other reason why they would care about the fate of Fairweather's.

Why had Edith left this household? She'd been making a good wage, and the duke seemed all right. He demonstrated none of the crawling sort of flirtation that came from a man taking pleasure in a woman's vulnerability. The Duke of Emory had seemed hardly to notice that Rowena was a woman at all.

I'm not going to talk about it, Edith had said to Rowena of her departure. *There's nothing to say*.

Which meant Edith was either afraid or ashamed.

Had she fallen in love with His Grace? Was *How to Ruin a Duke* embarrassing for her now that Emory's true character was revealed?

An hour and a half later, the pianoforte was back in tune, but Rowena's thoughts were no closer to harmony.

~

"'I NEITHER COULD THANK MY BENEFACTOR,'" read Nanny to Rowena, "'nor inquire how I was to repay him. I could not help feeling some inward sensations of horror.'"

"That's not what I'd feel if a mysterious man tossed bank drafts at me." By lamplight in the parlor, Rowena was sanding a new fingerboard for the broken-necked violoncello. The whole day had gone in travels about London, in tuning one pianoforte after another, and her repair work still remained. "'Inward sensations of horror'? Please! I'd kiss him on the lips."

"Hush," Nanny chastised. "There's going to be a necromancer soon. The title says so." Pulling the great magnifying lens to a handier spot, she continued, "'Having recovered from my amazement, I went to the table, took up the papers, and saw, with astonishment, that each of them was a draft for a hundred dollars.'"

"Only dollars? Not pounds? It might not be enough." Rowena squinted down the length of the fingerboard, holding the instrument's bridge beneath it. The curve of the latter would have to fit perfectly beneath the former, or the strings wouldn't lie properly.

"I can read this to myself if you're not interested," Nanny huffed.

"I'm too interested. More than I should be. I've been doing too much to forget the lease on the shop."

At the end of the month, the money would come due, or Fairweather's would cease to exist. The work of a century and more, gone under her guardianship.

She couldn't allow that to happen. She sanded harder.

Through the open doorway, she heard a knock at the shop door. Her ears were attuned to it, the promise of Simon Thorn's unexpected arrival. For several days, they'd been crossing paths at random times. She, to and fro from tuning pianofortes. He, popping in to change the shop window's display and share new bookings gathered from his meanderings through the orchestra pits of London's theaters.

"A caller for you. Time for me to go to bed, that's what that knock means." Nanny winked.

Rowena blushed, then pretended she hadn't. "It could be the fishmonger's boy. Alice will check."

"Twelve hours late, he'd be." Nanny heaved herself from her seat, grimacing as her knees and ankles popped. "I can tell you're not in the mood for *The Necromancer*. Maybe we'll read more tomorrow."

Rowena had to agree with this. She couldn't keep her mind on fiction. After kissing Nanny on the cheek and bidding the old woman an early good-night, she gathered up the pieces of her work and descended the stairs, laying out the fingerboard and bridge on her worktable before she passed into the foyer.

It wasn't Simon that Alice had admitted to the shop, wide-eyed and nervous-handed. It was their landlord, Mr. Lifford.

The maid's nervousness was entirely due to the man's role, not his demeanor, for Mr. Lifford had a gentle appearance. A man of perhaps forty years, he had been a clerk for years until he had the great good fortune of inheriting several properties along New Bond Street. He was prematurely stooped and gray and shortsighted, seeming still to carry the scents of paper and ink. But he was not meek, despite his mildness, and was never late in collecting the rents arranged by his ancestors with the ancestors of his tenants.

"Thank you, Alice." Rowena asked the maid to make tea, and Alice scurried off.

Lifford raised a thin, long-fingered hand. "No need for refreshment. I apologize for stopping by after hours. I did call earlier, but you were out."

"I've been out a great deal lately," Rowena explained. "Business has been good."

"I'm glad to hear it. I would very much like for you to keep this address."

"As would I." Rowena took a breath, plunged in. "Mr. Lifford, I have been thinking of how that might be possible. I cannot pay you in one lump sum, but I would be happy to pay you quarterly. Or even weekly, at three guineas per week. That would equal one hundred fifty-six guineas per annum."

He shook his head. "I'm sorry, Miss Fairweather, that won't do. I've been offered three guineas and a shilling per week for the space. If you can match that, very well. If you can pay me one hundred fifty per annum in a lump sum, now, that saves me the trouble of collecting each week."

Her heart plummeted. "I see."

Only an extra shilling each week, but what a difference it would make. A shilling a week represented any number of small luxuries: sweets and a library subscription and clean-burning beeswax candles for the workroom.

Could she afford it, those three guineas and that extra shilling, without cutting her lifestyle to the bone? If she did nothing but tune pianofortes...maybe. Yes, maybe she could. But then she wouldn't be a luthier anymore. She wouldn't repair instruments, and she'd certainly never build anything of her own.

She tried again. "Could I let only the ground and first floors? Would you be amenable to splitting the property?"

Lifford frowned. "No, I've no desire to run a rooming house, no matter how trustworthy the tenants. I'm afraid this building rents as a single unit. Besides, if I agreed, you'd still need a kitchen, and anyone in the attics would have to walk up through your shop.

"So," he concluded, "it has to be all or none."

All or none. All or nothing. Success or failure.

Save the shop. Run it as I've taught you, and all will be well. I'm relying on you. We all are.

Her father had entrusted her with his legacy. Surely he hadn't realized it would become a millstone.

"I will consider the weekly rate," Rowena said, even as her stomach felt icy and nauseated. Three guineas and a shilling every week; a financial burden every seven days. "Thank you."

"You've till the end of the month, but no longer. That's a week from now. At that time, I will either need payment or for Fairweather's to vacate this address. It's very desirable, and I'll have no trouble leasing it."

Yes, Rowena knew. She knew all that.

By the time Alice returned with a tea tray, Lifford had bid Rowena good night and let himself out. "Bring a tankard," Rowena told the maid. "And the brandy."

Idly, she wandered back into the workshop. She stroked the satin-smooth ebony fingerboard, the sharp-edged, intricately carved bridge. What if this was the last violoncello she repaired? What if her days never again held the surprise of what—of who—came through the door next? If she owed more than three guineas a week for the address alone, she'd have to accept the highest-paying jobs, not the most interesting ones. Pianofortes, one after another, forever.

Would that truly be saving Fairweather's? Would that be what her father had wanted—or what she did?

She was glad when Alice returned with a pair of pottery tankards and a bottle of brandy. Nanny took a medicinal nip every night, but Rowena rarely touched it. Tonight, though, why not? She splashed a little brandy into each tankard, then topped them with tea and added sugar. Handing one to the surprised Alice, she clinked their tankards together.

"To Fairweather's," she said, "whatever that means."

"Yes, miss," Alice said dutifully.

"You don't have to drink that if you don't want it." Rowena stared into the depths of her beverage, then took a sip. "It's good, though."

Alice curled protective fingers around the tankard. "I want it well enough, miss. I'll take it to my room. If that's all?"

May days were long, and sunset hadn't yet pulled all the blue from the sky. But morning came early, especially for a maid-of-all-work. "Of course, Alice. Thank you."

Once Alice bobbed a good-night and left Rowena alone, she sipped idly at her brandy-laced tea for a few minutes. Too tired to work, too busy to permit herself to sleep. It was an awkward in-between. Perhaps she'd try reading some of *The Necromancer* to weary her brain—but no, not even a book appealed right now.

The bell over the front door jingled a greeting. "Hullo, I didn't think it'd be unlocked," said a familiar voice.

Simon's voice. The only distraction she'd truly welcome at the moment.

"Simon?" Rowena thumped her tankard onto the worktable, then hurried into the front room. "Sorry, I must have forgot to lock the door when Mr. Lifford left. Stupid of me."

"I wouldn't put it that strongly, but I do want you to be safe." He smiled at her. "Hope I didn't give you a fright."

"No, it's quite all right. Why have you come?" Was that impolite? She didn't really care right now.

"Because I like seeing you."

She rolled her eyes. "You like everyone." No matter who came to the shop—whether a duke's footman or the merchant father of a daughter in need of town polish—Simon spoke to them as if they were equals, as if he'd never wanted to do anything else.

"I'm interested in almost everyone," Simon replied. "But I don't like everyone in the same way, or to the same degree."

She didn't want explanations. She wanted...what the devil did she want? Sympathy? Solutions? Oblivion?

All of it. None of it. "It's not a good time, Simon."

Concern softened his features. "Something has happened. Is it to do with the lease? Do you want to tell me about it?"

Did she? She supposed she did. It was good to tell someone who cared, who wasn't relying on her for their daily bread as Nanny and Alice were.

More than that: She truly did think of him as a partner. Someone she could rely on herself.

"Come to the back," she decided, locking the front door. "I'll tell you all of it."

So he followed her into the workroom, picking up the wandering Cotton and stroking the spiny-backed animal as Rowena explained Lifford's terms. After weeks of notice, she still couldn't quite believe the figure she had to meet.

She'd been prepared for another of the incremental increases built into the original lease. From a hundred pounds per annum to a hundred ten, perhaps. Or a hundred guineas, twenty-one shillings each instead of the nice common twenty per pound. A hundred fifty guineas? Extortionate!

But it wasn't, really. Here on Bond Street, she was surrounded by nobles, patronized by nobles, kept in business by nobles. So, properties commanded a noble rent.

"There it is," she concluded, "and the weekly rate is even higher. I have to look carefully at my accounts to sort out whether I can pay it. I can't lose the shop."

Simon crouched, setting Cotton on the floor. "Because your father told you not to?"

"My father, and generations before him, and...and what would I do? What else is there for a Fairweather?"

He gave the hedgehog a little nudge, setting the animal into snout-wiggling motion. "Anything you'd like there to be."

"Easily said for an able-bodied man with a nice accent. No. I'll have to think of some way to make this work."

Work, work, work. She picked up the fingerboard she'd been sanding earlier, then returned it to its spot. Was it finished? She wanted it to be. She wanted only to be done with it, to remove it from the list of things she needed to do. Poor violoncello; it deserved better.

At her side, Simon stood again. "Do you ever do something just because you want to?"

Oh yes, and that violin needed a new sound post. She looked over her racks of wood, built in and carefully sorted, to find a piece she could sand to fit. Spruce would be best. "I want to save this business. So yes, everything I do is because I want to."

"That's not what I mean. I'm asking if you ever do anything only for the joy of it."

"Read *How to Ruin a Duke*?" She laid hands on a spruce dowel. "Kiss you again, perhaps? I'd also rather like to go to Venice. Do you own a ship?"

"I don't," he said. "And I don't think kissing you again is exactly what you want right now either."

"I suppose not. Light that lamp, will you? I'll place this sound post. That'll make tomorrow's list of tasks shorter."

He lit the oil lamp she'd indicated, sliding it close to her side. Before she asked, he handed her a short, sharp knife and a pair of tweezers. "For cutting and placing the post."

Impressed, she said, "You've been paying attention."

"I have been." He puttered around the room idly while Rowena took measurements. "Look here. Can I tell you a story?"

"A *How to Ruin a Duke* kind of story? Or a story about you?"

"Both. It's about me, but it's got some ruin in it too. I just thought...I don't know. You seem troubled, and I thought it might help you to hear it. It's got problems you don't have to solve, just like in Gothic novels."

She wanted to look up, to look him deep in the eye, but instinct kept her head down and eyes on her work. If she watched him, he might go silent. "Of course I want to hear it."

So he told her, as he paced the room—watching where he placed his feet, she noted, to avoid Cotton—of his birth to a vicar and his wife in a village near Wolverhampton. When illness swept through the village, fourteen-year-old Simon had been orphaned.

Rowena cut the spruce dowel to length, wishing she could take his hand. "I'm so sorry. Losing a parent is terrible, and losing both abruptly must have been more so."

"It was a long time ago," he said, setting the subject aside. "A tinsmith in the village agreed to take me on as an apprentice. It was a kindness—Glennon Lines was a fair and kind master—and he said I could work off the apprenticeship fee by completing extra tasks. Sometimes I worked as a groom and sometimes as a maid, and Lines kept careful account."

Rowena had just picked up the dowel in her tweezers, and she bobbled it. "You were an indentured servant!"

"So are all apprentices," Simon replied. "And I learned many skills working for him. How to handle horses, how to talk to customers, how to clean virtually anything. But not..." He drew in a ragged breath. "Not enough about metalworking."

Rowena ignored the fallen dowel, ignored everything else, as Simon spoke on. About the older apprentice, Elias Howard, who treated Simon as a brother would. About the accident with boiling ore that Simon had caused.

"I don't quite know what happened," he said quietly. The lamp's light flickered over his face, limning every groove of sorrow. "All the times I've thought of it over the years, but memory shifts and changes. All I know for certain is the result: Howard was horribly burned on his right hand and arm."

"Your friend," Rowena said softly. "Your friend whom you try to help. You mentioned him the day we met."

"I didn't help him at the time," Simon said bitterly. "Once the surgeon had been called, I ran. I was fifteen years old then, and I ran and left my friend, and for thirteen years I've wondered what I could have done or should have done differently. He was only nineteen, and he lost the use of his right hand. His chance to become a master tinworker. He was courting a woman, and he wed her, but he's had lifelong health troubles."

Rowena splayed her fingers before her. Looked at her hands, her livelihood, and wondered what it would be like to lose the use of one completely. "Oh," was all she could think of to say. Any other words were closed off, her throat tight and heart hurting for the young man who had lost so much and the younger boy who blamed himself.

"So." Simon neatened the tools that didn't need neatening, probably to keep his back to Rowena. "Now you know. I think the world of your shop, and I wish I could help you. I'll do my best, and I won't give up. I can't, because Howard needs money. But I never stay anywhere for long because I hurt people."

He was repeating the cycle, she realized: part of an apprenticeship, and then he ran. Onward, across England, darting from town to town and skill to skill until at last he'd made his way to London. Here a man could get lost, could hide from anyone. Except himself.

"Why do you have to leave," Rowena asked, "just because you always have before? You could find a good place here in London. Surely your friend would be best served by you keeping a steady position with a good income."

Simon scoffed. "I had one—two, actually—and lost them."

"Playing the horn, you mean? Yes, but now you're here."

"Ah, but you can't afford to hire me. You told me so the day we met."

"I can't put a price on you," she blurted, and he turned to look at her at last.

"Now who's the incorrigible flirt?" He smiled. "Sweet of you to say so, but we both know my work here was a move born of desperation."

"Was, or is?"

"Was."

Your desperation, or mine? She did not know which of them had needed the other more.

Instead, she asked, "And what is it now?"

He caught his breath. In the sunset-warm light, the dim of the lamp, his eyelashes made touchable shadows on his cheekbones. "Now it's a dream."

Her heart went out to him, to the bleakness on his face. He could not carry such guilt if he had not cared deeply for his friend. "You cannot forgive yourself, can you?"

"Why should I when the harm I caused still exists?"

She understood this feeling, and her heart hurt. She realized how tender it had become for him, so that his pain could pierce it. She wanted to take him in her arms, and she wanted above all to ease the pain within him.

She took his hand, savoring its warmth and strength. "What good is guilt? Does it honor your friend if you feel guilty? If you don't allow yourself to make more friends? If you never settle?"

"No, of course not. Guilt doesn't honor him. I don't know how to honor him." Simon's fingers clung to hers, tightly intertwined. "I do the best I can. I send him money. I know it's not enough."

"What you do is enough for me." Rowena laid a gentle hand on his face, stroking the stubbly roughness and the hard line of his jaw. "It *is*. Thank you for trusting me with your story."

"You've told me yours." He sighed, shutting his eyes. "I wanted you to know mine. I wanted you to know what sort of fellow I am."

"I already knew." Her other hand, she laid over his heart. The quiet thunder of his heartbeat was unbearably intimate, his life beneath her palm. All they had to give was time, the precious gift they traded for coin. To help others. To support the life they wanted. To pay for the burdens they'd taken on.

But they had given time to each other for the sheer sweetness of it, too, for a touch and a kiss and a conversation of bitter, pure truths. Such time was precious, and Rowena could not allow it to end. Not yet.

"Simon." She brushed a kiss to his cheek. "Come upstairs with me. Let's do something for the joy of it."

CHAPTER SIX

"When he loved, and he never really loved but one, it was with so violent, so blind a passion, that he might be said to doat upon the very errors of the girl to whom he was thus attached."
From *Glenarvon* by Lady Caroline Lamb

He was in Rowena Fairweather's bedchamber, and it was more beautiful than the fireworks at Vauxhall. Her laugh, as she clasped his hand and shut the door behind them, was more tuneful than the sweetest arpeggio.

Simon could hardly dare breathe. "What do you want?"

He'd almost asked, *What do you want of me?* But that seemed too forward. He wouldn't beg to be essential to her—but if he gave her what she wished, maybe she would find him so.

"You," she said. "Kisses. You. In my bed." Her light eyes were frank and merry. "All of you, and right now, please."

The room was small, the bedstead generously sized and dominating the space. It was of sturdy wood and light curtains and a counterpane so invitingly velvety that he wanted to tug her down and roll all over it.

He did just that. "Have it all, then." Taking her hands, he flopped back onto the bed and yanked her atop him. She laughed, squealing about their boots marking the counterpane, so he drew her into a kiss until she quite forgot what she was saying.

When he broke the kiss for air, he felt glassy and buoyant. And then he cursed the boots and every layer of clothing that separated them. "Do you really want your boots off?" he asked.

"Eventually." Rowena moved atop him, driving him to distraction. "But at the moment, that is *not* my priority. I want your hands on me."

He grinned. "Any specific place?"

She placed his hands on her breasts. "This will do, for a start."

"Indeed it will." Through her gown and stays, he could feel the warm weight of her. She was the perfect shape, because it was *her* shape, and he thumbed her nipples until they grew hard and she gasped. It was nothing like touching her bare skin, though, and he coaxed her down so he could unfasten the back of her bodice and loosen the fabric between them. As he did, she remained straddling him, rocking her hips in a rhythm that drove him absolutely wild.

"The start is going to be the finish if you don't take pity on a poor celibate," he groaned.

She looked surprised. "I'm not a virgin. Are you?"

"No, but it's been some time." As he'd made his wandering way toward London over the years, there had been other women. But at this moment, he had no idea why.

Then he was jealous of the man who'd been Rowena's first. "Who else have you...no, never mind. It's not my business." His better nature came forth. He didn't want to know anything about the man or men she'd chosen in the past. That was done, and Simon was the one she had chosen today.

She didn't seem to mind the cutoff question, though. She shrugged, allowing her bodice to slip lower. "I gave myself to someone I thought loved me. I was wrong."

"He was a fool."

"You're sweet to say so. But I was the fool, not he."

With the same nimbleness with which she brought violin strings into tune, she unbuttoned Simon's waistcoat. When she tugged his shirt from his trousers, he almost forgot how to think.

Almost.

I gave myself to someone I thought loved me.

Rowena had invited Simon to her bed; she would give herself to him. Did this mean she thought he loved her? *Did* he love her? Did she love him?

Did it matter, if they were here now and both wanted this pleasure?

Yes, it mattered, he thought dimly as reason began to surrender to desire. It mattered very much. And if he'd known what love was—if he, an orphan, had known any love besides the old friendship that came with years of thwarted guilt—he would know in a flash how to respond.

Instead, he knew only that any man who'd given up the chance to be with Rowena Fairweather in any way was a fool, and the man who'd been in her bed and left it was the greatest fool of all.

But she hadn't asked a question about Simon's feelings, and when he kissed her, drawing deep of her taste of tea and sweetness, she didn't speak again. Not of who she'd been with, or what she had wanted from him. Not of anything at all besides "There" and "Again" and "Yes, more."

Simon played her slowly, tugging free her boots and peeling away her layers of clothing. Each layer gone revealed new places to kiss. Skin to stroke. Curves to admire. Blessings to count.

"You're teasing me," Rowena chided, rising up over him lovely and bare. "All that touching and stripping, and there you are fully clothed."

"Tease me back, then," Simon offered hopefully.

And she did, wearing a sly grin and nothing else as she tugged free his cravat, slipped his coat from his shoulders, wrenched his boots from his feet. She wasn't quick about the matter. Simon couldn't stop trying to touch her as she stripped him. He breathed the scent of her hair, kissing her neck or shoulders or chin or whatever he could reach. He was nearly drunk on her, nearly frantic, before she finished removing his clothing.

"Now we're even." She lay back on the bed, reaching up for him. In the moonlight, he could count every freckle on her nose. He could touch them all, kiss them all.

"We're not even until—" He bit off the words. *You're mine*, he'd been about to say. Because he was hers?

Oh damn. He was hers, all right. He was decidedly hers, and he had no idea whether she wanted him to belong to her or not. Not beyond this night.

"Until I bring you joy," he ground out as she drew him close and he seated himself within her.

They paused, gasping, then moved together, musicians in harmony. Each stroke of his body in hers plucked strings of pleasure deep within him. When she came with a cry, it was like the music of chimes. When he withdrew to spend outside of her cradling warmth, joy shot through him like the crash of cymbals.

Encore, he thought. *A million times. Forever.*

For a long, slow moment, they were silent beside each other. Through the window, a fat crescent moon smiled upon them.

Still breathing hard, he asked lightly, "Was it as good as a Gothic novel? Lightning-struck towers and skeletons and all that?"

Rowena took his hand in both of hers. "It was far better. I enjoyed your lightning-struck tower"—Simon choked—"but there was also a happy ending."

"I had no idea you were so able with erotic puns."

"I've had no idea about many things," she replied softly and nestled her head on his chest. He held her in the bed, eyes wide in the night-dark room as if that would help him see stars.

She had asked him to lie with her, which meant she thought he was worthy. Of her time, of her body, of a place in her bed. She gave him the right to kiss her lips, to touch her body, and he could not recall ever receiving such a gift.

Then Rowena stirred beside him, all warm tangled limbs, and sang softly.

"A brisk young man, diddle diddle
Met with a maid,
And laid her down, diddle diddle
Under the shade.
There they did play, diddle diddle
And kiss and court.
All the fine day, diddle diddle
Making good sport."

Simon laughed, tweaking her earlobe. "Our special song, 'Lavender's Blue.' Are those really the words? How scandalous."

"Yes, those are really the words. That's why I had to stop singing it to you the day we met."

"You were too shy?"

"Not at all. I thought *you* might be," she teased, and he couldn't let *that* stand, of course. He had to tickle her, to take her in his arms and kiss her up and down her neck until she squirmed free, laughing.

"Have you played your horn since that day?" she asked.

He hadn't. He hadn't even opened its case. He'd shoved it under the bed of his rented room, a room that cost four shillings a week, with extra for meals. He was living on savings, telling himself he was working at Fairweather's for Howard, to earn money for Howard.

But really, he was here for himself. After years of work, he was playing: changing the shop window, flirting with Rowena, taming the hedgehog. He was playacting at a life that didn't belong to him.

I want it, he thought. *I want her.* "Sing some more," he said, dodging her question. "Please."

Rowena obliged.

"Therefore be kind, diddle diddle
While here we lie,
And you will love, diddle diddle

My hedgehog and I."

Simon looked at her with skepticism. "Are *those* really the words?"

She blinked, all innocence. "They might as well be."

Love again. It belonged here in this room. It belonged with her, to her; it was a part of her. Simon felt like an outsider, with nothing but a child's memory of love. He wanted to be worthy of more, but he didn't know how.

But he could be kind. He could hold her, lie there with her to keep her warm. To bring her, he hoped, the joy she'd asked for.

Now that he'd met her, it seemed he was ruined for a life without music or joy. And both lay beside him, for as long as he dared grasp them.

WHEN ROWENA AWOKE in the morning, Simon was gone, but signs of him remained. The air in her room held his scent, a whisper of soap and bergamot. The mattress and pillow retained, faintly, the shape of his form.

And then there was her memory, which held every second of their conversation, their lovemaking, their embraces, their laughter.

He'd made her feel beautiful. Capable. Successful. What a gift it was, to know that she had only to grasp and what she wanted could be hers.

What a gift he'd given her, to draw pleasure from a body that had sometimes brought her annoyance and shame. To find joy in the way she was built, in the Rowena-ness of her.

Whatever he'd done in the past, whoever he'd been, he was a good man now, doing good things.

She bit her lip. He was an honest man, too, and he had always told her he was planning to move along. She mustn't try to keep him, no matter how good it felt to have him at her side.

Oh hell. She was falling in love with him, wasn't she? Perhaps she had even completed the process.

She would have to pretend she hadn't. That she'd involved only her body, not her heart, because Simon was clearly the property of his own past. A large part of him had never left the village in which he'd been apprenticed, and that same part had never moved beyond the day his friend had been injured.

Well. After all the help Simon had given her, she could help him in return. Sliding bare from her bed, she retrieved her lap desk and tied a robe about her. Settling into the indentation Simon had left in her mattress, she assembled paper, ink, quill, thoughts.

And then she inscribed a brief letter to the Howard family in... what was the name of the village? Something near Wolverhampton, with a flowery sort of name. Market Thistleton, that was it. She kept her letter short, knowing they'd have to pay to receive it. She said only that she represented Simon Thorn, that he missed them and would like to make contact again.

Had he told her that? No. But it was true nonetheless. A man didn't always have to use words to say what he meant. Especially not a man with eyes like Simon's, which had told her the first time they met that he liked to look at her.

That he liked her. Full stop.

She was tumbling beyond *like* to a place she hadn't intended to be, a place where she didn't want to be without him. A place where she wanted to heal his heart so that he could give it to her.

Once dressed for the day, she sealed the letter and placed it with other post, then tried not to think of it anymore. It was easy enough to distract herself with work, plunging into the accumulated tasks of the week. Tuning pianofortes, repairing violins, poring over her account books to calculate where margins could be increased and where pennies could be pinched. Counting her coins, studying her bank books.

This was dull work, though worthwhile. If she did more of it, she just might be able to afford the new lease. Three guineas and a shilling...if Lifford would accept the offered rate, she could match it.

She could save the shop. She could *do* this.

She could succeed. She would keep the address the *ton* had visited for a century. She'd keep her workroom, built specifically for luthiery, and the shop window that so recently had taken on its own personality.

It was a relief, sort of. She had expected to feel more relief. But as she whipped in and out of the workroom, to and from tuning pianofortes, untouched violins sprawled reproachfully on the work-table. The violoncello without its fingerboard looked like a strangled maiden, its poor neck askew. Simon had teased her once that she talked of instruments as if they were alive. She knew they were nothing but wood and varnish and string, of course, but she still felt in danger of failing them.

But she wouldn't. Numbers didn't lie. She wouldn't fail.

So passed the remaining days of May. Simon changed the shop window every day, lettering a new card each time. Rowena rebuilt the violin on display a bit at a time. When customers called with bookings, Rowena or Simon accepted the most lucrative jobs. For the first time in Rowena's memory, she turned aside work.

It was good to be busy. Right? It ought to have made everything easier, feeling as if she wasn't alone. She had only to repair and tune, and Simon managed the rest.

But it wasn't easier, because he wouldn't stay. He referred to his plans more than once. "Before I go..." or "After I leave..." So lightly, he spoke these words, as if they weren't weapons that slashed her heart.

So be it. She wouldn't ask him to stay, lest he say yes without wanting to. Each day, the coin mounted up, twenty pounds of it to be his—and then he'd be off again.

She tuned her pianofortes; she did not take him to bed again. He watched her narrowly, probably wanting her to ask, but she couldn't. She just couldn't.

Do you ever do something just because you want to?

It was a question of privilege, coming from someone who was sure of always taking more than he left behind.

She wouldn't give up—she'd learned that much from him. She wouldn't give up her body without attaching her heart to it. She was a parcel all wrapped in gut strings, all out of tune and craving his touch. And when he left, after he left, she'd be hopelessly jangled.

As it was, she was fine. Everything was fine.

On the last day of the month—a fine Monday, perfect for a new start—Lifford called at the shop.

Rowena made herself smile as she greeted the landlord. "I am ready to sign a new lease. Shall it be for another ninety-nine years, or something more moderate?"

Lifford did not smile back. "I'm afraid that's not possible, Miss Fairweather."

The sturdy wooden floors beneath Rowena's feet seemed to wobble. "I am of age and single, with no man in charge of my affairs. It's possible."

Lifford's mournful clerk's face looked regretful. "I've come to let you know that I've just been offered four guineas a week for this building. I can't turn it down."

"Four guineas..." She felt as if she'd been punched in the gut. "Who can afford such a rate?"

"Bond Street is more expensive each year. All of London wants to shop here, so all of London's merchants want to keep shop here."

"Yes, I know," she said faintly. "I've always thought it the perfect address."

"Yours is one of the finest buildings on the street. I've had interest for years, and I've put off the potential tenants while your lease held. But now..." Lifford trailed off, then asked, "I don't suppose you could match the offer?"

Four guineas? She would have laughed if she'd had air enough. "I could barely manage three guineas and a shilling," she choked.

Lifford nodded. "I thought that might be the case. I can give you a few days to vacate the premises, but I will need you out of the building by the end of the week." His expression was not unkind as he added, "I'm sorry for it, Miss Fairweather. But it's business."

It was indeed, as was her shop. And businesses rose and fell based on demand. One's skill. One's courage.

This shop was never intended to be run alone. It was a family establishment, and it was all Rowena had left of her family. For a century and more, people had come to this address to make their lives more musical. Now she would lose it. The address Simon had promoted. The building they'd carefully dressed to draw every eye.

It wasn't only business to her; it was her home. The only one she'd ever known. It was a refuge for an old woman who could scarcely move from her parlor. It was a haven for the beetles that kept a hedgehog plump and content. It was perfectly arranged, from the compartments built into the workroom to hold every type of wood to the racks for holding her tools.

And it wasn't hers anymore; it was all out of her grasp.

This was the end of Fairweather's.

CHAPTER SEVEN

"There is no more fatal symptom than when an open communicative disposition grows reserved."
From *Glenarvon* by Lady Caroline Lamb

If a man had a bed to sleep in, bread rolls and coffee to breakfast on, and a place he loved to go, he had no right to be in a foul mood. Simon knew this. But on the last day of May, despite counting up those small blessings, he was in a foul mood as he pushed open the door to Fairweather's at midday. When the little bell over the door jingled a greeting, he wanted to snatch it down and stomp on it.

This was the end. Good-bye came today, and it was nobody's fault but his own.

He pushed aside the velvet curtain, drinking the sight of the workroom with thirsty eyes. A perfect space for the work done here. A perfect home for the women who lived here.

"Good afternoon," Simon said to Rowena. She had her back to him when he entered and was counting off pieces of wood by size in the numerous built-in compartments.

"Hullo. One moment." She jotted a number onto a small bit of paper, then stuffed it into her pocket and turned. "Good afternoon to you. I've got a letter for you."

"For me? Is it from Botts?" He couldn't imagine who'd be sending him a message, unless it was one of his musical cronies seeking a booking with Fairweather's.

"No. It's not from Botts." From that same pocket in her gown, Rowena drew a sealed and folded missive. It had evidently come by post rather than being hand-carried by a messenger, for when Rowena placed it in Simon's hand, he had to squint to make out the direction through the post-markings.

And then he realized what it said. Where it was from. *Who* it was from. "It's from Elias Howard's family. How is it from Howard? How did he know... Why is anyone from Market Thistleton writing to me in London?" With nerveless fingers, he dropped the letter to the floor. He wasn't certain whether he wanted to pick it up.

Before he decided, Rowena snatched it up and pressed it into his hand again. Her smile was bright, her tone glassy, as she explained, "I wrote to them for you. I wanted them to know how much you miss Howard and still blame yourself for his—"

"You *what?*" Simon could have tossed the letter into the nearest fire. "I told you all of that in confidence! So you wouldn't feel alone in your worries!"

"Yes, well, I didn't want *you* to feel so alone. So I wrote, and you see that Howard is eager to make contact with you. He must have written back—"

"He can't write. I saw to that," Simon said flatly.

"—using his left hand," Rowena continued as if he hadn't spoken, "or had his wife write back on his behalf, as soon as your letter arrived."

"Your letter. Not mine."

"It comes to the same thing. Behold your reply."

Her smile was fixed and strange, but he couldn't think about that right now. He could only try to make sense of what she was saying, of the letter in his hand after so many years of silence. Silence he wanted, because he feared what Howard might say if given the chance to speak. It was better to fear he'd never be forgiven than to know it for certain.

He ripped the letter in half, cracking the seal and letting the inky page flutter to the floor in two pieces. "I don't want this. If I wanted to write to Howard, I would have done so anytime in the last thirteen years. You had no right to interfere."

Her cheeks flushed; her jaw set. "Interference? Is that what this is? Was it mere interference when you came to my shop and asked to remake my business dealings?"

Deliberately, Simon set his boot atop the fallen letter. "It was. You didn't have to say yes. That was your choice."

She muttered something that sounded like, "Maybe I shouldn't have," shoving wisps of hair back with quick, jerking gestures.

And then the fire seemed to go out of her. "I don't mean that. I'm glad I said yes. I hoped you would be glad about this too. I only wanted to open a door for you."

"I shut it a long time ago, and I want to leave it that way." Didn't he? What he *really* wanted was to erase the past, never to think of it again. But he'd never managed that. He'd never managed to stop missing his friend or regretting the harm he'd caused. Shaking his head, he added, "I'm allowed to feel guilty for something bad I've done."

"Not if it keeps you from living your own life!"

"This is the way I live," he said firmly, struggling for calm. "I've always been honest about that. Just because it's not what you would choose doesn't mean it's wrong."

Simon had always thought of himself as an inquisitive sort of person, one who always wanted to move on and learn something new. He wanted to help, he'd told Rowena once. He wanted to make things better.

Just now, he didn't want to do that. He wanted to block his ears; he wanted to protect himself. He was tired of helping others. He was tired of the burden of guilt and shame that he'd borne for years, all the way across England. It was poison for his heart, and she thought he'd want to read a letter about it. She thought he'd want to take that letter from her hand, a hand that had only ever been outstretched to him in grace and honesty.

She didn't understand. Maybe he hadn't allowed her to, and maybe he couldn't.

"I'm not trying to tell you how to live." Rowena pressed her lips together tightly as she unlocked a strongbox built into a hidden compartment in the workroom. With quick, cutting movements, she counted out bills. "Here." She thrust a handful at him. "Don't tear these in half and stomp on them. Twenty pounds, just as you wanted. You've more than earned it with your shop windows and your persistence."

He stuffed his hands into his coat pockets. "I can't take it from you. You need all your money for the lease." He took a deep breath. "I sold my horn. It'll be enough for now."

"You sold...but why? You won't make music anymore." Her brows drew together, an expression of puzzlement and sorrow.

"I don't need to." In his pocket, he felt the pawn ticket for the horn.

"You mean you don't have the right to pursue your own aims?" Rowena pressed.

He shrugged. It was done. There was no sense in discussing the why.

She slapped the handful of bills against her other palm. "So you'll do all you can to solve my problems, but you won't allow me to try to solve yours. Do you think you're the only one with any competence?"

His head jerked back. "God, no. I think I'm the only one who shouldn't have his problems solved."

"You're very special, then. Too special to allow others to care about you." Rowena looked at the money in her hand, then tossed it back into the strongbox as if she disliked it. Her back to him, she added in a muffled tone, "Or care for you."

Was she crying? He yanked his hands from his pockets and took a step closer to her—but then she rounded on him, and her eyes were dry. "If you won't accept my help, Simon, I don't want any more of yours. If you won't allow me to try to lessen your burdens, then why should I trust you to do the same for me? Is my love worth less than your pain?"

His knees went watery. "You love me?"

She slashed the air impatiently. "I could, if I thought you wanted me to at all."

He didn't know if he wanted that. He knew he hadn't earned it. "I'd stay, if I really thought I could help you."

She sighed, pressing the heels of her hands against her eyes. "If you really wanted to stay, you wouldn't think about obligation at all. You'd only think about me."

"I haven't the right to be that selfish."

Her hands dropped to her sides. Blue eyes, frank and troubled, pinned him. "I'm giving you that right."

He shook his head, taking a step backward. Toward the velvet curtain. Toward escape. "I can't take it. I wouldn't be able to live with myself. You should know that—you, who earns everything yourself."

"Love can't be earned," she said, "only granted freely." But she didn't sound as though she believed it. She sounded as though she had already given up on him.

"I think it can be earned," Simon replied. "As can trust. It can certainly be squandered."

She had trusted him to stay with her; she had deemed him worthy. It had felt like a gift, but just now it felt like a burden.

Was this how she felt about Fairweather's? Trust he'd never asked for, a legacy he'd never wanted. Yet, she did want the legacy to survive.

And he did want her trust. He just couldn't see how he could earn it long-term, any more than she could repair her beloved violins and still meet the terms of her lease. Not without a miracle. For her, the miracle had to come from without. For him, the miracle had to be much greater—it had to come from within.

"I have to go," he said through a throat tight with unspoken words. He shoved past the curtain, stumbled through the foyer, and slapped open the shop door, gritting his teeth against the cheerful parting jingle of the bell.

Hardly noticing the swirl of London crowds around him, he made his way back to his lodging house. It was a clean but plain building, devoid of personality and tradition. It was a place only to lay one's head and lock up a few belongings.

How had he let himself become satisfied with this?

Easing himself onto the bed, he looked around the rented room. There were no books to occupy him, no horn to practice. There was nothing to distract him from his own thoughts. In the past, he might have bought a bottle, gambled a bit on a game of cards, flirted with a barmaid. But now all he wanted was cream cakes. The only sort of card he cared for was the kind he lettered for the shop window. And he'd no desire to flirt with anyone at all.

How long he sat there, he didn't know. A knock at his chamber's door roused him at last. When he opened it with more force than grace, he was greeted by the familiar red-haired maid from Fairweather's.

"Alice?" Simon blinked at her, puzzled. "What are you doing here? Did you bring a message?"

"Of a sort." Fool that he was, he hadn't noticed she was holding anything until she thrust a massive paper-wrapped package at him. Without another word, she curtseyed and turned on her heel, strolling away.

Mystified, Simon shut the door and placed the parcel on his bed. As soon as he untied the twine, he realized what was inside.

His horn case. Popping open the latches, he saw the brass instrument—shining and intact as if it had never left his possession.

Somehow, Rowena had redeemed it. How had she known where he'd sold it? He patted his coat pockets. No pawn ticket. It must have fluttered from his pocket in her workroom.

He lifted the bell, wondering at the heft of the cold metal. He hadn't thought the instrument would be his again. He hadn't thought he'd mind if it wasn't, but here he was choking on emotion like a child given a beloved toy.

What was this? Papers, rolled up and tucked into the bell of the horn. Simon tugged them free, heart thumping wildly.

Here was the letter he'd torn in half and discarded. And here was a note from Rowena.

All right, he'd read the damned letter from Market Thistleton. He spread the pieces out flat, lining up the torn edges.

It was brief, and he was surprised to be disappointed by that. A few courtesies of greeting, a willingness to communicate with Mr. Thorn "in any way he sees fit." It was signed simply "Howard."

Had Elias Howard himself written this? Signed this? What was the feeling behind the tidy script? Was there any feeling at all?

Carefully, Simon refolded the pieces and tucked them into the pocket of the case where he sometimes carried sheet music. Then he opened the message from Rowena. It was even shorter than the letter, a mere four words.

Go make it right.

Maybe she had understood, after all. This was a good-bye, but it was also a farewell. *Fare well. Have music. Be forgiven.*

He would never deserve someone like Rowena—no, correction, he'd never *think* he deserved someone like Rowena—and would never be able to enjoy life without doubt and guilt, unless he went to Howard. Put the money in his hand, saw the operation completed, and apologized. Begged for forgiveness.

Could he do it? After all this time?

Until he bought a ticket to Market Thistleton, he hadn't been sure he really intended to go. Before the coach departed, he had just enough time to pack a satchel and buy a copy of *How to Ruin a Duke*. Something to read along the way. A distraction from the everyday, as Rowena had described it.

And he was off, away from London. Traveling northwest to Staffordshire like a bird flying home after a long winter. Unlike a bird, free and fresh, he'd spend the four-day journey in a cramped carriage full of odoriferous strangers. The thought was distracting enough that he'd wedged himself into his seat, the horses clopping off for the journey's beginning, before he realized he had neglected to ask Rowena about the final terms of the lease. What would the fate of Fairweather's be?

He could guess: She wouldn't give up. She'd keep the building, the business, the name. She would manage it all. Hadn't she offered him everything he'd asked, to see him packing? She'd made it possible for him to leave, just as he'd always told her he wanted to.

He ought to be happy about that. He was on his own, unfettered and free to try whatever he wanted. He could be anything.

But for a little while, he'd been a part of something valuable. He'd been Rowena's, and how grand it had been.

AFTER DISPATCHING Alice with the pawnbroker's ticket, papers to tuck in the horn, and a banknote, Rowena made her way upstairs to the parlor. As she'd expected, Nanny was ensconced on her favorite seat.

"Last day of May." Nanny peered over her spectacles. "How do we stand?"

Probably she referred to the lease, but a different matter was foremost on Rowena's mind. "Simon has left."

"Ah." Nanny sank against the back of her seat. "That's a shame, that."

"He was always preparing me for it. He promised that he would." Rowena swallowed, her throat tight. "He kept every promise he made to me. That one was no different."

"It's all right with you, then?"

"Of course it's not all right. I wanted him to stay. Forever." Boneless, Rowena sank to the floor at Nanny's feet. They had sat this way on many evenings throughout Rowena's childhood, as one read to the other, or as they talked about matters light or difficult. It seemed impossible that Rowena would not always be able to sit before this chair, pick at the threads of this carpet, confide in Nanny.

Just as Nanny had on hundreds of occasions before, she ran a gnarled hand over Rowena's hair. Stroking the thick locks, a soothing gesture. "You love him. Does he know?"

"He does. Nearly. I...admitted as much, then tried to take it back." How embarrassing, to share one's heart and have it not matter in the slightest. "I can't make him stay. I don't want to be an obligation to him."

A lease of ninety-nine years in human form. A building too large, too costly to manage. From the first, Simon's presence in her life had been tied to the fate of Fairweather's. She had hoped to keep them both.

"We've lost the lease," Rowena admitted, closing her eyes as Nanny continued stroking her hair. "Lifford was offered four guineas a week. There is no way I can match that."

"Ah," said Nanny again. "So the temptation was removed, then."

"Temptation?" She lifted her head, looking up at Nanny curiously.

"Yes. Temptation." The comfortable old face smiled. "The temptation to invest in something when its time was past. The temptation to give too much of yourself to something you don't love."

"To Fairweather's," Rowena realized. "As it is now." She hadn't thought of it as a temptation, but as a burden. Perhaps those were two sides of the same coin—a coin no one wanted to receive, as it represented unbearable obligation.

Nanny nodded. "How long have we before we need to leave?"

"A few days. Lifford said he'd give us until week's end."

"Not long," mused the old woman. "But not impossible to work around. What will you do?"

Rowena looked around at the familiar parlor, with its worn furniture and scattered family portraits. She thought of the workspace—its grand table, its racks of wood, its tidy tools. The smells she'd known all her life—the sweet cut wood and the oils for her tools and lamps. She'd never lived anywhere else. She'd never wanted any other life.

In a few days, all of it would be gone.

Her father would have hated this, grieved this. He had wanted her to persist, for Fairweather's to survive just as he'd known it. But she was the last Fairweather, and she was alone, and she couldn't manage anymore as she had when there were two of them.

But just because all would be gone didn't mean all was lost. Now that change was forced upon her…it was fine. In a way, she was relieved.

"I have an idea," she told Nanny. "Even though I'm on my own, I think it will be all right."

"That's my girl." Nanny smiled, resting a hand on Rowena's head. "And you're not on your own, you know. You have me and Alice and your friend Edith. And a sometime cook."

"And Cotton," said Rowena. "Five women and a hedgehog. How are we not ruling the world already?"

She laughed, because the alternative was crying.

In truth, there were blessings on the reverse of most misfortunes. If Rowena had not been born with a little hand, Nanny might not have fought so fiercely for her to learn the family trade.

If Edith had never been left to her own devices, she'd never have come to work for the Duchess of Emory as a companion—and Rowena would never have met the truest friend she'd ever possessed.

If Simon Thorn had not been blackballed as a horn player, he would never have returned to Fairweather's.

And if Lifford had never raised the rent beyond Rowena's ability to pay, she would never have attempted to live a life other than the one laid out for her ninety-nine years ago.

Simon had been wrong, after all. Sometimes giving up was the right thing to do. Sometimes trying a different approach wasn't the answer; walking away was.

Because sometimes an ending gave way to the beginning of something even better.

CHAPTER EIGHT

"It is a duke's privilege always to be in the right! While you or I,
gentle reader, cannot navigate the cataclysmic currents of life
without often pleading for pardon."
From *How to Ruin a Duke* by Anonymous

After four long, jolting, weary days, Simon descended from the coach
on a street that seemed hardly to have changed in thirteen years.
There was the grocery, there the butcher, there the dressmaker and
milliner. And the church at the far end of the main street, its steeple
freshly painted white.

Simon had spent his early years in the small vicarage behind the
church, the only child of his parents. They were buried in the
churchyard, and he strode in that direction to pay his respects.

Was he postponing his visit to the tinsmith's workshop, or to
Howard's house? Probably. But he also owed his respects to Father
McCrone, the widower who now served Market Thistleton as vicar
and who had been Simon's only correspondent in the village for
years. To Father McCrone, he sent money for Howard. From the
vicar, he received bits of news.

He was pleased, as he pushed open the gate to the churchyard, to see the vicar there. The churchyard was peaceful and green, with headstones both new and worn with age. Flowers adorned many graves, while ancient trees shaded the space, leaves whispering comfort in a slight breeze.

McCrone was clipping at a vining plant and didn't notice Simon until he'd drawn near. The old man, still hale and strong, squinted at Simon from beneath an unruly thatch of white hair. "Help you?"

"You already have," Simon replied. "I'm Simon Thorn, Father."

"Simon Thorn." The vicar dropped his clippers. "In the flesh. Well, now. This is a surprise."

"It surprises me too. But it was time."

"Past time, I think." Stern gray eyes regarded him for a long moment, then McCrone clapped Simon on the back. "Yes, past time. Sorry I didn't recognize you, but then, you've changed a fair bit since you were last here."

"You haven't."

"I know, I know. I've looked old my whole life. Now my years have caught up to my looks." With a grace that belied his statement, the vicar stooped to retrieve his clippers, then trimmed off another leaf with a flourish. "Come to visit your parents?"

"And a few of the living." Simon took a deep breath. "Father, can you grant me absolution before I call on the Howard family?"

McCrone examined a rogue bit of vine, then clipped it off. "You've always had it for the wanting of it. Is your heart finally ready?"

"I think it is. It might be." Simon told McCrone about the letter from Howard. He left out Rowena's role, though the merry twinkle in the old man's eyes showed he suspected there was more to the story.

"I heard about that," said the vicar. "I hear about everything, and Howard doesn't get a lot of mail from London."

"Did he write the reply himself?"

"He did indeed." McCrone pushed at the clippings with his foot, making a neat pile of them. "Going to see him next? At this hour, you might find him at the workshop."

Simon blanched. "The...tinsmith's workshop?"

"Well do you know it." McCrone eyed Simon narrowly. "Will you permit yourself that absolution or not?"

Hell. Simon had never wanted to return to the tinsmith to whom he'd been apprenticed. He didn't want to see Howard there, struggling with tasks that had once been simple for him. He didn't want to be faced with the contrast between what was and what had been.

But he hadn't come all the way to Market Thistleton only to turn back. "I'll try," he told the vicar.

McCrone didn't look entirely pleased by this, but he didn't press the matter. "Your parents' roses are blooming well," was all he said. Gathering up the clippings, he bade Simon a good day and left the churchyard.

Alone amongst the sun-dappled graves, Simon made his quiet way to his parents' plots. They had both died of a fever, separated by only a day, and they rested now beneath the same stone. Behind it, a sturdy rosebush leafed and bloomed.

"It's still here." Simon set down his satchel, reached out a forefinger, touched a ruffled red-pink flower. He had planted the bush when it, and he, were no more than sprouts. "I'm glad it's been with you this whole time. Mum. Dad. I wish I'd been able to be here too. But... I'm not sorry about the way matters turned out."

He wouldn't have made a good vicar, but he'd tried to be a good whatever-else-he-was. He told them about Rowena, about her shop and the letter she sent. Why he was here now.

In the gentle breeze, the roses nodded, listening.

The loss of his parents was so old that it had faded, grown comfortable. He could shrug on the missing of them like a familiar robe, wrapping himself in memory—then lay it aside again fondly when it was time to leave. "I love you," he told them both. "Wish me luck, all right?"

When he left the churchyard to turn toward the shop where he'd once been apprenticed, he felt more peaceful. This was how his life had progressed: the vicarage, the churchyard, the tinsmith's workshop where Glennon Lines had taken in an orphan and tried to make a metalworker of him. Simon had failed at that, but he'd found other successes in his life. It was time for absolution.

From the front, the tinsmith's shop looked like most others: a neat window displaying shining wares and a counter and shelves within to display yet more. At the rear of the store, these items were forged and formed, and it was to this workshop that Simon went.

The metallic odor was strong, as was the blast of heat from a forge as large as a blacksmith's, hot as the maw of hell. Here sheets of tin were formed into cooking vessels and storage containers. Tin was punched into lanterns and tugged into kettle spouts and brushed in a molten layer over iron pots. It was snipped and sheared and soldered and hammered. Tin, tin, tin.

The workshop, with all its organized clutter and myriad tools, reminded him of Rowena's. He'd always admired the skill of those who worked with their hands; it was proof that they had something to offer the world. This was why he'd been so willing to apprentice himself to Lines.

That, and the fact that he'd had nowhere else to go.

At the benches and tables, people worked using everything from massive hammers and anvils down to the most delicate nippers and narrow chisels. One of the workers, a stripling boy, was unfamiliar to Simon and was likely an apprentice. Lines himself, a man bulky from labor, had grown a luxuriant mustache. It, like his hair, was the exact shade of the silvery metal with which he worked.

Lines came forward when he noticed Simon. "Thorn! I heard you might be coming back to see us. Or have you come back to finish your apprenticeship?"

Simon reared back in dismay. "God, no. No. That's not why I'm here."

Lines laughed, scratchy and belly-deep. "And that was always going to be the answer, accident or no. You're not a *things* sort of person, Thorn. You're a *people* sort of person."

Simon frowned. "That's vague."

"Not to the people you work with." Lines looked about his work-shop with satisfaction, then clapped Simon on the back. "Not everyone needs a kettle, Thorn. Sometimes people just need the help of another person."

"I hadn't thought of it that way." He hadn't even come looking for forgiveness and understanding from his former master, but here it was. "I do intend to pay you back the apprenticeship fee," Simon assured the older man. "Once Howard is cared for."

"Hmm." At this last statement, Lines looked skeptical. "Howard is already cared for, but you needn't take my word for it. He'll be back from an errand in a few minutes and you can see for yourself. As for the fee, I let that go when you left. I reported to the justice of the peace that I'd agreed to the ending of the apprenticeship."

Simon blew out a tense breath. "Thank you for that. You had every right to come after me for the remaining years of my service."

"Thorn. Please. I never intended to prosecute you for the accident, which it clearly was. And"—amusement crimped the old stern features—"you weren't that good of an apprentice. If you'd stolen or embezzled from me, I'd have gone after you, but all you left with was the clothes on your back. I couldn't begrudge you that, after all the work you'd done for me."

All Simon could do was thank him again, heartily and heartfelt. There was no time to do more than this before a silhouette filled the doorway.

"Howard!" called Lines. "Here's your visitor."

"Hullo, Thorn," came the voice from the sun-shadowed figure.

Until this moment, Simon wouldn't have thought he remembered the sound of Elias Howard's voice. It was easy to let memory blur with time and distance, so that a former friend and almost-brother became no more than the embodiment of guilt. But when Howard spoke Simon's name, it was as if a stored safe of recollection was unlocked, and the contents that spilled forth almost brought Simon to his knees.

Sandwiches shared during a quick break from work. Howard's comforting hand as Simon, newly orphaned, cried out his grief. A patient, corrective word in the absence of Lines. Taking the top bunk because Simon was restless and might fall out of bed.

"Howard." Simon almost choked on the word, it was so weighty.

"Come out and speak with me," came the familiar voice, and there was no question that Simon would obey.

An old wooden bench stood against the outside of the workshop. Here Howard settled, and Simon sat as far away as possible, settling his satchel beside the bench. Then he let himself stare, his first look at Howard in thirteen years, since the man's fight for survival had been joined by a physician.

He had never been handsome, but he had a good face, kind and pleasant. It had hardened and roughened, but he still looked like himself, thank God. Oh, the hair was thinner, the eyebrows thicker. But mostly the change was to his right arm. In the rolled-up shirt-sleeves that all the tinworkers wore, the scarring was obvious. The hand had a cramped, frozen look, the fingers contracted.

"You're staring at my arm," Howard said.

"Yes." Simon didn't try to deny it. "I hurt you. I need to know how badly."

"You did hurt me. But you can't always tell how badly someone is hurt just by looking at his body."

All right. He'd ask. "How badly are you hurt?"

Howard sighed. "Simon Thorn, you puppy. My hand's in a sad state. It hurts me every day, and I have to see a physician for it, and someday I might have to have it amputated. But I can still work with tin; I've sorted out my own way. And I still became the person I wanted to be." He shot Simon a sideways glance. "I hope you haven't brought more guilt money."

Simon thought of the bills he'd brought along, the money from selling his horn before Rowena bought it back for him. "It's...not guilt money. It's *helping* money." And he had to ask another question. "How have you been able to do what you wanted to?"

"Time, hard work, the love of a good woman. I married Ellie Schofield as soon as I arose from my sickbed. Surely the vicar told you? McCrone's been keeping you informed, hasn't he, when you send him money with your newest address?"

"He has. But I thought..."

"But you thought Ellie couldn't possibly have wanted to marry me still?" Howard's voice went hard. "That there was nothing to love about a man with a damaged arm and hand? That she'd have married me out of pity?"

Simon thought of Rowena. "No. There's as much to love as ever. A person's worth doesn't come from their hands."

In Rowena's case, her hands created beauty, and that gave them a beauty all their own.

He'd thought that any man who had Rowena and left her was a fool, and the man who left her bed was the greatest fool of all. Well, what did that make him? He was four days away from her now, and... and by God, he loved her. He'd been waiting for years to love her. How had he never realized it?

"I'm a fool," Simon murmured.

Howard grunted. "Good of you to realize it," he said, but sounded mollified. "You're not only talking about me, are you?"

"I'm not. But that's the most urgent right now. Howard, I just couldn't believe I hadn't ruined everything. You were like a brother to me, and I wanted you to be well and happy, but..."

"You thought you'd ruined my life. Thorn, you ass." Howard chuckled. "You don't have the power. I suppose I could have let the accident ruin my life, but that would have been my doing, not yours."

"Do you forgive me?" Simon's voice sounded hoarse and slow to his own ears. "I haven't earned it. I could never earn it."

"Forgiveness can't be earned, you sapskull. It's a free gift."

This was what Rowena had said about love, and Simon had not

believed her. He should have. He wished he had, that he'd agreed with her at once.

Howard continued, "Now, a body might be more likely to give it based on how you act. If you'd never shown a bit of remorse, I might have been far angrier. But you were a child doing your best. It was an accident. You never meant to cause harm."

More likely to give it based on how you act. He had acted as if he wanted to be forgiven; he knew that. It had always been the deepest, most impossible desire of his heart.

Until recently, when his familiar guilt became mixed with desire. Hope. Longing for something sweet and true, not merely for the lifting of pain. He'd wanted Rowena, a life with her. Had he acted as if he wanted it? She'd all but said she loved him, then wavered as he tossed her feelings aside.

Howard seemed to take Simon's silence for doubt. "You need to hear the words, then?" His familiar features, now rugged with the addition of thirteen years, creased with an expression that was not quite a smile. "I forgive you, Thorn."

He put his hands on Simon's shoulders—one unmarred, then, deliberately, the twisted and scarred hand—and looked him in the eye. "I forgive you. I forgave you long ago."

Simon had expected to feel forgiveness in a wash, like a baptism. Or like a weight lifted, like floating with glee. But instead, it was relief. It was the easing of an old knot. It was a slow, bubbling lift in his spirits.

It was remembering who he'd always intended to be. Maybe who he'd already become without even realizing it.

It was gratitude. It was grace.

Howard clapped Simon on both shoulders, then withdrew and looked at him knowingly. "Bodies heal more easily than hearts, don't they? I expect you've suffered more than I since the first months after the accident."

Simon nodded, the movement halting. He thought he'd fled to

freedom, but he had never truly been free. He'd shaped his life around leaving, fleeing, guilt, atonement.

Rowena was the only one who knew the truth about Simon and still thought he was worthy, he thought. But it seemed Howard had extended him the same grace. And those two—both with their challenges, their determination, their unwillingness to give up—gave Simon courage. He wanted to be better for them.

And he wanted to be better for himself. He didn't want the sort of life where he was always on the run. He wanted to plant roots, to grow the sort of life he'd never dared imagine for himself. One where he belonged in a place.

To a person. In a family. Doing meaningful work.

"Father McCrone mentioned," Howard drawled out, "you're a musician."

"I—yes, sometimes." Simon blinked at the turn of subject. "I played the horn for a while. I worked in a luthier's shop, too."

"I've a daughter. Amelia. She's twelve years old and loves music." Howard eyed Simon speculatively. "If she stays in this village, she'll do no more than offer lessons on the pianoforte for a pittance."

"Would she like doing that?"

"She might." Howard looked away, across the main street. He squinted into the afternoon sun. "But I don't know if I like that for her. She should try...more."

"As you never had the chance to?"

"As I never had the *inclination* to," Howard corrected. "If I'd never had the accident, I'd still have finished my apprenticeship and stayed here. I just would have finished it sooner. And you'd have left. You simply would have left later."

"I wouldn't—yes, I would have," Simon agreed. He'd always wanted something different.

Howard smiled. "You were always going to leave and wander, but maybe you'd have felt you could come home when you wanted to."

"You saw all that?"

Howard waved his hand. "All of it. I'm a homebody. You're not. At least, not for village life."

"I just needed to find the right place. And I think...I think I have. I think it could be home."

"In London?" Howard turned sharp eyes upon Simon. "Then why are you still here?"

"Because I wanted forgiveness."

"I told you. From me, you have it." So readily, the words came from the older man. "Now, how about from yourself?"

It had taken this: chastisement, a smile, the tale of a home and wife and daughter. Out of guilt, Simon had paused his own life and set himself to wandering. But Howard had not allowed the accident to do the same to him. He had everything he'd ever wanted.

If anyone's life had been ruined that day in Lines's forge, it hadn't been Howard's. How selfish Simon had been, to send money and not give anything real. What a coward he'd been—not only to run away, but to cut off all communication from a man he'd once considered a second mentor. A man he'd admired and called friend.

He wouldn't live that way anymore.

"I've all I want," Howard added, "except your friendship. But I can write perfectly well with my left hand, and I can even muck through a bit with my right. Father McCrone wouldn't tell me where your letters came from, and you were always moving on. But if you'll write to me yourself, I'll write back."

"I will."

Howard nodded, then extended a boot toward Simon's satchel. "Is that a copy of *How to Ruin a Duke?*"

Surprised, Simon looked down at his stashed belongings. Indeed, the book was poking from beneath the leather flap of the traveling bag. "It is. I read it along the way. I know a lady with a fondness for it."

"Do you, now?" Howard's eyes crinkled, knowing.

"I do. She's the luthier I mentioned."

"She's a lot more to you than that, judging by the look on your face. Well, if you've already read your book, you can leave it with me. Everyone's been talking about it, and I haven't got a copy. I want to know how it ends."

Simon handed over the volume. "It ends in seduction and scandal, of course. But the amusing part is the journey, not the destination."

"I've always thought so." Howard smiled, the old familiar smile that made his eyes into crescent moons. "Keep Amelia in mind if that lady of yours wants an apprentice. Not as a favor you'd do out of guilt, but as a favor you'd do a friend. I've been setting aside the guilt money you sent. It could serve as an apprenticeship fee."

There was little more to say then except good-bye, a series of good-byes that felt like farewells. Or *au revoirs*, as the French said. *Until we see each other again.* This wasn't the end, wasn't a door closed on the past. It was the continuation of a path Simon had once lacked the courage to walk. Now he strode it with gratitude.

And he took his place on a coach returning to London.

The four days seemed just as long as they had on his journey northwest, but this time he felt much lighter. So light he could have run alongside the carriage. So light he could have played a tune to the sky. *Lavender's blue, diddle diddle…*

When he arrived in London, tired and travel-worn, he didn't return to his lodgings. He made his way at once to the familiar corner of Bond Street, thronged as ever with London's wealthy and influential. There was no place he wanted to be but Fairweather's. No face he wanted to see but Rowena's.

But Fairweather's was gone. Closed. Abandoned. The painted sign had been scraped and covered over with flat white. The shop window was empty.

With the curtain gone, Simon could see the bare workroom. No tools, no wood, no hedgehog. No Rowena.

She had given up, after all.

CHAPTER NINE

"There is nothing so difficult to describe as happiness... It is easier to
enjoy it than to define it."
From *Glenarvon* by Lady Caroline Lamb

"The business name is *Fairweather's*," Rowena instructed the sign
painter with a touch of exasperation. "It's spelled like the word 'fair'
and the word 'weather.'"

The painter, a well-meaning but careless man, had already
jumbled the spelling once. Fortunately Rowena had caught him after
he painted *Ferrywheater's*, a name surely pulled from his imagination, and made him begin again.

"The spelling is f-a-i-r," she added. "As in, 'It's fair for you to
repaint the sign at no cost.' And w-e-a-t-h-e-r. The kind of weather
that comes from the sky."

"Not the sort of *whether* that implies doubt," a voice behind her
chimed in.

She went stiff, startled like a doe. She knew that voice. She hadn't
expected to hear it again so soon, maybe not ever.

But here it was. Here *he* was.

A smile spread over her face, seeping through her whole self. "Simon Thorn." She turned to face him, tempted to throw herself into his arms—but stopped. "You look worn to a thread! Are you quite well?"

He was hollow-eyed and stubbled, his clothing rumpled and in need of freshening. "I'm well, all right. I've just been traveling for eight of the last nine days."

Had she been smiling? Now she was beaming. "You went home!"

"No, this is home. London is home. But I did go back to Market Thistleton."

"And how was your journey?"

His expression was more pensive than happy. It was peaceful, even through weariness. "I'm forgiven. I wish I'd been ready to be forgiven a long time ago, but I wasn't done blaming myself. I'll never be done wishing I hadn't hurt my friend, but that's not the same thing as shame or guilt."

"I'm glad you've found peace." She hesitated, then admitted, "I thought you might stay there if you did."

"I went where I needed to go. I came back to where I want to be." His eyes creased with humor. "Though it took me longer than expected. I had to track you through a violinist at the Mallery Lane Theater. Thank the Lord you'd given the musicians your new address."

"Yes, the move came as a surprise." She explained about the abrupt hike in the weekly lease rate. "I'd learned about that shortly before your letter came from Howard."

"And you never said a thing? You are a goddess of stoicism."

"Hardly." She laughed, then caught sight of the sign painter, just beginning to brush the second half of her name above the door. "W-e-a-t-h-e-r-apostrophe-s, remember?" she called to him, relieved when he nodded.

"As you can tell, we're still getting settled into the new space," she told Simon. "I must have spent every second of our grace period in the Bond Street house looking for this one. It's smaller than the old building, but I quite like it. And the rent is a dream."

Simon grinned, nudging her with an elbow. "Well done you. Moving the shop when you thought you couldn't or shouldn't. What changed?"

"Circumstance, for one." She considered. "And I was inspired by my father, in a way. And also by *How to Ruin a Duke*."

"By that book?" His elfin brows lifted. "How did that delightful drivel inspire you?"

"Alliteration! That's well done you."

Simon bowed. "We'll take turns accomplishing mighty deeds. Though I admit, yours are far mightier."

Laughing, Rowena explained, "Through that book, someone has earned a fortune by the work of their own hands. It reminded me that there are many ways to do that, not only my father's. Once the possibility of the Bond Street lease was gone, I felt...unburdened. Because the Bond Street address was a burden. It kept me from living or doing the work I want to do."

"Too many pianofortes," Simon said wisely.

"And not enough of everything else. Violins and repairs and..."

"Moonlight kisses?" he suggested.

"Must they happen only in moonlight?" Rowena asked innocently. When Simon's jaw dropped a little, she laughed. "I know I'll lose some business, not having a tonnish address anymore. Not being where customers have found Fairweather's for a century. But I'll tune all the pianofortes I must to communicate the new address, and that's really all I can do for now. The workshop's not settled for repairing or building yet."

"But it will be?"

"As soon as my hands can make it so." She held a picture in her mind of how she wanted it to be: compartments for the wood currently stacked in random rooms, racks for the tools she'd neatly oiled and wrapped in heavy cloth. And a cushion, of course, for Cotton. It would be nearly like the workroom she remembered, but not quite. Everything would be arranged for her, within reach the way she wanted it.

She added, "If the Fairweather name is the draw, and not the address, then the name will be a draw elsewhere, don't you think?"

"I absolutely think so. The name, and the fine work you do."

"Then that's my family's true legacy. Not a building."

Save the shop, her father had told her. *Run it as I've taught you, and all will be well.*

"I thought," she told Simon after sharing her father's final words with him, "that he meant I had to run it just as he had. But what he taught me was to use my skills and my judgment. And so I have."

Simon looked interested. "Is that what he meant?"

"I think it is *not* what he meant," Rowena said dryly. "I think he wanted things to continue as they always had. But it's up to me to decide now, isn't it?"

"It is, and look what you've done. It's wonderful."

"Well." At the warmth of his words, she suddenly felt shy. "I hope it will be."

Was Simon blushing too? Was he scuffing his boot against the pavement? The moment had shifted, tipped. It wasn't all business. With the word *wonderful*, it had become something more.

"If you're amenable..." Simon coughed. "I know you don't want an assistant. But if you'd like a carpenter, I'm a fair one."

"One of the million jobs you've had in the past?"

"Exactly. I'm not saying I can build a house for you, but I can miter and nail and plane. If it would help you set up your workshop sooner, I could stay."

"I don't need a house," Rowena said. "And I'd love for you to stay. As long as you're willing." There. She'd extended a hand. Would he reach out? Would he take it?

He cleared his throat. "About that. Staying. Right. It depends on you. I wondered if you might have me."

His bashfulness was adorable. She had to prolong it, even as delight bubbled within her. "For what?" she teased. "For dinner? For a fortnight? For a sales campaign?"

He poked her in the ribs. "Minx. For a husband, I mean. For life. My home is in London, Rowena, and more specifically, it's with you. You helped me sort out my poor muddled heart, and as it turns out...it's yours."

She had to press a bit more, had to know. "How can I be sure? More important, how can *you* be sure?"

He waved a hand, as if this were the simplest question imaginable. "Because the only things I tired of were, well, *things*. The man to whom I was apprenticed helped me realize that I'm not one who attaches to things. I attach to people. I've never wavered in my sense of loyalty to my old friend Howard, and that was out of guilt. Motivated instead by love, imagine how tightly I feel tied to you. How tightly I *want* to be tied to you. If you'll allow it." He took a deep breath. "If you'll marry me."

"Oh," she said faintly. She looked up at the painter, frankly eavesdropping from his perch on a ladder.

"Your evergreen line." When she didn't say more, Simon pressed her for an answer. "Is that all you have to say? 'Oh'?"

She bit her lip. "I was thinking...we shall have to repaint the sign. Or can I call the shop Fairweather's anymore if my last name is Thorn?"

He whooped, taking her in his arms and swinging her in a circle. When he set her back down again, she still didn't feel the pavement beneath her feet. She couldn't feel her hands, her face. All she could feel was a swooping joy that, at last, at last, they'd found their way to each other, and there they'd stay.

"Now, why should your name change?" Simon answered, still holding her in an embrace. "My last name isn't serving me any particular purpose, and yours is. If you'll have my hand, I'll have your name. We'll both be Fairweathers. How about that?"

She'd heard of the elite adopting new names for the sake of an inheritance, but never of a husband taking his wife's name for a shop. But...why not?

"I'll have it," she decided. "And all of you. Simon, I'm so glad you came back. I love you dearly."

"As I love you." He pulled back, smiling at her gently. "Were you ever going to tell me?"

"Why, I just did. But I wasn't going to chase you. I didn't want to force you to my side."

"Wise, independent, wily woman. I don't deserve you. Will you tell me all the time that you love me?"

She grinned at him. "I can do that." And rising to her toes, she caught his lips with a kiss.

ONE YEAR LATER

"Prinny—no, I ought to call him George IV now—entertains far more than the former king." Rowena shuffled through invoices, noting the stamps. *Paid. Paid.* Thank the Lord, *Paid.* "And he's paying his royal luthier a bit. Isn't that lovely?"

Yes, she was carrying on a conversation by herself again, but now she had *two* good listeners. Cuddled on a cushion beside Rowena's desk, Cotton dozed, sated after gorging on crawling insects for several hours. At Rowena's other side, in a rocking cradle, month-old baby Howard blinked up at her blearily. His eyes, as light as Rowena's when he was born, were now turning the lovely rosewood color of his father's.

"You're fighting sleep again, little fellow," she chided her son. "I suppose I can't blame you. The world is a fascinating place."

The dear baby. She hadn't ever thought of herself as particularly maternal, but when she's realized she was with child, both she and Simon had fallen in love with the little one they nicknamed Sprout. Howard was born with a wild fuzz of black hair, a curious gaze, and ten perfect fingers. Not that it signified what his hands looked like, really. He could become a luthier no matter what. Or, if he chose, he could become something entirely different.

"Maybe you'd like to tune pianofortes like your father," she suggested, winning herself a worried furrow of baby brows. "No, I'm serious. He loves it. He'll be back any moment and can tell us all about how it went." She regarded the clock on the study mantelpiece with some doubt. "Well, maybe he won't be back at any moment. I'd have been done two hours ago, but he's not as quick."

"Kkhhhhgg," contributed Howard.

"Not as quick *yet*, that's true. He'll soon catch on. Ah! There's the door now." Through the open study door, Rowena heard their manservant, Jafferty, greeting Simon downstairs.

Though business had slowed a bit since Fairweather's moved from Bond Street, the lower rent still left them with more available funds—as did the stipend from George IV that had been paid each month since George III, the poor mad monarch, passed away in January.

They'd hired Jafferty soon after their wedding, greatly lessening Alice's workload. The former maid-of-all-work now served as upper housemaid and an occasional lady's maid to Rowena. Other servants had been hired for the house and to help Cook, now employed in the house rather than for a mere three days per week.

Rowena's favorite use for their free funds was the help she'd been able to give Nanny. After arranging a pension, she and Simon had found a block of rooms nearby for Nanny and her old friend Mrs. Newland in a house formerly owned by a man who used a wheel-chair. Instead of the steps that were so difficult for the aging women, one reached the ground-floor rooms with a gentle ramp from the street. Rowena also gave Nanny a magnifying lens for reading, and she'd bought the two women a subscription to a circulating library.

"It's too much," Nanny had protested, her round face marked with tears.

But it wasn't. When someone had shown a body how to live a

confident life, the least one could do in return was give her the means
to enjoy the books she loved.

Rowena and Simon were also setting money aside for the future.
One day the king might halt the stipend. One day Rowena and
Simon might choose to stop working. Or they might need to for
reasons of health, like Mrs. Newland and Nanny. Or there might be
more children.

"Though not yet, please," Rowena said to Howard, melding
thought and conversation. "You're a delight, but you don't sleep
nearly enough. Babies are supposed to nap during the day. You've got
to work on that."

"Mg," replied the baby. Cotton dozed on.

Simon rapped at the doorframe. "Hullo, dears. Rowena, want
me to finish reconciling the accounts? You could work on your
violin."

"What a lovely offer." She rose from her chair and gathered her
husband in her arms, inhaling his fresh scent of soap and bergamot—
and of cut wood and coal smoke, the smells of a Londoner who'd
spent hours in the luthier workshop and then walked outdoors. "I'll
happily turn over the accounts to you, though I've nearly finished.
Your skull cracker personage might need to pursue only one or two
outstanding debts."

"Excellent." Simon gave her a hearty kiss on the lips, then
grinned with unholy mischief. "It's nice to be manly and aggressive
every once in a while."

Besides skull-cracking, which in reality consisted of assertive
individual reminders, Simon had taken on most of the shop's other
administrative tasks. He made clever advertising cards for the
windows. He visited theaters to consult with the orchestras' string
players—and sometimes, even, he played his horn. He checked print-
makers' shops for the latest fashions and scandals and made window
displays based on them.

And most happily for Rowena, he'd learned to tune pianofortes
over the past long, laborious year. Today marked the first occasion

he'd done the tuning completely on his own, after the couple had carried out dozens of tunings together.

"How did the tuning go?" Rowena asked. "I hope you didn't find it deadly dull."

Simon laughed. "Not at all. I liked it, though it took me twice as long as you'd have needed. I'll improve eventually. And the footmen gossiped with me the whole time, and the housekeeper brought me tea and biscuits."

"How lucky of you! I rarely get tea. The gossip is by far my favorite part of tuning a pianoforte."

"If that's the only part you like, you needn't do it anymore. Eventually I'll get quicker at the job, and I'll pass along all the interesting news I hear. Such as a few rumors about our new majesty. Lady Templeton's footman says the king is renovating Buckingham House for his use as a palace, and he's planning a month of festivities for his coronation. He'll be needing a lot of string players, and they'll be needing a lot of repairs."

"Wonderful news. Though the coronation's about a year away, so we shouldn't count those chickens yet."

"Aaaaa," added Howard.

"Speaking of chickens." Simon released his wife, crossed to the cradle, and swooped up the baby. "Look who's stayed awake again, hmm? Go on, Ro, work on your violin. I've got this little one, at least until he's hungry."

One more kiss for each of her fellows, and Rowena was off. Down to the ground floor, where the formal parlor had been fitted to her specifications as a workshop. Here she carried out all the repairs, her time freed by Simon's work on other aspects of the business. And when she'd caught up on repairs, she worked on her violin—a slow process as she experimented with each wood, each varnish. She even tinkered with dimensions, as Guarneri had once done.

At present, she was working on a new piece: a small platform to position the chin, so the instrument wouldn't need to be pinched in place between the chin and shoulder. If she could get the material and position and size correct, the left arm would be freed to extend brightly up the whole length of the strings.

Just because something had always been done a certain way didn't mean she couldn't try something different. Maybe it would turn out wonderfully; maybe it would be a disaster. But it would be her way, and she wouldn't have to do it alone.

She had a loving husband and a distracting but darling baby. She had the help of trustworthy servants. She had an apprentice, even. Thirteen-year-old Amelia Howard attended a prestigious London girls' school, Mrs. Brodie's Academy for Exceptional Young Ladies, then stayed in Rowena and Simon's Marylebone house over the weekend to work with Rowena on Saturdays.

It was a full home, a shop serving its purpose. It was everything Rowena had always wanted Fairweather's to be.

Of course, she still kept her library subscription. When she and Simon read Gothic novels together, they knew that whatever happened in the books was ridiculous—but whatever happened in life, they could handle together.

ABOUT THE AUTHOR

Theresa Romain is the bestselling author of historical romances, including the Matchmaker trilogy, the Holiday Pleasures series, the Royal Rewards series, and the Romance of the Turf trilogy. Praised as "one of the rising stars of Regency historical romance" (*Booklist*), she has received starred reviews from Booklist and was a 2016 RITA® finalist. A member of Romance Writers of America, Theresa is hard at work on her next novel from her home in the Midwest.

To keep up with all the news about Theresa's upcoming books, sign up for her newsletter here or follow her on BookBub.

Visit Theresa on the web at http://theresaromain.com * Facebook * Twitter * Pinterest

If this story has put you in a novella state of mind, read on for an excerpt from Theresa's foodie historical, *The Way to a Gentleman's Heart*—found in the novella duo *Mrs. Brodie's Academy for Exceptional Young Ladies*.

EXCERPT FROM THE WAY TO A GENTLEMAN'S HEART

From THE WAY TO A GENTLEMAN'S HEART, ©2018 by Theresa Romain

Eight years ago, impoverished gentleman's daughter Marianne Redfern fled her Lincolnshire home when her first love was forced to wed another. At Mrs. Brodie's Academy, she learned the arts of cookery and self-defense—and as head cook, she can manage her staff, feed hundreds, and take down thieves. But she has no defense against Jack Grahame's unexpected arrival two weeks before a dinner that will secure the academy's fortunes.

Now a wealthy widower, Jack still has a wicked twinkle in his eye and a place in Marianne's heart. Before long, he's at her side in the kitchen all day and the bedchamber all night. But forgiveness doesn't come together as easily as a sauce, and the wounds of the past could ruin Jack and Marianne's chance at a future.

"Scale of dragon, tooth of wolf," chanted Marianne Redfern as she kneaded dough for the next day's bread. "Witches' mummy, maw and gulf of the ravined salt-sea shark..."

She trailed off when she noticed her assistant, Sally White, looking at her with some alarm. "Did you...are you making a new kind of bread, Mrs. Redfern?"

Mrs. The honorific always made Marianne smile. She'd never been wed in her life, but as cook at the exclusive Mrs. Brodie's Academy for Exceptional Young Ladies—and a young cook in addition, at age twenty-eight—she was due the status and protection of a fictional husband.

"Just amusing myself, Sally," she reassured the girl. "Shakespeare's got the right rhythm for kneading, but you won't see me feeding our girls any of those ingredients."

She liked the wayward sisters of *Macbeth*, the three prophetesses who drew a king's notice when they predicted his rise—then his doom. There was a certain man whose face she liked to imagine in the dough when she punched it. She didn't want to bring Jack Grahame to his doom, exactly, but when a woman had once had a lover's notice, it was difficult to be cast aside.

Since then, she'd become a bit wayward herself. Though she had no magic but that created by a stove or an oven, carried out with grains and meats and vegetables. Bespelling only for the length of a bite or a meal.

It was enough. It had become enough.

Satisfied with her dough, she turned the worked mass over to Sally. "Divide this part into rolls for the second rising, this into loaves, and cover it all. Put it in the larder so it will proof slowly. It'll be ready for baking in the morning, and the young ladies can have fresh rolls for breakfast." At Sally's nod, Marianne patted her on the shoulder. "Very good. I'll be on to the sauces."

Sally had been cook's assistant in the kitchen of Mrs. Brodie's Academy for only a week, having moved up from the post of kitchen maid when Marianne's previous assistant married the butcher's son. Marianne could teach any girl who wanted to learn, and indeed Sally did, for she had dreams of heading her own kitchen someday.

Katie before her had been a fair worker, but her heart hadn't been in cookery. She'd wanted the kitchen post only because she was in love with the boy who brought the meat. For three weeks they'd called the banns, yet Katie had said nothing to Marianne of her plans to marry. As soon as the parish register was signed, she sent for her things—and that was that, with no notice.

Love, love. It made people so deceptive. Yes, it was a good match for the girl; as wife to a butcher's son, she'd never go hungry. But even better than making a good match was knowing a body could take care of herself, come what might.

That was the purpose behind Mrs. Brodie's Academy for Exceptional Young Ladies, and it applied to everyone, from the headmistress herself to the youngest scullery maid. Along with the usual French and drawing, the students learned forgery and how to hold their own in a fistfight and God knew what else. The servants were welcome to take the same instruction after their daily work was done, if a teacher would agree to it. And for a little extra pay—no one could accuse Mrs. Brodie of being an ungenerous employer—most of the teachers were willing indeed.

Marianne had arrived here eight years before, new from the country and without even rudimentary skills in the kitchen. She'd worked as kitchenmaid and then assistant under a fine cook, Mrs. Patchett, until that good lady had retired to Devon to live with her son and grandchildren on a family farm. From Mrs. Patchett, Marianne had learned how to use and care for knives, how to clean and chop produce, how to choose the best fish and fowl and meat, and above all, how to provide three meals a day for seventy-five teachers and students, plus the army of servants who kept the school running smoothly.

It was difficult work, and hot, and physical, and sometimes dull. And Marianne would do it forever rather than return to Lincolnshire. After eight years here, two as the head of the kitchen, she had never been stronger, faster, more skilled. She could split a sheep's head, knee a presumptuous man, and stir a sauce of stock and cream to keep it from splitting—all at once and without turning a hair.

She had made something quite fine of herself, though the Miss Redfern who had first come to London might not have been so impressed. That young woman knew nothing but silk and song and embroidery and manners.

Marianne glanced at the clock that beamed from the corner. Eleven o'clock already, and most of the preparations were finally done for dinner at six. That was the main meal for the students; their midday repast was a simple one of breads and meats and cheeses, eaten between their lessons. She and Sally could assemble that in another hour, and the footmen would arrange platters for the young ladies in the refectory.

There was just enough time to begin a pastry for tarts before Marianne started the slow-simmering sauces. Tarts would be more special than a simple dessert of fruit and cream, and the young ladies deserved a treat now that they were nearly done with their spring term. The early apricots Marianne had bought that morning were fine and sweet; she could make do with them. It still smarted that she'd failed to win the first strawberries of the season from a greengrocer who'd wanted to charge the earth. Not that they'd have made tarts enough for all the students, but she had a weakness for strawberries.

"Sally," she called. "I need you to work with the apricots once you've stowed the bread."

When the answer yes'm came in reply through the open door of the larder, Marianne turned to her book of receipts and looked up her favorite ingredients for a tart pastry. How much flour ought she to remove, substituting almonds? One part ground almonds to ten parts flour might do the trick, enriching the delicate flavor of the apricots with melting sweetness.

She peered into the canister where she kept the nuts, pounded to powder and ready for use. Almost empty! She cursed. It was one of Sally's tasks to keep a good supply of pounded almonds, but if Marianne didn't direct her, the younger woman couldn't be expected to remember every detail of their stocks. They needed another kitchen maid to fill Sally's old role, and soon. Mrs. Brodie's annual Donor Dinner—Marianne couldn't help but think of it in capital letters—was in a fortnight, after the term ended, and there was no way a single cook and assistant could prepare two formal courses and assorted desserts for one hundred people.

Well. She'd recruit the scullery maids to chop and peel if she had to, and she'd jug and stone and jar and press as much ahead of time as she could. And for today's tarts, butter alone it would be in the pastry, and that would keep the cost of today's meals down too. Mrs. Brodie was never mean with her kitchen staff, allowing Marianne all the budget she liked. Even so, the gentleman's daughter who'd once spent several pounds on a single bonnet now measured out ground almonds in cautious spoonfuls and haggled to the ha'penny over the price of lettuce or fish. When it wasn't her own money she was spending, she was more responsible with it.

Again, the face of Jack Grahame came to mind, and she wondered fleetingly if he'd felt the same about his father's money. The money that had been needed, and that she'd had none of, and that had split them apart.

Money. Money. Money. This time, there was no dough for her to punch.

So she turned her thoughts to the tasks before her, the ones she did every day. She checked the joints slowly roasting in the ovens, confirming that the coal held out. She pulled out the ingredients for the sauces she'd make for dinner; she sifted shelled peas in her hand and approved the amount. These could be cooked shortly before the dinner service. They'd boil in a flash and be finished with fresh cream and...something else. Something surprising and flavorful. Chopped shallots maybe, fried crisp in lard and scattered like beads over the top. Yes, that would do well.

Now back to the tarts. Sally had finished with the bread, and at the other end of the long worktable, she was settled with a great pile of apricots. Clean, cleave, discard the stone, set aside. The halved fruits went into a huge bowl, piling up quickly.

"You've a good rhythm for that work," Marianne told the younger woman. "Thinking of Shakespeare? Scale of dragon, tooth of wolf?"

Sally blushed. "Little Boy Blue. It's a nice old rhyme, that. My mum taught it to me and my sisters."

Marianne smiled as she dug her hands into the flour and butter, now coming together smoothly. "I have sisters too. Haven't seen them in a long while, but I remember learning those old rhymes with them."

But where is the boy who looks after the sheep?
He's back in Lincolnshire. Do not weep...

No, that wasn't right. That wasn't right at all.

A knock sounded then on the door to the tradesmen's entrance. The kitchen was a few rooms away, but the servants' quarters were quiet at the moment. The footmen were likely upstairs, while Mrs. Hobbes, the housekeeper, would be making the rounds of the students' chambers as the maids were cleaning them. She'd a keen eye and would come down hard on any maid who hadn't done her work well. Her husband, the old butler, had grown hard of hearing in recent years. If he were polishing silver in his pantry with the door closed, he wouldn't hear a Catherine wheel going off two feet away.

"Are we expecting another delivery, ma'am?" Sally asked with mild curiosity.

"Of kitchen goods? Not until I do tomorrow's shopping." Marianne eyed her butter-covered hands, then the pile of apricots her assistant had left to split and prepare. "I'll answer that door. Back in a moment, Sally."

She wiped her hands on her apron and wound her way past the servants' stairs, their hall, and the housekeeper's room. Unfastening the door to the area, she lifted her brows, prepared to scold a lost delivery boy for interrupting her work.

But it wasn't a delivery boy at all.

Her startled brain took a moment to understand the sight before her. The thoughts went like this:

Oh! It's a man.

A handsome man.

He looks familiar. Does he work for the fishmonger?

No, he's not holding fish. Strawberries! He got those strawberries I wanted of the greengrocer. Look at him holding them, juicy and red, in that little basket. Does he work for the greengrocer?

Of course not. I'd have noticed him there.

No, he looks like...like...

And then she knit all the pieces together, and her jaw dropped.

"Jack," she said faintly. "Jack Grahame. Why are you here?"

"Marianne. I brought you strawberries," said the man she'd loved and hoped never to see again.

When he held out the little basket, she took it, bemused. She looked from the strawberries to the face of her first lover, her only lover, dressed as fine as ever and handsome enough to be in a painting. Then back at the basket. And then she remembered that her hands were greasy from butter, her apron had a bit of everything she'd cooked today upon it, and her hair—her long dark brown hair that he'd once run his fingers through, lovingly—was sloppily confined under a cook's cap, and her cheeks were flushed from the heat of the ovens.

Ah, hell. If one's long-ago love showed up unexpectedly at one's door, it ought to be at a time when one looked one's best. But Marianne was a cook now, and a cook was what she looked like.

She lifted her chin. Closed her hands around the basket of strawberries. Did he remember she liked them, after all this time? Bright as rubies, and she'd rather have them than gemstones.

"Well. Thank you," she said with as much dignity as she could manage. "Is that all? As you're here, you know I'm working as a cook. And since you were always a bright fellow, you must guess I've got to get back to work."

"Since you asked, I'd like to come in and speak to you. Do the strawberries win me a little of your time?" His brows were puckish, his mobile mouth always at the edge of a grin.

So he *did* remember. "Time enough for you to say you're sorry for keeping away so long." She tried not to sound as soft as she felt, but her own words betrayed her.

The humor on his face melted. He looked at her with grave gray eyes and said, "I'm not here to apologize, Marianne. But I do want your forgiveness."

Like it? Order your copy of THE WAY TO A GENTLEMAN'S HEART!

WHEN HIS GRACE FALLS
BY GRACE BURROWES

Dedicated to those fallen upon hard times

CHAPTER ONE

"A duke cannot, of course, be *ruined*, except by his own folly, and
what an entertaining spectacle that can be!"
From *How to Ruin a Duke* by Anonymous

"She is the personification of gall, the embodiment of presumption,
and a walking temple to betrayal." Thaddeus, Duke of Emory, made
a precise about-face at the edge of the library's carpet. "I'd sooner
share my coach with a viper than admit this family ever employed
Lady Edith Charbonneau. Stop swilling all the good brandy."

Thaddeus had been scolding and lecturing his baby brother for
more than twenty years, not that Jeremiah had ever listened.

"A lady's companion has a difficult lot," Jeremiah said, draining
the last of the spirits from his glass. "Have you considered paying
Lady Edith off? I'd be happy to act as intermediary."

Thaddeus made another about-face before the portrait of the
previous duke. "That's quite generous of you, but she hasn't
demanded to be paid off. She hasn't even acknowledged her authorship of the damned book. And what sort of woman titles a book, *How
to Ruin a Duke*? She and I barely spoke during the whole of her

tenure as Mama's companion. What she knows about dukes wouldn't fill a toddler's porringer."

The mere sight of Lady Edith's compilation of drivel—already sold in a bound edition—made Thaddeus want to roar profanities and throw the book at the nearest fragile object. He'd been the object of satire before—every peer was—but he'd never so badly misjudged a woman's character.

He'd liked Lady Edith, rather a lot, and he liked very few people indeed.

"What she knows about *you*," Jeremiah said, "handsomely fills nearly three hundred pages. Have you read it?"

"I wouldn't admit it if I had." Much less admit that he'd read it several times, word for word. Alone, of course, because on occasion—rare occasion—the author managed a humorous turn of phrase that provoked a begrudging laugh.

Jeremiah opened the book to a page at random and ran his finger along the prose. "'His nose is of majestic proportions, and those ladies in a position to comment knowledgeably—said to number in the scores—claim other aspects of the ducal anatomy are in proportion not only to His Grace's magnificent proboscis, but also to his considerable conceit.' This can't possibly be aimed at you, Emory. Your conceit surpassed considerable before you reached your majority. At the very least, your conceit qualifies as stupendous."

"Unlike your sense of humor." The footmen had positioned a spray of daisies on the mantel, a half inch off center. Thaddeus corrected the error and realized the flowers were nearly out of water.

"Again, Your Grace, I suggest with all deference that if you'd simply wave a handsome *sum* at the woman, your handsome *person* would no longer be the subject of her literary maunderings. I'll search her out, handle the details, and nobody need ever acknowledge the source of the money."

Now that was a fiction approaching the absurd. Jeremiah was so inept at managing his funds, his allowance was disbursed every two weeks rather than quarterly. He was a good soul, but too generous with his friends and too reckless with his bets.

No misanthropic spinster would ever write a satirical tome about Jeremiah. Being a charming, impecunious courtesy lord had its advantages.

"Will you join Mama and the ladies for the carriage parade?" Thaddeus asked, using the pitcher on the sideboard to water the flowers. The day was glorious as only London in late spring could be.

"Isn't it your turn, Your Grace?" The polite form of address became mocking when Jeremiah adopted that tone.

"I rode with them yesterday and the day before," Thaddeus replied, returning the pitcher to the sideboard. "The ladies prefer your escort because everybody likes you."

Jeremiah saluted with his brandy glass, which was full again. "You really do need to work on your flattery, Emory."

"I am a duke. I need not flatter anybody. I'm simply speaking the truth. You are not only received everywhere, you are *welcomed* everywhere." While Thaddeus had long since reconciled himself to merely being invited everywhere.

He and Jeremiah both had the family height, blue eyes, and dark hair, but Jeremiah had perfected the air of a man amused by life's contradictions. Thaddeus could not afford that posture, which only made the damned book all the more vexing.

"I do have a certain modest social appeal," Jeremiah said. "I admit it. If I'm to squire Mama and the ladies about, I suppose I'd better change into riding attire. What pressing engagement prevents you from joining us?"

A dozen pressing engagements. The house steward was in the boughs over some comment the sommelier had made about the dampness of the cellars. The kitchen staff agreed with the sommelier, the footmen had aligned themselves with the house steward, and the maids were stirring the pot as maids were ever wont to do. Mama expected Thaddeus to make peace among the warring parties—a task that Lady Edith had somehow managed from time to time—but really, the cellar *was* damp. All London cellars were.

"My afternoon is not my own," Thaddeus said. "And it's your turn, Jeremiah." They had a schedule, so the escort tribulation was evenly divided between them, but the schedule was usually honored in the breach, and the breach was invariably on Jeremiah's part.

"Give my regards to whichever merry widow is claiming your time, Emory."

The tailor—a short, bald, nervous fellow who had no acquaintance with merriment that Thaddeus could divine—claimed that a final fitting for Thaddeus's new frock coat was absolutely imperative, the third such final fitting for that one garment.

The Committee for the Relief of Aged Seamen hadn't disbursed this month's funds, mostly because Thaddeus hadn't yet bullied them into it.

No less than four bills pending in the Lords required a judicious application of ducal persuasion in the direction of various earls and other tedious fellows, all of whom wanted to be seen having dinner with Thaddeus at his clubs.

"I will tend to the press of business," Thaddeus said, lining up the decanters on the sideboard in order of height. "Tending to the press of business is, after all, why I was born."

"Mama might attribute your birth to other causes." Jeremiah took a considering sip of his drink. "According to a certain scribbling spinster, your chief pursuits are nearly breaking your neck in wild horse races, consuming vast quantities of liquor, and disappointing mistresses after you've made their wildest erotic fantasies come true."

"No wonder I am usually in need of a good nap." In truth Thaddeus hadn't any mistresses to disappoint. At the beginning of the Season, he'd promised himself to engage the company of some friendly widow who didn't mind an occasional frolic, but that had been several months ago, and the press of business had interfered with even that pursuit.

"Enjoy the carriage parade," Thaddeus said, striding for the door.

"I have an appointment with a certain publisher whom I hope will lead me to Lady Edith's doorstep."

"You intend to confront her ladyship directly?" Jeremiah set down his glass on Grandpapa's desk. "Is that wise, Emory? She can turn even an innocent meeting into more grist for her mill. Perhaps I should go with you."

This genuine fraternal concern was part of the reason Thaddeus continued to support his brother. Jeremiah spent money like a sailor in his home port for the first time in two years. He wiggled out of social obligations, and his naughty wagers were legendary in the club betting books.

But he was loyal to Thaddeus, and if a brother could have only one redeeming value—Jeremiah had many, in truth—loyalty was the one that would most easily earn Thaddeus's esteem.

"If I can locate Lady Edith," Thaddeus said, reversing course to put the empty glass on the tray on the sideboard, "then perhaps I will have you accompany me when I call upon her, but first I must find the woman."

Jeremiah gave the library's globe a spin, letting his index finger trail along the northern hemisphere. "Is there some urgency about this errand, Emory? Society is having a good laugh at our expense, but this is not the first such book to be published, nor will it be the last."

When Lord Jeremiah Maitland was the voice of reason, pigs might be spotted fluttering into the branches of the plane maples.

"I'd rather it be the last such book published *about me*. The author is said to be working on a sequel, and if I allow a second book into print, Mama will disown me."

"Would that Mama disowned me. Why is it your fault that somebody has decided to immortalize your exploits for the delectation of bored clubmen?"

Thaddeus made for the door once again. "Immortality by way of infamy and ridicule is not a goal I aspire to. Shouldn't you be changing into riding attire?"

"Explain to me why you take such grievous exception to a harmless spoof. I always have time to lend a friendly ear to my dearest older brother."

This was true, oddly enough. "In the first place, the exploits are unfairly portrayed, as you well know. In the second place, the book is being read by far more than the younger sons and idlers lounging about the clubs. In the third,"—Thaddeus got out his pocket watch to compare the time it kept to the eight-day clock on the mantel—"this dratted book has Mama concerned for my prospects."

The two timepieces were in gratifying synchrony.

"Your *prospects*?" Jeremiah spluttered. "Mama thinks no decent woman will have you, a poor old homely fellow with only what—six or is it seven—titles to your name and a different estate to go with each one? Perhaps our dame is suffering a touch of dementia. We certainly can't let that get out or the sequel will devolve into a trilogy."

"This isn't amusing, Jeremiah. What decent woman wants to ally herself with a man who's the butt of a three-hundred-page joke?"

Jeremiah strolled for the door. "The book is merely a nine days' wonder, Emory. Shall I place a wager on who will be the topic of the next such tome? I nominate old Windham. He was supposedly a rascal in his youth."

"No wagers, if you please," Thaddeus said, preceding Jeremiah out the door. "That rascal has three grown sons who'd skewer you without blinking if you maligned their papa, and then the in-laws would start in." Besides, Thaddeus both liked and respected Percival, His Grace of Windham, who had passed along more than a few insightful suggestions regarding the care and feeding of parliamentary committees.

"I fancy a bit of swordplay, now that you bring up skewering," Jeremiah said. "Shall we make an appointment at Angelo's?"

Nice try. "You shall change into your riding attire. I will send a footman to the stables to tell them you'll need your horse."

Jeremiah stopped at the foot of the staircase that wound up in a grand sweep around three-quarters of the octagonal foyer. Of the house's public spaces, this was Thaddeus's favorite. Marble half-columns created a series of niches wherein reposed classical urns, dignified busts, and splendid ferns. Ancestors scowled down from the portraits on the walls, and the mosaic on the floor—the family coat of arms—hadn't a single flawed or misplaced stone.

"One must concede the author has shown initiative," Jeremiah said, foot on the first step. "Don't you agree? She is enterprising enough to write all those pages, to find a publisher, to turn common human foibles into entertainment. That's not something just any idle fribble could do, Emory."

Jeremiah sounded genuinely admiring or perhaps envious.

"If another such book comes out, and I become a running joke from year to year, no duchess I could esteem would bother marrying me. That leaves *you* to secure the succession, my lord, meaning your bachelor days would be over."

"Good gracious, Emory. As dire as all that? Then be on your way, by all means. Nothing must be allowed to jeopardize my bachelor-hood. The good ladies of Mayfair would go into a decline and I would have to join them."

His lordship scampered up the steps all merriment and laughter, though Thaddeus was certain that Jeremiah's last expostulation was only half in jest.

LADY EDITH CHARBONNEAU sat on the hard chair, her outward composure firmly in place while she raged inside. Two years as companion to the Duchess of Emory had resulted in the ability to maintain her dignity, if nothing else. Little good that would do her when she had no roof over her head.

"My lady, I do apologize," Mr. Jared Ventnor said, from the far side of a desk both massive and battered, "but at present I am not in the business of publishing books of domestic advice. Have you tried Mr. MacHugh?"

"Mr. MacHugh has all the domestic guidance authors he needs. He suggested I proceed by subscription, but Mr. Ventnor, I am a lady by birth. I cannot be seen importuning my friends to support my publishing endeavors. The result would label my literary aspirations charity, and I will not be made into an object of pity." Moreover, the goal of Edith's considerable writing efforts was to earn money, not to perfect her begging skills.

When male authors drummed up support for a book yet to be written—much less published—that was business as usual. A woman in the same posture met with a very different reception.

Mr. Ventnor rose. "Leave me some of your writing samples. If I can't publish you, I might think of somebody who can once I have a sense of your voice and tone. Reading for entertainment is becoming stylish, and whoever can write the next *How to Ruin a Duke* will be assured of a long and lucrative career."

If I never hear of that book again... "Might I consider my writing samples and send you the best of the lot?"

Ventnor was rumored to be a decent sort. He had a wife and family, he paid his authors honestly—not a given, in London's publishing community—and he met with impoverished spinsters when he doubtless had other things to do.

And yet, paper was precious. Edith had only the single final copies of the samples she'd brought, thinking to pass them over for Mr. Ventnor's perusal while she'd waited.

"You may send them along," he said, offering his hand to assist her to her feet. "But promise me you will show me something. Too many authors claim they seek publication, and when I ask for a sample, they fuss and dither and delay, gilding the lily—or tarnishing it, more likely—until their courage has ebbed to nothing. Send me something within the week."

"I can make you that promise, sir."

He was mannerly. Edith gave him grudging respect for that. As an earl's daughter, she'd met many mannerly men. Only those who offered her courtesy when nobody compelled it earned her admiration. Ventnor could have been rude rather than kind, and Edith would nonetheless have applied to him for work.

He walked with her to the front door, past all the editors at their desks and clerks with their green visors. The air of industry here was unmistakable and fascinating. An earl's daughter was raised to be an ornament, idling from one entertainment to the next. A lady's companion might be kept busy, but she could not *look* busy.

These fellows gloried in their work, and in the challenge of making a business successful.

"Have you considered finding another post as a lady's companion?" Mr. Ventnor asked, passing Edith her cloak. "My in-laws move in polite society at levels above what a mere publisher can aspire to. I could ask my wife to make inquiries through her sister."

He really was kind, and Edith really did want to smack him with her reticule. She'd learned to keep a copy of the first volume of *Glenarvon* in her bag the better to deter pickpockets and presuming men. Heaven knew Lady Caroline's book had few other redeeming qualities.

"I have had my fill of being a lady's companion," Edith said. "It did not end well." She put her Sunday bonnet on and tied the ribbons loosely. The day was fine, and even a poor spinster could enjoy a beautiful spring afternoon. "Companions are not generously compensated, and they are pitied when they aren't held in contempt."

By polite society. The servant class, much to Edith's surprise, had been far more tolerant and welcoming.

Ventnor bowed over her hand. "Send me those writing samples, please, and I will consult my family on your behalf. Necessity sometimes compels us into situations we'd otherwise avoid, but circumstances unfortunate on their face can end happily."

He spoke as if from experience, when to all appearances he was a contented and prosperous man.

"If you say so, Mr. Ventnor, though necessity has landed many a decent woman in ruin. Good afternoon and thank you for your time." Edith let herself out into the lovely day, the sun a benevolence and the London air enjoying a rare freshness. The day was a lie, promising pretty flowers and blossom-scented breezes rather than the stinking oppression of the coming summer.

A pretty lie, like much of polite society.

Edith set off down the walk, abundantly aware that she had not even a footman to accompany her. Women of the lower orders moved about as they pleased, but their freedom made them less safe. As a companion to a duchess, Edith had been safe on the streets, something she'd taken for granted.

She ought not to have said that part about decent women being brought to ruin to Mr. Ventnor, though the word haunted her. That silly book—*How to Ruin a Duke*—couched ruin in terms of stupid pranks, idiot wagers, and pleasures of the flesh. Those venalities were hardly ruinous to a duke.

True ruin meant horrors that gave Edith nightmares. Debtor's prison for Foster, worse for Edith herself.

She was so sunk in dread over those familiar worries that she didn't see the oversized lout who plowed into her right on the walkway. The instant after he'd nearly trampled her, she caught his scent, a particular blend of grassy and floral fragrances.

Such a beautiful, warm fragrance for such a chilly, self-possessed man.

The Duke of Emory steadied her with a hand on each of her arms. "I do beg your pardon, ma'am. I was at risk for tardiness at my next appointment and one is loath to inconvenience another who has—"

She stepped back, her reticule catching His Grace a glancing blow that he seemed not to notice. "Hands off, Your Grace. Please watch where you are going. Last I heard, gentlemen were to yield the way to ladies, but then—"

"You," he said, glaring down the ducal beak. "The very person who has authored all of my difficulties."

Emory was a monument to aristocratic self-possession, but unless he had changed very much in the past six months, he wasn't given to rudeness or wild fancies.

"Your difficulties are the envy of those who must work for a living. Excuse me, sir." She tried to maneuver around him, but for a big man, he was nimble.

"I do not excuse you. I hold you accountable for a wrong done to me and to my family, and I intend to seek retribution from the perpetrator."

"Then call him out." Edith dodged left only to again be blocked by a wall of fine tailoring exquisitely fitted to the ducal person. "That's what Lord Jeremiah would do." Then his lordship would probably delope, have a drink or six with his opponent, and go carousing onto the next potentially fatal lark. No wonder the duchess had been a woman easily vexed.

"Alas," Emory retorted. "My detractor, who stands before me in the most horrid shade of pink I have ever beheld, is a female. One cannot call out a female, which said female well knows and likely exploits at every turn."

"Are you tipsy, Emory?" Many wealthy men were seldom sober, but Edith had put Emory in the seldom drunk column. "Fevered, perhaps? Have you suffered a blow to the head? That must be it."

"I have suffered a blow to my reputation, and well you know it."

This conversation was attracting notice, which Edith could ill afford. "I'll thank you to spare me a litany of the slights you image yourself to have suffered, Emory. Having already earned the notice of a satirist, you should be reluctant to accost women on the street, much less lecture them about your supposed miseries. Good day."

She made it past him, but he fell in step beside her.

"Have you no escort, my lady?"

"Why would I need an escort when I can fly from one destination to the next on my broomstick?"

The hordes of pedestrians made way for Emory, and thus for Edith. Even an indignity as minor as getting jostled on the street had been an adjustment for her, an insistent reminder that she'd come down in the world, far down. She hated that Emory could see what she'd been reduced to, and resentment gave her tongue unladylike sharpness.

"And there," Emory said, "we have a pathetic gesture in the direction of the feeble wit that has apparently inspired you to make a living with your pen." He tipped his hat to a dowager mincing along on the arm of a young man. "You should have an escort because a lady does not travel the streets alone."

"And who made up that rule?" Edith mused. "Instead of limiting a woman's movements to those times when some hulking bullyboy is available to escort her, why don't gentlemen of goodwill simply cosh the heads of the parasites who presume to assault the gentler sex in broad daylight? Fellows styling themselves as gentlemen could have a jolly time bloodying noses and wielding their fists while the ladies accomplished their errands in peace. But no, of course not. Englishmen could not be half so sensible. The ne'er-do-wells wander freely, while the ladies are shackled to the company of dandiprats and bores, all in the name of keeping the ladies from harm."

Emory remained at her side right up to the corner. "What the *hell* is wrong with you?" He spoke quietly, and if Emory had one virtue—even his mother allowed that he had at least five—it was that he rarely used foul language in the hearing of any female.

Traffic refused to oblige Edith's need to cross the street. "What the *hell* is wrong with me?" Cursing felt fiendishly good. "I was nearly knocked on my backside by male arrogance bearing the proportions of a mastodon. That same mastodon has insulted my only warm cloak, and he has made me a public spectacle while accusing me of behaviors that he apparently disapproves of. You clearly need a change of air, Emory. I intend to turn north here, I suggest you strut off to the south."

She made a shooing motion.

He caught her hand and put it on his arm. "Literary notoriety has gone to your head. Her Grace would despair to hear you spouting such ungenteel sentiments. Perhaps you are the one in need of a change of air, my lady."

Traffic cleared and as the crossing sweepers darted out to collect horse droppings, His Grace accompanied Edith to the next walkway.

"What I need, sir, is a decent meal, peace and quiet, and to be rid of you."

"You do look peaked. All that flying about on broomsticks must be exhausting, but then, ruining dukes probably takes a toll on a lady's energy too. Perhaps your conscience keeps you awake at night?"

He sauntered along, tossing out insults like bread crumbs for crows, while the crowds parted for him as if he were royalty. He was merely 42nd in line for the throne and the last person Edith wanted to spend time with.

"Are you ruined?" Edith asked, untwining her hand from his arm. "You look to be in obnoxiously good health to me."

Both Lord Jeremiah and His Grace of Emory were attractive men, viewed objectively. Lord Jeremiah was the classically handsome brother, with wavy brown hair styled just so, a mouth made for drawling *bon mots*, and a physique that showed the benefit of regular athletic activity. His demeanor was congenial, his manner relaxed and gracious when in polite surrounds.

He could be an idiot, but he looked like a lord ought to look.

Without Lord Jeremiah as a contrast, Emory would have passed for handsome as well. Next to his younger sibling, though, the duke was two inches too tall for the dance floor, his hair a shade too dark and unruly for proper fashion. Those shortcomings might have been overlooked, but he was without his brother's charm.

And polite society valued charm exceedingly.

Edith had respected Emory when she'd been in his mother's employ. The duke paid well and punctually, and he did not bother the help. She'd learned to appreciate those traits. She could not, however, recall any occasion when Emory had relented from his infernal dignity, which made the book written about him hard to credit.

"Where are we going?" Emory asked after they'd crossed another intersection.

"You may go straight to perdition." Edith had another three streets to travel before she'd be home. The thought of some bread and butter with a cup of tea loomed like a mirage on the horizon of a vast desert.

"I find it odd that your pen has sent me to social perdition, and yet you offer me nothing but insults."

He wasn't making any sense, or perhaps hunger was making Edith light-headed. "Did you apologize for nearly running me down? For insulting my cloak? For attaching yourself to me without my permission? For accusing me of hatching some scheme to add to your enormous heap of imaginary miseries? For insulting my appearance?"

That last had hurt. Edith had never been pretty, but she'd troubled over her complexion and taken care to always be tidy. If she was looking peaked, that was another step down from the serene pinnacle of feminine grace an earl's daughter should have inhabited.

"Well, you are peaked," Emory observed. "You look like you've lost flesh since leaving my employment."

"Your mother's employment." All of Edith's dresses were looser, as were her boots.

"Are we in a footrace, my lady? I am compelled to say this is not the sort of neighborhood I'd expect you to frequent."

The neighborhood was respectable. Five streets on, it would become shabby. "Nothing compels you to say any such thing, Your Grace. You toss that barb at me out of a mean-spiritedness I do not deserve and would not have attributed to you previously. I know I left your mother's employ—"

"My employ."

"—without much notice, but I had my reasons. If you would please take yourself off, I would be much obliged."

She marched on with as much speed as dignity allowed, though Emory remained at her side. Perhaps that was providential—she was overdue for some kindness from providence—because before she'd gone six steps, her vision wavered, her boot caught on an up-thrust brick, and she was again pitched hard against the duke.

CHAPTER TWO

_____

"His Grace lacks the two essential qualities of a gentleman about
Town—wit, and a tailor with an imagination."
From *How to Ruin a Duke* by Anonymous

For a woman who could spew three hundred pages of unrelenting
calumny, Lady Edith felt like eiderdown in Thaddeus's arms. When
he'd first collided with her outside the publisher's offices, she had
nearly bounced off of him like one of those lap dogs that doubles its
perceived dimensions with an abundance of hair and yapping.

She was too slight for the pink atrocity of a cloak she wore, and
she did look pale and tired. Success as a satirist was apparently a
taxing business.

"Is this a ploy?" he asked her, a hand under her pointy elbow.
"Are you attempting to extort my sympathy by feigning weakness?"

Furious blue eyes glared up at him. "I am not weak, I am famished. I
have not eaten since the day before yesterday. I wanted cab fare for my
appointment with Mr. Ventnor in case it rained. A woman resembling a
drowned rat hardly inspires confidence in a prospective employer."

Not a drowned rat, but a cornered cat. One who hadn't seen regular meals or a warm fireplace in some time. *How to Ruin a Duke* was rumored to be in its fifth printing. Lady Edith's appearance and the success of the book were facts in contradiction.

Thaddeus was constitutionally incapable of ignoring facts in contradiction.

"Perhaps a meal will improve your manners," he said, guiding her several doors down the street. The neighborhood was going seedy about the edges, but the inn looked respectable enough.

"I cannot be seen to sit down to a meal with you in public." The edge of ire had left her speech. She was reciting a rule rather than scolding him.

Her scolds had been impressive, considering she'd presumed to scold a duke who could ruin her.

"You march around London," he said, "like a supervisor of the watch. You neglect adequate nutrition. You insult a peer of the realm without batting an eye. You can share a trencher with me at an obscure establishment such as this. The pubs and inns always have the best food, and as it happens, I am hungry as well."

She closed her eyes, doubtless marshalling some sham of martyrdom.

"My objective was to seek you out today," Thaddeus went on. "I was surprised to find you at Ventnor's, because he is not your publisher. I thought perhaps he could send me in the right direction though. Instead I find my quarry landing almost literally at my feet. This has put me in a better humor."

She opened her eyes. "One shudders to think what your version of a poor humor is. I will eat with you, for two reasons. Firstly, because I need food. Secondly, because I suspect you will not leave me in peace until you've aired whatever daft notions have resulted in your pestering me with your presence."

Clever alliteration had been a signal characteristic of the prose in *How to Ruin a Duke.*

Thaddeus held the door for her. "I will leave you in peace—on this occasion—if you will share a meal with me."

She swept past him, as dignified as the queen mother, into the gloom of the common. Her pink cloak caused some stares, or perhaps Emory's height and attire were gaining the notice of the patrons. The working classes were notably shorter than the aristocracy, and Emory was tall even among his peers.

Lady Edith was tall as well, something he'd liked about her. She wasn't a wilting, vapid, fading little creature who could barely waft through a Beethoven slow movement before drifting to the garden for a nap in a hammock. Mama had been in a much better mood during Lady Edith's tenure as a companion, and the entire ducal staff had been less prone to insurrections and feuds.

"You will have a steak," Thaddeus said, choosing a table well away from the window and from any other patrons. "Steak is the best thing for restoring vigor. You will need your vigor if I'm to ruin you."

She unpinned her bonnet, the millinery adorned with a tired collection of feathers and silk flowers.

"Will this be a literal ruination or figurative? Lord Jeremiah struck me as more the ruining kind. You, on the other hand,"—she perused him in a manner more frank than flattering—"you have the arrogance for true villainy, but your dignity wouldn't allow it. Shrieking virgins, swoons, dramatics, I don't think you have the patience for them."

A serving maid came over to the table, her apron tidy, her cap neat. Thaddeus ordered steak all around, a small pint for Lady Edith and summer ale for himself.

"You condescend to consume ale," Lady Edith said, unbuttoning her cloak. "I, on the other hand, would rather have had a good, restorative pot of China black. Don't worry. The ale will not go to waste, though my goodwill where you are concerned—which used to be substantial—has apparently been squandered."

She drew off her gloves, revealing pale, slender hands with an ink stain near her right wrist.

"I have puzzled over your motive," Thaddeus replied, removing his hat and setting it on the bench beside him. "You left our household of your own volition, and while Her Grace was not pleased with the short notice, she wrote you a decent character. You've apparently spent the entire intervening six months plotting revenge against us for some fictitious slight. I cannot fathom what that slight might be."

He tugged off his gloves, prepared to hear that an underbutler had started a false rumor regarding her ladyship's use of hair coloring —her hair was golden—or a maid had purposely scorched her ladyship's favorite cloak. Any justification was better than believing he himself might have given Lady Edith cause for offense.

"I do not want to ruin you," he said, when the serving maid had bustled off. "But I cannot ignore ongoing literary character assassination."

"Surely it is beneath the consequence of a duke to ruin a mere failed lady's companion."

Her ladyship was either not afraid to be ruined, or she did not take the threat seriously.

"I could do it. All it would take is mention in my club of a rumor or two. A hint, an aside, and you would never be received in polite society again." Thaddeus did not want that outcome on his conscience, but to whom did he owe greater allegiance? A former companion who'd apparently acquired the disposition of a dyspeptic hedgehog or his own family?

How could he have been so wrong about her?

Lady Edith gave the humble inn a slow perusal, then she swiveled her gaze back to Thaddeus. "My father died up to his ears in debt from his gaming and wagering. My step-mother followed him within months. I attribute his demise to an excessive fondness for spirits, while the countess passed away due to a surfeit of mortification.

"Polite society did nothing to aid us," she went on. "Our worldly goods were sold before Papa was cold in the ground, my step-brother's dog led off by a neighbor while the boy cried his heart out all the way down the drive. We were passed from one relative to another, until the last of the aunts died. I pray for her eternal rest every night, because she at least wrote to your mother on my behalf before expiring."

The pink cloak and the worn feathers took on a new significance. "So you hate all who are well to do?" Though again, facts in contradiction caught Thaddeus's notice. A lady fallen on hard times should not have left her post on a whim.

"I loathe hypocrisy, Your Grace, and a society that pretends to be polite while laughing behind their painted fans at anybody who suffers misfortune, a society that blames children for their parents' bad judgment, deserves not only contempt but divine judgment."

The serving maid reappeared with a pint and a small pint on a tray along with half a loaf of sliced bread and a plate of butter pats.

"A pot of China black," Emory said, "with all the trimmings."

The maid put the offerings on the table, bobbed a curtsey, and moved away.

"They'll serve adulterated tea," he said, letting the foam on his ale settle.

"No, they won't. The publican's wife will not allow weak tea to be brought to your table."

"What makes you say that?" The ale was quite good. The bread smelled fresh from the oven.

Lady Edith put a table napkin on her lap and bowed her head. "For what I am about to receive, I am most sincerely grateful. Would that all going without such fare soon have reason to pray similarly. I would also appreciate it if the Architect of All Worldly Affairs could see fit to serve His Grace the truth regarding that awful book. Amen."

Would a woman who gave thanks for bread and butter find it morally acceptable to wreck another's social standing, and then mislead her victim while she said grace?

She took up her knife and spread a liberal portion of butter on a slice of bread. "With regard to the tea, you need have no fear of being cheated. Your boots cost more than most of these people would see in a year. Your sartorial splendor would blind the angels. Your height proclaims your blue blood, and you would send watered down tea back to the kitchen, making more work for any who sought to cheat you."

She was right, also fond of butter, apparently.

Her ladyship took a delicate nibble of her bread. "You won't ruin me, because I don't deserve ruin, though it stares me in the face without your good offices to help it along. I gather you think I wrote *How to Ruin a Duke*."

Her expression as she consumed a humble slice of buttered bread was enraptured. No expensive courtesan had ever gazed upon Thaddeus with that blend of soft focus, quiet joy, and profound appreciation. Thaddeus left off swilling his ale, fascinated by the transformation. Lady Edith was, he realized, not a plain woman, but a woman who'd learned to *appear* plain.

Severe bun, no cosmetics, no jewelry, clothing far from fashionable, nothing flirtatious or engaging about her. She set out to be overlooked, or perhaps that succession of begrudging relatives simply hadn't included anybody who might have shown a young girl how to present herself.

None of which must sway him from his course. "I know you wrote that dratted book. Nobody else could have."

She hadn't set down her bread since taking the first bite, but she did pause in her consumption of it.

"Do you think, if I'd written such a wildly popular novel, I'd be subjecting myself to a meal in the company of a titled buffoon who cannot be bothered to consider facts?"

"I always consider facts."

The food arrived, smelling divine and requiring a hiatus in the skirmishing. Thaddeus's objective mattered to him—he would secure her ladyship's promise to stop publishing satire aimed at him or his family—but good English beef was not to be ignored.

Lady Edith ate sparingly of the meat, and only half of her potato. She added both milk and sugar to her tea and drank two cups in quick succession. When she'd poured her third cup of tea, she sat back. Her cheeks had acquired a bit of color and the battle light was back in her eye.

"We should order a sweet," Thaddeus said, which was inane of him, but he did not care to resume hostilities quite so soon. Lady Edith had suggested a contradiction—literary revenue and straightened circumstances—and she had a point.

Maybe.

"I have eaten all I can manage for now," she replied. "The belly loses the habit of digesting substantial meals."

Two slices of bread, half a potato and a few bites of beef was not a substantial meal. "Then I will order a sweet, because I am an arrogant, ungentlemanly buffoon with the appetite of a mastodon."

"Suit yourself." She gestured with her teaspoon. *As you always do.*

Splendid. She could now insult him without even speaking.

"If you didn't write the blasted, blighted book, who did?" And since when was alliteration contagious?

"Let's see...." She peered into the teapot. "Your butler knows every secret associated with your entire family back for at least five generations and he's nearing retirement. Your mother is at the end of her patience with both of her sons for different reasons, and she's quite well read. Maybe she thought to shame you into holy matrimony. Your cousin Antigone is angry with you because you would not approve her match to that fortune-hunting rake, Sir Prancing Ninny."

Sir Prendergast Nanceforth. "I'd forgotten about that."

"Last year, you were rumored to be considering a marquess's daughter for your duchess, but decided not to offer for her when she turned out to have a fondness for wagering. She might not be your greatest admirer."

"One wagering fool in the family is one too many." Thaddeus had forgotten about the marquess's daughter too.

"You don't want to ruin me. Now you can ruin her instead."

"I don't have time to ruin you for any but the most pressing reasons," Thaddeus said, motioning to the serving maid. He ordered lemon cake with orange glaze and fresh raspberries—two servings.

Lady Edith poured herself the last of the tea, though it had to be cold by now. "I told you I haven't room for any more food."

"Fear not," Thaddeus replied, starting on the lady's pint. "Nothing goes to waste when a mastodon sits down to dine. I not only don't have time to ruin you for my own pleasure, the undertaking would be inefficient."

More milk and sugar went into her ladyship's teacup. "The horror of an inefficient duke boggles and bewilders the imagination."

"The book has been selling for the past month," Thaddeus went on. "The damage has been done. If I were to ruin you now simply for having written the dratted thing, that would be an act of revenge, and revenge on a woman for a jest in poor taste would not reflect well on me." Especially not revenge that sat about for a month re-reading the damned book and pondering options.

"So the ducal arrogance will spare me from ruination. My relief beggars description, especially considering I *did not write that wretched book*. I could not have written it."

The maid brought the dessert to the table, handsome portions liberally topped with fresh fruit and preserves. She set down one bowl before her ladyship, the other before Thaddeus.

"Try a bite," he said. "I'll eat what you don't finish." He expected a lecture about ignoring her wishes and wants.

Instead, the lady picked up her fork and speared a fat red raspberry.

"Why should I eliminate you as a potential author of the book?" he asked.

She put the single berry into her mouth. "I miss fresh fruit. I miss it more than strong tea." She ducked her head and speared another berry.

Her admission was troubling. Irksome. A distraction, possibly. "Why could you not have written *How to Ruin a Duke*? You've a lady's education, you observed my family at close quarters for two years, and likely heard all sorts of tales from the staff. My mother and Lord Jeremiah have also been known to spin the occasional entertaining bit of family lore. Am I to believe ladylike sensibilities alone stopped you from airing my linen in exchange for a small fortune?"

She took a bite of cake this time, dabbing it in the preserves. "Of course not. If I'd been ingenious enough to write such a tale, we'd be having a very different conversation in a very different venue, but I wasn't. To make public what should remain private is an act of desperation and the thought of debtor's prison should make the stoutest soul tremble. I wish I had written that book. If you were foolish enough to race from London to Brighton under a quarter moon, then the world deserves to be entertained by your foolishness."

Nobody had ever referred to Thaddeus as foolish before. He did not care for the term, and yet, that race had been stupid beyond all description, despite the fact that he'd won by a five-minute margin.

And Lady Edith was also correct that debtor's prison was worse than a death sentence. While the debtor slowly rotted from the inevitable ravages of consumption, he or she was charged exorbitant sums for basic necessities. Between disease and despair, a sad end was inevitable.

"You admit to being sufficiently desperate to go after the lure of dangled wealth," Thaddeus said, ignoring his dessert. "So why shouldn't I attribute authorship of that vile book to you?"

"Because," she said. "I have no patience with dangling modifiers, and what ruin isn't visited upon the fictitious Duke of Amorous is inflicted by the author on the English language. If I set out to ruin you, Your Grace, I'd at least do it in the king's proper English."

VERBALLY BRAWLING with Emory enlightened Edith on one point: She finally understood why young men delighted in pounding each other to flinders in the name of pugilistic science. All of her worry, all of her ire at a fate she and Foster had done nothing to earn, found a target in the person of the duke who was ignoring his sweet while he argued with a lady.

Maybe this was why gentlemen were prohibited from engaging in disputes with women—because the ladies could too easily learn to enjoy winning those arguments. Where would masculine self-regard be then?

"I have silenced you," Edith said, savoring another fat, tart raspberry slathered in sweetened juices. "Have a care when you step out of doors, Your Grace."

"You fear for my welfare. I am touched, Lady Edith. Moved in the tenderest profundities of my heart. What occasions your concern, when my social disrepute does not?"

"Low-flying swine. If ever an omen augured for their appearance, your silence does. You should not waste your sweet."

He moved the bowl of lemon cake closer and made no move to pick up his fork. "You make a jest of me and then scold me, but your point fails to prove that you didn't write *How to Ruin a Duke*. A skilled writer can affect any number of less-skilled mannerisms in her prose."

"I liked you better when you held your tongue. These raspberries are delectable, and one shouldn't spoil good food with harsh words."

The duke gazed across the common, apparently at nothing in particular. An older couple sat at a table by the window sharing a meal in silence while they each read from a newspaper. A trio of young men did justice to a pitcher of ale closer to the door. Two maids were wiping down empty tables, and a boy with a tray collected dirty dishes.

A scene like this would have fascinated a younger Edith for its plebian details. Nobody here carried a parasol, despite the brilliant sunshine outside. Nobody wore silk or lace at this establishment, but for the lace adorning His Grace's cravat.

"Your conclusion," Edith said, "that an author of some skill penned the book, eliminates your cousin Antigone as a suspect. She can barely write her name."

His Grace buttered one of the four remaining slices of bread. "Her gifts lie more in the direction of social discourse and water colors."

Gallant of him, to defend a chatterbox who'd never had a governess worthy of the name. "Antigone knows everybody and is liked by all. She might have collaborated with a co-author."

The duke made two bread and butter sandwiches, using up every last dab of butter. "Now you toy with me. If we bring co-authors and collaborators into the equation, half of Mayfair might have written that infernal tome."

A pot of strong tea and some real victuals had taken the edge off of Edith's foul mood, enough that she could make a dispassionate inspection of the man across the table.

Emory carried a vague air of annoyance with him everywhere, a counterpoint to his luscious scent and fine tailoring. He doubtless had reason to be testy. His mama was a restless and discontented woman by nature, given to meddling and gossip. His younger brother was the typical spare waiting to be deposed by a nephew.

Lord Jeremiah was a fribbling *bon vivant* for whom Edith had no respect, though she'd liked him well enough on first impression. His lordship had the gift of making anybody feel as if they were the sole focus of his attention and always would be. Perhaps fribbles developed that skill early.

His Grace's extended family called upon him mostly when they wanted something—a post for a young fellow completing the university education Emory had paid for, entrée at some fancy dress ball to which Emory would be invited as a matter of course.

Never had Edith seen or heard the duke complain regarding his duties. He groused at length about the king's financial irresponsibility, he lamented without limit the idiocy that passed for Parliament's governance, and he had pointed opinions about women who wore enormous hats.

But on his own behalf, he never complained, and he wasn't complaining for himself now. *How to Ruin a Duke* was affecting his family, and Emory took their welfare very seriously indeed.

"A co-author bears thinking about," Edith said. "Your mother's circle includes the set at Almack's, and they've all but banished Lady Caroline for her literary accomplishments. If Her Grace wrote *How to Ruin a Duke*, she could hide behind the skirts of a collaborator or hack writer."

His Grace next began slicing up the uneaten portion of Edith's steak. Perhaps he was one of those people who had to keep his hands busy, though in two years of sharing meals with him, she'd never noticed that about him.

"Lady Caroline had worn her welcome thin in polite society long before she took up her pen," Emory observed, "and for the viciousness of her satire, she deserved banishment. At least whoever decided to lampoon me left the rest of my friends and family unscathed."

"Which again suggests your mother, a cousin, or a rejected marital prospect. The author's ire is personal to you, Your Grace."

He finished slicing the meat and set down the utensils. "Sir Prendergast made a scene at Tattersalls." This recollection inspired Emory to a slight smile, more a change of the light in his eyes than a curving of his lips. The only time Edith had seen him truly joyous was on the occasion of becoming godfather to some new member of the extended family. No man had ever looked more pleased to have his nose seized in a tiny fist. No baby had ever been more carefully cradled in his godfather's arms.

The ceremony had gone forth, with the duke caught variously by the nose, the chin, or the gloved finger, and Edith feeling oddly enchanted by the sight.

"Perhaps Sir Prendergast is your culprit."

"He found another fortune to marry. Once his bruises healed, I made it a point to introduce him to a few cits who wouldn't mind seeing their daughter on the arm of a gallant knight."

Edith's lemon cake was half gone. She stopped eating, lest she regret over-indulging. "Generous of you."

"Prudent. He dwells in the north now."

"Which does not rule him out as your nemesis."

His Grace raised a hand and the serving maid scampered over. "If you'd be so good as to wrap up the rest of this food, I'd appreciate it."

A common request, but the maid looked as if she'd never been given a greater compliment. "Of course, sir. At once."

"All of it," he said. "Every morsel, and some plum tarts and cheese wouldn't go amiss either. You know how hunger can strike two hours after a decent repast, and good food shouldn't go to waste when a man of my robust proportions is on hand to enjoy it."

"Quite so, sir. Exactly. Waste not, want not. Ma says the same thing at least seventeen times a day. Eighteen, possibly."

The maid gathered up the plates while Edith tried not to watch. This was the best meal she'd eaten in ages, and Emory wasn't having the leftovers boxed up for himself.

"Thank you," she said, when the maid had bustled off to the kitchen.

His Grace looked at Edith directly, something she could not recall happening previously. Emory stalked through life, intent on pressing business. At the ducal residence he'd often been trailed by a secretary, solicitor, footman, steward or butler, all of whom followed him about as he'd lobbed orders in every direction.

At table, Emory tended to focus on the food, the wine, the appointments in the room.

On the dance floor, he was so much taller than most of his partners, he usually stared past their shoulders.

The full brunt of his gaze was unnerving. His eyes were brown, the deep, soft shade of mink in summer. They gave his countenance gravity, and Edith well knew those eyes could narrow on the deserving in preparation for a scathing setdown.

His gaze could also, apparently, be kind.

"Hunger makes me irritable," he said. "I cannot think as clearly, I cannot moderate my words as effectively, and we mastodons require substantial fare on a regular basis. If you've finished, I'll walk you home."

That was as close to an apology as a duke was likely to come, but Edith did not want him to walk her home. Foster might be there, and that would occasion questions such as only a nosy younger sibling could ask. He left the house each day "to look for work," but no work ever found him, and matters were becoming dire.

"That courtesy is not necessary, Your Grace. I appreciate the meal. Have you exonerated me of literary crimes against your person?" Edith never had borne him ill will—just the opposite—and no sane woman wanted a duke taking aim at her.

"If you were clever—and you are—you would toss out other candidates to throw me off the scent."

He stood and offered Edith his hand, still bare because they hadn't yet put their gloves back on. "What would my fate be, if I admitted to authorship of *How to Ruin a Duke?*"

"I'd offer you a substantial sum to return to your needlepoint and gothic novels. We would sign an agreement giving me all right, title, and interest in any further literary works written by you or based on your recollections of my household, and society could move on to its next scandal."

His idea of a substantial sum would doubtless be enough to see Foster commissioned as an officer, but then what? A lady—a woman raised to privilege—had few means of earning any coin at all, and Edith regarded writing as her best option for remaining a lady in any sense.

She took his hand and rose. "I cannot accept that offer, Your Grace. As it happens, I was calling on Mr. Ventnor precisely because I hope to become established as an authority on domestic matters in homes with some means. Signing away my ability to earn a living would not be prudent."

The duke left a pile of coins on the table—a generous sum—and collected a sack from the beaming serving maid.

"You are a shrewd negotiator," he said as he held the door for Edith. "Perhaps you called upon Ventnor because you seek more lucrative terms upon which to write a sequel to the first volume."

"A sequel?" Edith blinked at the bright sunshine and still—still— she had the impulse to open a parasol out of habit. "Somebody is at work on a sequel?"

"You needn't sound so pleased. Why haven't you a parasol?"

The meal had fortified Edith, put her back on her mettle. "I pawned all of my parasols months ago."

"And your good cloak as well, apparently, and yet you disdain to take my coin." The insult to her cloak was half-hearted, and His Grace's pace down the walkway more leisurely.

"Honesty rather than pride prevents me from taking your money, sir. I did not write *How to Ruin a Duke*. You could buy the rights to ten books from me, and I'd still not be able to prevent that sequel from being published."

His Grace fell silent, which was a mercy. The day was too beautiful and the meal had been too lovely to resume bickering. Edith made no further attempts to send Emory on his way, because the truth was, she liked having him at her side.

Even on this pretty day in this mostly decent neighborhood, Emory's escort made her feel safer and a little bit more the respected lady she'd been raised to be.

"NEVER WAS a correspondent more conscientious than you, Mama." Jeremiah kissed the duchess's cheek, which affection she pretended to ignore, though he knew she enjoyed the little touches.

The woman should remarry. She had taken good care of her appearance and held a lavish dower portion, though what mature man of sense would willingly take on a widowed duchess prone to managing and carping?

"A lady does not neglect her letters," the duchess replied, dipping her pen into the ink. "You would do well to stay in touch with some of your university friends, my boy. Life is long and the associations we form in our youth can be some of the dearest we ever enjoy."

What associations had Mama formed in her youth? She longed to become one of the patronesses at Almack's, but Emory had scotched such a notion the few times it had come up. Emory had a positive genius for finding the flaws in other people's plans, though in his defense, becoming further entangled with the pit of vipers at the assembly rooms would have made Mama miserable.

And when Mama was miserable, both of her sons were miserable.

Jeremiah flipped out his tails and took the chair opposite Mama's escritoire. "Most of the fellows I went to university with are either married or have bought their colors. The ranks here in London are thinner by the year."

She put down her pen and sat back. "And does marriage or an officer's uniform turn a man illiterate? Particularly when a fellow is posted far from home, society news can bring great comfort. This business with that nasty book, for example, is just the sort of incident most of your set would find hilarious be they in London, Lower Canada, or India."

Jeremiah found it hilarious, though the book was refusing to die. Five printings already, and Emory looking delectably frustrated for a change.

"His Grace is trying to find the author," Jeremiah said. "I can't tell if he means to sue the fellow or pay him off."

Mama capped her ink and sanded the letter, her movements unhurried and graceful. "What makes you so sure the author is a man?"

"Because the incidents recounted are true, and they mostly happened in male company."

She wrinkled her nose, not as splendid a proboscis as Emory

boasted, but a nose that could charitably be called aristocratic. "Even
that bit about the gin? I cannot imagine my firstborn consuming gin,
much less wagering on such a feat."

"It's true, all of it," Jeremiah said, "though the author omitted
some extenuating circumstances. I don't believe Emory has touched a
drop of gin since."

"Then a suit for defamation cannot be brought." Mama seemed
relieved about that.

Jeremiah was relieved as well, because litigation could only pour
fuel on the flames of gossip. Poking fun at a titled man who enjoyed a
reputation for unrelenting seriousness was one thing, miring a family
in scandal was quite another.

"Emory is not one to change his mind once he's come to a decision," Jeremiah said. "Why do you say he won't sue?"

"Because truth is a defense to any claim of defamation, young
man. To tell lies about a person is to slander him, to share the truth is
entertaining. Publishers know that, and while they might push the
boundaries of decency, they avoid lawyers at all costs. I see you are
dressed for riding. Are you accompanying me to the park today?"

He'd come to beg off actually. A few hands of cards or a visit to
Madam Bellassai's establishment always made for a pleasant
afternoon.

"Emory pled the press of business. He did not inquire as to
whether my own business might also obligate me elsewhere."

"On such a lovely day? Jeremiah, what business could you
possibly have to attend to?" Mama smiled at him as if he'd made a
jest. "Your cousin Antigone has accepted an invitation to ride with
me, and she's bringing that lovely Miss Faraday."

Mama was nothing, if not relentless. "Miss Faraday and I would
not suit."

"She's rich, agreeable, pretty, and pragmatic, Jeremiah.
You'd suit."

"How will she like a remove to India, Mama? I'm told the heat
alone can kill a woman of delicate constitution. They have snakes

there longer than the train of the monarch's coronation cloak, and diseases that can debilitate a woman for the rest of her days if they don't steal her life outright."

Mama patted his arm. "Such a flair for drama you have. Until Emory has his heir and spare, you won't be posting to anywhere half so exciting as India, even assuming His Grace does buy you a commission, which we both know he's refused to do."

"He has other heirs," Jeremiah said, not for the first time. "Cousin Eldridge and Cousin Harry."

"They are eight and eleven years old respectively, and a pair of reckless little scamps." Mama poured the sand from her letter into the dust bin beside the escritoire. "Until I can find a match for Emory, he will not be swayed. Trust me on that. Perhaps you might use the time with Miss Faraday to extol your brother's virtues if you can't see fit to impress her with your own."

Emory underestimated Mama, and Jeremiah had the sense she preferred it that way. She had a gift for strategy, and Jeremiah had six married female cousins to show for it.

"I'm to sing Emory's praises? That will be a short chorus, Mama. I love him without limit, but from the perspective of a lady, he's not exactly brilliant company."

Mama folded her letter and dripped claret-colored wax onto the flap. A rosy fragrance filled the air, the sealing wax being scented with her signature perfume.

"Emory is a duke, he need not be charming." She pressed a signet ring into the hot wax and set the letter on a stack of four others. "I suspect he envies you your social skills. You could give him a few pointers."

"One has tried, Mama. As you say, he's a duke. I will sing his praises up one carriageway and down another, but the poor fellow is as dull as last year's bonnet trimmings when in the company of females." And that, very likely, was precisely as Emory intended.

Mama rose on a rustle of velvet. "So it's only in the company of you fellows that he ever cuts loose. A mother does wonder. I don't begrudge either of my boys the occasional lark, but if half of what's in the dratted book is true, then there's a side to Emory I would never have guessed at. I'll meet you out front in twenty minutes."

She patted Jeremiah's cheek and glided away.

He waited until she'd quit the room before he rifled her outgoing correspondence. Every letter was to a male relative or acquaintance of longstanding—three of Jeremiah's uncles, a cousin of Mama's, the bereaved spouse of one of Mama's late friends. Each letter was a single sheet and folded such that no writing was visible on the outside.

Her Grace was up to something. Had Jeremiah more time, he would have broken the seal on one of the letters, read the contents, then resealed the epistle using his own ring. He loved his mother dearly, but he knew better than to trust her.

Time to share a meal tête-à-tête with an uncle or two. Jeremiah replaced the letters in the same order Mama had organized them and went down to the front door to await his penance. He used the time to ponder what he could say to Miss Faraday about his brother that would be honest and cast the duke in a positive light.

"Emory takes the welfare of family seriously," Jeremiah murmured, tapping his top hat onto his head. "He takes everything seriously, including silly little books intended only to entertain and poke fun."

But then, when a book went into five printings, perhaps the book, and its author, should be taken seriously.

CHAPTER THREE

"The only good duke is a married duke, and even that kind is prone to
wandering."
From *How to Ruin a Duke* by Anonymous

Thaddeus strolled along at Lady Edith's side, while he mentally
wrestled with facts in contradiction.

She had quit a lucrative post of her own volition and had done so
without first securing another position. Why behave so rashly? Why,
with a character from Her Grace of Emory in hand, hadn't Lady
Edith found another post of comparable status?

Why reside in this frankly shabby neighborhood if she was the
author of the most popular novel since *Waverly*? On the stoops and
porches, Thaddeus saw only an occasional pot of struggling heart-
sease, most of which looked as if a cat had slept curled atop the
flowers and weeds. A single crossing sweeper shuffled along the
street, doing a desultory job of collecting horse droppings, and a small
grubby boy sat cross-legged beneath a street lamp.

Why hadn't Lady Edith applied for support to the present holder
of her late father's title? Every man who came into a lofty station did

so knowing that dependents and responsibilities went hand-in-glove with his privileges.

Why should Lady Edith have to *ask* for support from the head of her own family?

"Who holds your father's earldom now?" Thaddeus asked as Lady Edith stopped at a side lane.

"A second cousin," she said. "We'd never met prior to Papa's death. You want to know why I'm not kept in a rural hovel like any other poor relation. The answer to that is none of your concern but simple enough: Papa left his heir an enormous pile of debt, a barely habitable country estate, and the bad will of all our neighbors. His lordship had nothing to offer me but the post of housekeeper without pay, and for my brother, perhaps a similarly uncompensated post as undergardener. Working for your mother, I was able to at least save back most of my wages."

"You have a brother?" Had she kept that a secret? Thaddeus took an interest in his employees and should have known this about his mother's companion.

"I do, and I live on this lane, so we've reached our destination."

Lady Edith wasn't looking anywhere in particular. Not at any one of the humble doorways on the narrow lane, not at Thaddeus's face, and certainly not at the sack of food he held in his left hand.

"I'll walk you to your door. Where is your brother now?"

"This isn't necessary, Your Grace. I know how to find my own dwelling."

"What you do not know is how to set aside your pride. If I wanted to find out where you live, I'd simply ask the crossing sweeper and then verify his information with that filthy boy trying to look idle and harmless beneath the street lamp while he doubtless dreams of ill-gotten coin. Tell me more about your brother."

Thaddeus refrained from adding, *I might have work for him.* In the first place, a brother who allowed his sister to come to such a pass as this might be unemployable, and in the second, facts not in contradiction still weighed against Lady Edith's protestations of innocence.

She knew the ducal family's dirty linen. She used language effectively. She grasped how polite society loved to gossip. She desperately needed funds. Very few people fit all of those descriptors. An army of servants might also know family lore, but those servants were either illiterate or not literary. Half of polite society had a gift for tattle, but not a one of them would willingly engage in labor for coin.

Lady Edith led Thaddeus to the fourth door on the left side of the lane. The street ended in a cul-de-sac, with a crumbling, lichen-encrusted fountain in the center of the circle. Once upon a time, this would have been a quaint, tidy address, a place prosperous shopkeepers moved to when their children grew old enough to take over the family business.

Now, these houses were teetering on the edge of neglect. A few had boarded up windows, a sure sign somebody was trying to reduce taxes at the cost of their eyesight. Brick walkways had heaved and buckled under decades of English weather, and a large brindle dog of indeterminant pedigree napped on the sunny side of the decrepit fountain.

"You are not to feed this steak to that wretched canine," Thaddeus said, passing over the sack. "This food is not charity, but rather, a token of appreciation for your insights regarding the mystery before me. I would never have thought to consider Antigone or Mama, or a co-author. You were about to tell me of your brother."

"I was about to wish you good day, and good luck finding the author of your misfortune. My thanks for the food." She tried to hold the sack and open her reticule at the same time.

"Is this brother a wastrel like your father was?"

"No, he is not. Foster is a wastrel of a completely different stripe. He does not drink to excess, he's not prone to wagers, but he had only a gentleman's education." She produced a key, which only made balancing the reticule and the sack of food more complicated.

"Allow me," Thaddeus said, taking both items and leaving her with the key. "If you set that food down, yonder hound will abscond with the lot."

"Galahad is fast asleep."

"Galahad is doubtless fast as a bolting rabbit when it comes to snatching a meal."

The lock squeaked and with some effort, Lady Edith pushed the door open. "I'll take those," she said, holding out her hands.

"This reticule weighs more than some cannonballs. Whatever do you have in here?" Thaddeus grasped the middle of the reticule, a quilted affair slightly worn at the bottom. "Is this a book?"

"*Glenarvon*," she said, "for weight, and to keep the papers I brought with me from being crushed or wrinkled."

"You have a bound copy of *Glenarvon*?" Another fact that weighed against her innocence.

"Half of London has a copy of Lady Caroline's tale and this was a gift from a friend who enjoys a good yarn. My brother was considering turning it into a play at one point. I'll wish you good day, Your Grace." She stood in the doorway, her faded millinery and pink cloak adding a poignant note to the dignity of her bearing.

"Might I come in?"

"That would be most improper."

"No, it would not. I am your former employer, we are well acquainted, I won't tarry long, and if you prefer, we can remain before your front window for all the world to gawk at. That said, I would rather not conclude this conversation where all the world can also hear our every word." All the world being, at the moment, one somnolent dog.

"Then will you go away?"

"Do you know how rarely people tell me to go away?" They might wish him to the Shetland Islands, but they would never say that to his face.

"Not often enough, for you don't appear to grasp the meaning of the words." Lady Edith stepped back and held the door open.

Thaddeus's first impulse was to peer about at the interior, to sniff the air, to generally behave with ill-bred curiosity. Lady Edith would pitch him through the window if he offered her that insult, so he stood just inside the door, where—indeed—he was visible from the street through the window.

"Why would this brother of yours be turning *Glenarvon* into a stage play?"

"Because nobody has yet, and the book was wildly popular." She set her packages on a rickety table with a cracked marble top. "Foster considers himself an amateur thespian and has a gentleman's ability with letters. He abandoned the project because the work is quite long for a staged production. If that's all you needed to—"

"He fancies himself a writer?"

"He's eighteen years old, Your Grace. He fancies himself a writer one day, an explorer the next, a documenter of England's vanishing folklore the day after that."

"Be glad he's not keen to buy an officer's commission and ship out for the jungles of India." Mama had emphatically forbidden Thaddeus to approve that course for Jeremiah, though his lordship longed to buy his colors—or have them purchased for him.

"We cannot afford to buy Foster new boots, much less a commission. When I left my post with your mother, Foster was homeless. He held a job as tutor to a stationer's sons, but the boys accused him of teaching them naughty Latin verses. Foster was turned off without a character and not even given the wages he was owed."

Most boys were born knowing a few naughty Latin verses. Jeremiah had them memorized by the score. "How long ago was this?"

"Six months."

So why would she then also render herself unemployed? "Where is Foster now?"

Her chin came up. "Looking for work."

Perhaps he was, or perhaps he was slumped over a bottle outside the nearest gin shop. A man prone to inebriation could run up all sorts of debts in no time at all, and even an author enjoying lucrative earnings could soon see her wealth dwindle to nothing.

"Your Grace, I do not mean to be rude, but I have been more than patient with your accusations. I did not write that blasted book, and if your interrogation is at an end, then you really should be going."

He should. This was her abode, he was a guest, and he'd overstayed his welcome. He bowed. "Thank you for your time. Good day."

She held the door for him, and then he was back out in the afternoon sunshine, enduring what looked like a pitying gaze from the hound by the fountain.

"Facts in contradiction, dog. They vex me."

A thick tail thumped once, then the beast sighed and went back to napping. Thaddeus tarried in the neighborhood for a few moments, taking stock of Lady Edith's situation and considering possibilities.

For the three minutes he'd been in her house, he'd remained politely in her foyer, if the cramped space near her front door could be called that. A parlor had sat off to the left of the foyer, a worn loveseat, mismatched reading chair, and a desk the sum total of the furnishings therein. The carpet, a faded circle barely six feet across, might have been woven in the days of Good King Hal, and the andirons hadn't been blackened within living memory.

The desk though, had been tidy and ready for use. The blotter had boasted a stack of foolscap, a standish, a bottle of sand, and spare ink as well as a wooden pen tray. Perhaps Lady Edith did have literary aspirations...

Or perhaps her brother, the gentleman of letters without portfolio, had turned the recollections of a duchess's companion into a popular satire regarding her former employer. That theory fit the facts, or most of them, and wanted further study.

ONCE UPON A TIME, Foster would have occupied the loveseat like a proper young gentleman, eager to slip any commonplace into a polite conversation. When he'd come into Edith's life as a shy four-year-old, she—who'd reached the age of fourteen without any siblings —had been enthralled with him. He had been so little, dear, and earnest.

Also lost. A small boy without a father was easily lost, which Papa, to his credit, had tried to rectify. His manner with Foster had been avuncular and affectionate, if somewhat offhand. Then Papa had died without making any provision for his fourteen-year-old step-son, and Foster's earnestness had faded into moodiness and impulsivity.

Now, he lounged on the loveseat, half-reclining, one leg slung over the armrest, morning sun revealing the adult he had become when Edith had been too busy humoring a cranky duchess.

"Breaking bread with a duke," he mused, one stockinged foot swinging. "Any chance of getting your old post back?"

"I would not accept my old post if Emory begged me on bended knee." Though the only time Emory would go down on one knee would be to propose to his duchess. He'd observe all the protocol— flowers, cordial notes, the carriage parade—which only made the tales told about him in *How to Ruin a Duke* more difficult to believe.

"You might have no choice but to apply for your old post," Foster said, "though I could come by some coin by the end of the week. Not a lot, but some, and it could turn into steady work."

His eyes were closed. He'd been out quite late, as was his habit, leaving Edith home alone and fretting.

"You won't tell me the nature of your employment?"

He smiled without opening his eyes. "Not yet. You'll be appalled. Tell me more about Emory's predicament."

Edith drove her needle through the toe of Foster's second pair of white stockings. Darning his stockings had become an almost daily chore, and yet, what sort of work would he find if he couldn't leave the house attired as a gentleman?

"You want to gloat at His Grace's misfortune. He isn't distressed for himself, Foster, he's distressed for his family."

"I'm distressed for my family. Those plum tarts were divine,

Edie. We shouldn't be depending on a duke's charity to keep us in plum tarts."

"I'll pawn my earbobs."

Foster scrubbed his hands over his face and sat up. "You shall not part with your mother's earbobs. You've accepted Emory's charity and that's bad enough."

"Not charity." His Grace had been quite firm on that point. "Appreciation for my insights. The duke prevented a fortune hunter from compromising Miss Antigone Banner and Miss Antigone did not appreciate her cousin's meddling. His Grace had forgotten that. I also pointed out that the duchess might be trying to inspire her son to take a bride, and now that I think on it, the duke also has several boy cousins at university who might consider publishing that book a lark."

"Where are my boots?"

Edith knotted off her thread. "Wherever you left them. I suspect within three yards of your bed." Foster's entire bedroom was barely three yards square.

"Did you mention those boy cousins to the duke?"

"I did not. Emory is loath to think ill of his family." That was not quite true. The duke was loath to admit his family's faults. Not quite the same thing.

"The whole book doesn't make sense to me," Foster said, rising. "You described Emory to me in detail on many occasions. His religious fervor for reform, his disdain for the frequently inebriated, his exasperation with Lord Jeremiah, and yet, the fellow in *How to Ruin a Duke* is a sot who makes foolish wagers and takes even more foolish risks."

An eighteen-year-old might be impulsive and broody, but loyalty to his gender had not yet afflicted him with the blinders he'd acquire later in adulthood.

"You put your finger on a troubling point." Edith snipped the thread right at the knot and rolled the stocking into a cylinder. "The Emory I know never sang other than to move his lips in church to a lot of dusty old hymns. The ruined duke accepted a bet to sing *God Save the King* at midnight outside Almack's."

Foster tugged at his shirt cuffs, which were an inch shorter than fashion required. "And he won the wager. Did Emory imply that the incidents recounted in the book never happened?"

Edith thought back over yesterday's conversation. She'd been so peevish at the time, so out of sorts and mortified, she'd mostly been intent on getting free of Emory's company.

"He never once claimed the book's narrative was untrue, now that you mention it." And the rest of Foster's point—that the ruined duke bore little resemblance to the duke Edith knew—was also puzzling.

Foster used the mantel to balance himself for a series of slow demi-pliés, such as a fencer might make prior to a match.

"You should take pity on a wealthy peer and help Emory solve his mystery, Edie. He'll bumble about like a drunken footman in a china closet, overlooking the obvious, offending the blameless, and getting nowhere."

A slow pirouette followed the pliés, the movement accenting Foster's height and the muscles he'd been developing in recent months. Such grace should have been on display at Almack's, not that Edith had ever applied for vouchers.

"I'm not offended that he'd question me," she said. "I am a logical suspect." Though so too was His Grace's friend and fellow duke, Wrexham, Duke of Elsmore. Elsmore's reputation was one of scrupulous integrity—his family was involved in banking—but then, Emory enjoyed the same reputation.

Or he had, prior to the book's publication. And who knew what constituted a jest among dukes?

"Who else might have written that book, Edie?"

She took up the second stocking and examined it for tears or holes. "Emory has countless opponents in the Lords, which means countless more MPs don't like his politics. His younger cousins at university would know all the family stories, as would any close companion to Lord Jeremiah. Emory went to public school and university with peers and heirs, and many of them might enjoy a joke at His Grace's expense."

Foster swung his leg like a bell-clapper, his bare foot brushing the floor. "Now you think the author is a man?"

"I don't know. All the incidents recounted are the sort of idiocy men get up to when unchaperoned by ladies. Are you training to be a dancer, Foster?" Male dancers were few and usually French.

"I am not, but I do enjoy watching dancers rehearse and perform. Emory should pay you to solve his mystery. Send him a note, tell him you've had a few more ideas. He'll be back on our doorstep like Galahad on the scent of a meat pie."

The last of the cheese and bread would be Edith's fare for the day, unless she walked to market and spent the coins she'd hoarded for coach fare the previous day.

"Mr. Ventnor wants me to send samples of my work." A silver lining, though delivering those samples meant another trek through the London crowds.

"Then send them, you must. Perhaps you could interest him in a sequel to *How to Ruin a Duke*. Surely you know tales regarding Lord Jeremiah or the duchess that the public would enjoy?"

The second stocking was still in good repair, and thank heavens for that, because Edith hadn't much thread left.

"What makes you think of a sequel?"

"*How to Ruin a Duke* is wildly popular, Edie. I wish you *had* written it. You've a way with a pen, you know the material, and polite society hasn't exactly treated you well. I'm just a common orphan, grateful for the charity your family has shown me, but you are a lady in more than name. You ought not to be hoarding cheese to have with your cold potatoes."

Rare temper colored Foster's words, though he switched from the swinging, loose sweeps of his leg to tracing a wide half-circle on the floor with his pointed toe.

For all his sleek muscle, he was skinny, now that Edith took the time to observe him in morning light. "Take the cheese and the last plum tart with you when you go out."

"I'll take some of the cheese, but you shall have the plum tart. You earned it by enduring Emory's company."

"The duke was unfailingly polite." Though unfailingly high-handed too. Edith didn't much mind the highhandedness when the result was good food in the house for the first time in ages. "Foster, you aren't up to anything untoward in your efforts to find employment, are you?"

He sauntered away from the mantel, pushing his hair from his eyes. "If I could find a situation as a cicisbeo, Edie, I'd take it, but English society hasn't the breadth of mind to tolerate such arrangements."

How bitter he sounded for a man of barely eighteen. "Don't compromise your honor for my sake, Foster."

He collected the stockings from her. "I won't if you won't, Edie. If that duke comes sniffing around again, he will mind his manners, I don't care how lofty his title is. Extract some coin from him to solve his mystery, but if he thinks to take advantage of your circumstances, I'll write a theatrical that makes *How to Ruin a Duke* look like a collection of dessert recipes. I'm peddling a script for a play, and so far, the reception has been very positive. Drury Lane promised me a decision by week's end."

"A play?"

"A farce. Something to make people laugh when life doesn't go their way. I'll be out late."

Again. "Best of luck with the play. I'm sure it's brilliant."

He bowed, then left the room with a dramatic flourish, waving the un-darned stocking for comic effect.

Foster had a way with a pen, he'd heard all of Edith's recollections of life in Emory's household, and Foster would know which pubs to frequent to chat up His Grace's footmen and grooms.

Oh, dear. Oh, drat and damnation. Edith put away her sewing, went to the desk, and took out pencil and paper.

∽

"THE BOOK SHOULD HAVE BEEN a nine days' wonder," Thaddeus said. "A bit of tattle for those moments when Prinny refuses to oblige us with a scandal."

"Which moments are those?" Wrexham, Duke of Elsmore asked, lounging back in the club's well-padded dining chair. "Pass me the wine. It's quite good. I'm sure the author is thrilled to be enjoying weeks rather than days of notoriety."

Thaddeus set the Bordeaux near Elsmore's plate. The wine was good, though too fruity to be an an optimal complement to the *boeuf à la mode*. "That brings us back to the question: Who *is* the author?"

Elsmore topped up both glasses. "You won't let this rest."

"If you were the butt of an ongoing scandal, one that threatened to escalate, would you let it rest?"

"Of course not, but scandal that touches me touches my bank and my darling sisters. You have neither sisters nor a bank, so why not enjoy being perceived as something other than the Duke of Dullards?"

The schoolyard nickname had followed Emory ever since he'd taken successive firsts in Latin. "I have a brother and a mother, and the last thing Jeremiah needs is a reason to dismiss me as a good example. Half the incidents in the dratted book were situations he embroiled me in."

Elsmore held his wineglass up to the candles in the center of the table. "What does he say about possible authors?"

Thaddeus pushed the bowl before him aside. The fare was delicious, but what was Lady Edith dining on this evening?

"Jeremiah is vastly entertained by the whole situation. Maybe an impecunious friend plied him with spirits on occasion simply to hear his lordship expound on matters best kept private. From there to cobbling together a book takes only time and a well stocked desk."

Elsmore took Thaddeus's unfinished portion and poured it into his own bowl. "Lord Jeremiah seems to be friends with half of London. What are you doing with that bread, Emory?"

"I put butter on it."

"And then you made a butter sandwich with another slice. I can say honestly that in all the years I've known you, which are getting to be more than either of us should admit, I've never seen you make a butter sandwich at table."

"I don't know as I've ever made a butter sandwich before." Thaddeus had been thinking of Lady Edith having to choose between hackney fare and a proper meal. "I met with my mother's former companion yesterday. We shared a luncheon."

"Lady Edith?"

"The very one. She might be the author of the damned book." Thaddeus took a bite of his butter sandwich, because he could not very well stuff it into his pocket with Elsmore looking on, nor could he have it sent to her ladyship with compliments from His Grace of Dullards.

"Does her ladyship hate you?" Elsmore asked.

"I don't think so." Thaddeus hoped not, in fact.

"Then she doesn't."

"You're an authority on females now, Elsmore, and you such a legendary bachelor?"

"I am blessed with three sisters, a mama, plus aunties and female cousins without number. I am an authority on *disgruntled* females. Why do you believe Lady Edith wrote the book?"

"After my conversation with her, I'm fairly certain she couldn't have." Bread and butter was good food. Thaddeus had stuffed his maw with it countless times and never appreciated just how good.

"Because she doesn't hate you? You should consider courting her."

Elsmore had been at the wine enthusiastically, but he was a good-sized fellow whom Thaddeus had never seen drunk.

"Court her simply because she doesn't hate me? Town is full of women who don't hate me."

"You hope. Lady Edith could make your dear mama laugh, something I daresay you and Lord Jeremiah don't do often enough. Not a quality to be overlooked by a bachelor duke battling undeserved scandal."

Thaddeus took another bite of his butter sandwich. "Her ladyship carries a copy of *Glenarvon* in her reticule to use as a club." He liked knowing she'd taken that precaution, but he detested that she had to racket about London without so much as a footman to see to her safety.

"Best possible use for that tome. I suppose a lady's companion hears all the family tales belowstairs, doesn't she?"

"Lady Edith is also well read, and more to the point, she hasn't another post. She would need the money such a story should be earning, and if she's not trotting after some crotchety beldame, she'd have the time to do the writing."

Elsmore gestured with his fork. "Maybe she came into an inheritance. Women do."

"She ate as if famished, Elsmore, as we used to eat at public school, watching the food on our plates lest it disappear before we could consume it. I had the kitchen send the leftovers along with us when I walked her ladyship home. That food did not go to waste."

Elsmore set aside his now-empty bowl. "You carried leftovers across London like some ticket porter? That is a fact in contradiction to everything I know of you, my friend. If Lady Edith is truly short of funds, perhaps she'd accept an arrangement that benefits both parties."

Thaddeus's own thoughts had wandered in that direction, late of a solitudinous night. He did not castigate himself for noticing an attractive female, much less one who put him in his place as easily as she dropped a curtsey.

"Her ladyship would fillet me if I even hinted at such a proposition." Which made her refreshingly different from the widows and duchesses-in-waiting who all but sat in Thaddeus's lap to gain his attention. The odd thing was, Lady Edith, in her horrid pink cloak and tired bonnet was more interesting to him than any heiress or courtesan had ever been.

Her ladyship could talk about something other than the weather, fashion, or gossip. She had common sense and a tart tongue, and how had Thaddeus all but failed to notice her for the two years she'd been a member of his household?

But then, he knew how: She'd taken consistent, well thought out measures not to be noticed. A quiet manner, drab attire, unremarkable conversation. Just as she'd weighted her reticule with a hidden means of defense, so too had she avoided catching Thaddeus's eye.

"Not that sort of arrangement," Elsmore said, lowering his voice. "Lady Edith knows your family and your social circle, she would respect your confidences, and you've already explained the problem to her. Offer her something she values in exchange for her assistance tracking down the author of *How to Ruin a Duke*. You could doubtless find her another post, for example."

Thaddeus didn't want to find her another damned post, didn't want her once again consigned to the conundrum of being neither servant nor family, but having the burdens of both statuses.

"I doubt she liked being Mama's companion, but she does fancy herself as an author of domestic advice."

Elmore finished his wine. "Offer to sponsor those aspirations. Have a word with a publisher on her behalf. You're a duke. The publishers have to be polite to you."

"Lady Edith wasn't polite to me." She'd twitted him, truth be told.

"Then you'd best pay a call on her before she accepts a post in Lesser Road Apple. She's making you smile and inspiring you to fashioning butter sandwiches. She also had you traipsing about London with a sack of comestibles like her personal footman."

"True enough." And—most telling of all—she and her situation had kept Thaddeus awake half the night. "You have a point, Elsmore. That doesn't happen often, so we should remark the rare occasion when it befalls us. You do have a point."

CHAPTER FOUR

"If the Duke of Amorous asks you to dance, you should smile, curtsey, and run like the devil."
From *How to Ruin a Duke*, by Anonymous

Rainy days were particularly vexing to Edith. Her half-boots did not keep her feet dry, she had neither umbrella nor parasol, and yet, if she wanted to procure something to eat, then go out, she must. Foster had sallied forth to do whatever he did of an early afternoon, while Edith had put off a trip to the nearest bake shop as long as she could.

"It's not a downpour," she muttered, donning her cloak. "More of a drizzle. Barely qualifies as rain."

And yet, a London drizzle had a chilly, penetrating quality that wilted bonnets and spirits alike. She decided against her bonnet and instead took down the only other choice, a wide-brimmed straw hat left over from when she'd spent an occasional morning in Her Grace of Emory's flower garden.

Edith tied the ribbons firmly under her chin—the wind was gusting most disagreeably—and gathered up her reticule.

"There and home in no time," she said, gloved hand on the door latch.

A stout triple knock had her leaping back. Did bill collectors knock like that? She wasn't behind on anything that she knew of, but Foster's finances were mysterious to her.

Edith cracked the door to find a very wet Duke of Emory standing on her front porch. "Your Grace. Good day."

"Might I come in? This deluge shows no signs of abating and I seem to have misplaced my ark."

Water dripped from his hat brim, and the fragrance of his shaving soap blended with the scent of damp wool and... fresh bread?

"I am home alone," Edith said, stepping aside. "You shouldn't stay long."

The temperature was dropping and the wind picking up. She really could not leave him on the stoop, nor did she want to let the house's meager heat out by standing about with the door open.

"I will stay only long enough to complete my business. I brought food." He held up a sack as Edith closed the door behind him. "You will accept the sustenance. I am hungry, I missed my nuncheon, and you would not be rude to a guest, would you?"

"Not until after we've eaten." Edith took his greatcoat from his shoulders. The garment had three capes and weighed more than her entire wardrobe combined. "I can't even offer you tea to go with the food, though."

"No matter. I brought hot tea as well."

Edith was torn between pleasure at the thought of another meal, dismay that Emory should again have evidence of her straitened circumstances, and—how lowering—pleasure at the simple sight of him. He was a connection to a better time, and as high-handed and imperious as he could be, he was also a gentleman.

He held doors for her.

He escorted her home when he'd no obligation to do so.

He'd thought to bring her food, and he'd arrived on foot—no

carriage, even in the rain, which meant no coachman, grooms, or footmen on hand to speculate about the purpose of the call.

"We can eat at my desk," Edith said. "I don't keep the fire in the kitchen lit, so the front parlor is the warmest room in the house."

His Grace did not peer around, wrinkle his nose, or otherwise indicate that a shabby little sitting room in any way offended his sensibilities. He passed Edith the sack of food, which weighed nearly as much as his coat had.

"I have another suggestion." He lifted the side table, carried it into the parlor, and set it down before the loveseat. "That should suffice."

Edith was too interested in the food to scold him for moving furniture without first asking permission. She withdrew a loaf of bread—still warm—and a crock of butter. A larger crock held beef stew seasoned with basil. The duke had also brought a wedge of cheese, tarts, what looked like a shepherd's pie, and—bless him—a flask of tea.

"The tea has sugar in it," he said. "I hope that will serve?"

"I'll find us some cups." Though all Edith had were mugs and they didn't match.

"No need for that. We'll share. Shall we sit?"

She took one side of the loveseat, he took the other, a cozy arrangement with a man of his proportions. The chop shop, bake shop, or pub where he'd procured this feast had sent along utensils and bowls, and in a few moments, Edith was consuming the best beef stew she'd ever tasted.

"Wherever did you find this? It's delicious."

"I have my sources. Try the tea." He uncorked the flask and passed it to her.

"I'm to drink from the flask?"

"That's the usual approach. Tally ho and all that." He tore a portion of bread from the loaf, buttered it, and sopped it in his stew.

Edith tipped the flask to her lips, the hot, sweet tea a benediction on such a dreary day. She passed the duke the flask and felt slightly naughty to be sharing it with him. One small step past the bounds of formality reassured her that a few choices yet remained to her, however modest the resulting indulgence.

Emory tossed back some tea as if parlor picnics were a frequent item on his schedule.

"Still hot," he said, buttering another chunk of bread. "I cannot abide tepid tea." He passed Edith the bread reinforcing the sense of casual intimacy.

More than the tea and the food, the duke's unexpected companionability made the meal a pleasure. Nobody warned a lady that poverty was a lonely undertaking. Edith did not call on those who had known her as the duchess's companion. One didn't presume, in the first place, and her wardrobe was no longer up to that challenge in the second.

"I'm told one usually consumes buttered bread," the duke said. "Preferably while the bread is fresh, but save room for a pear tart."

"I adore pear tarts."

"One suspects you have a sweet tooth. Your secret is safe with me. Don't let your soup get cold."

"Not a chance of that happening. Have you discovered who wrote *How to Ruin a Duke?*" And why would a man who could dine at the finest clubs or command his own French chef to prepare him delicacies choose instead to share this meal with Edith?

Now that the worst of her hunger was sated, the odd nature of the call itself troubled her.

"I have not found the author yet, but I might be getting closer. More soup?"

Edith could have consumed the entire crock but that would leave nothing for supper. "A pear tart would serve nicely."

Emory sliced her a wedge of cheese and held out the basket of tarts. "Before we discuss specifics relating to the book, I have a proposition to put to you."

Edith had picked up the flask, the pewter warm against her hand. Her insides, however, went queasy and cold.

"A proposition, Your Grace? A *proposition*? You come here when I am likely to be alone, bringing me much needed sustenance. You pretend to enjoy a meal with me, merely so that you can offer to do more damage to my good standing than any book has done to yours." She shoved the basket back at him. "Please leave."

He took a pear tart and left her holding the basket. "Your imagination has got the better of your common sense, my lady. I can procure the favors of the six most sought-after courtesans in London *at the same time* if I please to. What I seek from you is a rarer skill than what they offer, also of more value to me."

Edith was angry, but also caught in a confusion of contradictory emotions. She had long since noticed Emory's broad shoulders, his sardonic humor, his vigilance where his family's wellbeing was concerned. She knew he genuinely liked Italian opera and also enjoyed a ribald farce. He gave generously to charities and was incensed at the cost royalty inflicted on the national exchequer.

He was, in other words, a good man, if lamentably short of charm. He was also *attractive*. Not in the flirtatious, polished manner of his brother, but in a robust, unapologetically masculine sense. The notion of the duke sharing a bed with a half dozen courtesans put that attractiveness before Edith with startling vividness.

And yet, he was offering her some sort of proposition? "Half a dozen, Your Grace? *At the same time?*"

He took a bite of pear tart. "One doesn't discuss such topics with a lady, but I have it on good authority that more than two at once becomes taxing from an organizational standpoint. Shall we return to the matter at hand?"

The duke's expression was perfectly composed, and yet, his eyes danced.

Edith set aside the basket of pear tarts. "I'm prepared to listen to your proposition, but I will not be insulted in my own home."

"Nor do I offer you any insult. Quite the contrary. Do have a tart. They're quite good."

"Do stop giving me orders, sir."

The smile broke over the rest of his features, from his eyes to his mouth, dimples grooving his cheeks. "Why my mother ever let you go is yet another vexing mystery."

"She had no choice, Your Grace. I was determined to leave. I had had enough of service, and though she offered me an increase in salary, my mind was made up."

The duke wasn't buying that load of wash, but Edith had no intention of providing him a more honest version of the facts. He would not believe her any more than the duchess had.

"A discussion for another time, perhaps," he said, the smile fading. "Her Grace was much happier when you kept her company. We were all much happier, come to that. And now we are *unhappy* in part because of this damned book. You are ideally suited to help me solve the mystery of its authorship."

Edith bit into a pear tart, and oh ye dancing muses of Epicurus, the taste was divine. The crust was a buttery marvel of perfectly cooked pastry, the pears redolent of some elegant vintage sacrificed in the name of a perfect reduction, and the spices both subtle and complex.

"I am in love," she murmured. Perhaps poverty made the palate more discerning, perhaps she had never had a proper pear tart before. "I am in love with this recipe. I'd like to publish it, but first I'd like to eat the rest of that basket of tarts, slowly, one at a time, in complete silence."

Emory regarded her, a half-eaten tart in his hand. "They are good."

"They are incomparably delectable." She took another nibble, and the first was as ambrosial as the second.

The duke watched her enjoying her sweet, his expression thoughtful. "If I promised you an endless supply of these pear tarts would you agree to help me find the author of the dratted book?"

Edith spoke without thinking. "If you agreed to supply me with pear tarts like these, I'd promise you nearly anything."

His smile reignited, blazing from naughty to a degree of wicked merriment that rivaled the pear tart for its scrumptiousness. "You'd promise me *anything*, my lady? Anything at all?"

"I HAVE DONE SOMETHING DARING," Antigone whispered.

Jeremiah was trapped in the family parlor with the ladies, a penance that had befallen him because of the rain. No riding out this afternoon, no carriage parade, no pleasant stroll over to Mrs. Bellassai's establishment, not that he was welcome there again—yet.

"You have doubtless done something foolish," Jeremiah said. "Tell Cousin Jere your sins, and I'll do what I can to sort them out."

"I made a list," Antigone said, "of every silly prank I ever got up to."

"A long list indeed." Uncle Frederick was at the piano, twiddling away at Mozart. The music provided privacy for Antigone's confidences, and kept Uncle from descending into the usual litany of his own youthful follies.

"My list is interesting, not merely lengthy," Antigone said, scooting closer. "How many young ladies of good breeding have knotted their sheets into a rope and escaped the manor house to dance at midnight under a summer moon?"

In Jeremiah's estimation, that stunt was probably a rite of passage, akin to a youth's first experience of drunkenness. "But did you climb the rope back up to your bedroom undetected?"

Antigone glowered at him over her embroidery hoop. "Of course not. What do you take me for? I came in through the scullery as any sensible woman would."

"And perhaps at some point, you stole a bottle of wine from the pantry of your finishing school, and you and your five closest friends grew tipsy on one glass each?"

The glower became a frown. "We took to stealing a bottle every Saturday night. Cook went into the village to see her sister, and we knew where the pantry keys were. Nobody ever said anything, so we concluded the wine wasn't inventoried."

Jeremiah patted her arm. "The cook tippled, meaning she claimed to use much more of the wine in her recipes than was necessary. Rather than expose her own pilfering, she overlooked yours. At public school, the errand of purloining libation from the wine cellar is assigned to the newest boys. They feel daring and bold and provide a needed service."

He yawned, the weather making him drowsy. Then too, he'd been up late the previous evening.

"Well, I can promise you no public school boy ever stole his papa's cigars and smoked them in the orchard."

"Antigone, dearest, if a boy—any boy, from the royal princes to the drover's pride and joy—has a father who indulges in tobacco, that boy eventually steals from the humidor and coughs himself silly trying to learn to smoke. He ends up light-headed and sick to his stomach, and his dear father ignores the lad's reeking clothing. Some traditions cut across all classes."

Antigone stabbed her needle through the fabric and set aside her hoop. "You are being awful."

"I'm being honest. Why have you prepared this list of follies?"

"So I can attribute each one of them to somebody I dislike and write a wildly popular novel. I will be famous and have lots of money and everybody will wish they'd thought of it first."

Oh, dear. Jeremiah was torn between laughter and terror, for Antigone was stubborn beyond belief. "You do know that Lady Caroline's reputation never recovered from penning *Glenarvon?* She was never allowed back into Almack's, and many fashionable doors remained closed to her. Is that what you want?"

"Nobody ever liked Lady Caroline; besides, I'll write as if I'm a man recounting my sister's mistakes."

An interesting ploy. "And if your identity should be revealed?"

Uncle Frederick thumped away at the pianoforte, taking a repeat that Jeremiah was sure the composer hadn't included in the score.

"Nobody will find out who the author is," Antigone said, leaning near. "Emory has been trying to determine who wrote *How to Ruin a Duke*, and if *he* can't unearth that information, with all his resources, then no anonymous author need worry for her privacy."

Valid point, damn the luck. "How will you manage the vast sums that come pouring into your coffers in exchange for penning this disaster? You aren't yet even permitted your own pin money that I know of."

Antigone turned innocent blue eyes on him. "I was hoping I could count on *you* for that sort of assistance. I know you can be discreet when necessary, and I'd be willing to share a bit of the proceeds with you."

"Do you know what Emory would do to me if I in any way aided you? Do you know what he'd do to you?" Though, thundering choruses on high, what if Antigone enlisted the aid of one of her throng of admirers?

"His Grace can't stop me. Do you know, I'm glad somebody wrote that awful book. Emory is a plague on my freedom. When he's preoccupied with his literary troubles, he hasn't as much time to interfere with my life." She paused to look around the parlor. "I got a letter from Sir Prendergast."

Real alarm replaced Jeremiah's amusement. "I do not want to hear this."

"He's a very resourceful fellow. I'm sure the footmen thought the letter was from a former schoolmate. The penmanship was all flourish-y and the paper was scented with lemon verbena."

Uncle's sonata transitioned into the slow movement, thank the merciful angels.

"Sir Prendergast is a very married fellow, Antigone. He ought not to be sending you anything, ever."

She fluffed her skirts. "He's unhappy. He wrote to apologize to me for all the trouble and disappointment he caused. I thought that quite gallant."

If Jeremiah scolded her, she'd sulk as only Antigone could sulk.

The next time Sir Prancing Ninny wrote to her, she'd tell no one, until some daft elopement was in train—or worse.

"Antigone, do you recall the incident in *How to Ruin a Duke* where His Grace planted some fellow a facer behind Carlton House?"

"Very unsporting of the duke, but who will tell the likes of Emory that brawling nearly on the street isn't the done thing?"

Carlton House's grounds were not 'nearly on the street,' which was beside the point. "Emory drew the other fellow's cork because that man was making ungentlemanly comments about a lady. The lady is of good birth, and this bounder presumed to announce that he could lift her skirts on the way to Gretna Green, and the woman's family would have to accept him as her husband."

"What has that tale to do with me, Jere?" Murmured over the rippling chords of the adagio.

"The idiot announcing his perfidy was Sir Prendergast. Emory could not call him out, because they are of such different stations. I suspect that's all that saved Sir Prendergast's life. Prendergast was boasting about a young woman's ruin, all but on the street, as you say. Now you tell me he's writing to you, probably pilfering his wife's perfume to disguise his letter. Burn that letter, Antigone, and I will inform the gallant knight that you see his wicked lures for the selfish schemes they are."

"You are making this up. Sir Prendergast would never say such things about a proper lady. Maybe she wasn't quite proper. Did you or Emory ever think of that? Not every woman has the scruples I've been raised with."

Stubborn, stubborn, stubborn. "*I was there*, Antigone. Prendergast didn't realize he would be overheard by your cousins. He clearly mentioned the lady's name when he bragged to his cronies."

The sonata shifted into a minor key, appropriate for the rainy day and this hopeless conversation.

"Sir Prendergast was in love with me," Antigone whispered. "I know he was, and maybe he still is. He had to marry that woman, and

I understand that a gentleman needs means. But he would never have run off with some female just to get his hands on her settlements. You don't know anything about love because you're too busy being a... a libertine."

Said as if libertines were so vile as to exceed even the criminals and sinners filling Dante's *Inferno*.

"Antigone, dearest, please believe me when I tell you that it was your name Sir Prendergast bandied about so carelessly. Had anybody other than Emory been present, you would be enjoying a long respite at the family seat under the watchful eye of three aunts, two companions, and a brace of mastiffs. Emory handled the matter quietly for your sake."

Jeremiah braced himself for an explosion, but Antigone instead went still. "*My name?* Sir Prendergast bandied *my name* about in that manner?"

"If you believe nothing else I ever say, please believe I'm being honest with you now. You had a narrow escape."

She was quiet until the slow movement concluded. When Uncle embarked on a lively trio, Antigone took up her hoop again.

"Maybe Sir Prendergast wrote that awful book. He would hate Emory enough to do such a thing." She stabbed the fabric with her needle and pulled the thread taut. "Who else would take an incident like that and turn it into a reproach against our duke?"

"Weren't you just saying Emory was overdue for a set-down?"

"A set-down is one thing, but whoever wrote that book went beyond a set-down. I hope His Grace does find the author and draws his cork too." She paused in her stitching. "There's something else you should know."

"No more secrets, please. I've heard my quota for the year in the past quarter hour." And shared a secret or two as well.

"Well, you can hear one more, because Emory has seen fit to avoid this gathering. I think Her Grace is working on a book. She's been making lists, consulting her spies, and collecting stories. When we drove out the other day in Hyde Park, she was positively glowing over some tidbit she'd gleaned from Lady Westerfield. The scandals that woman has been privy too would probably fill ten books."

Jeremiah experienced a sensation that he associated with the early phases of inebriation when the quality of drink was particularly poor. A sense of events spinning beyond his control while he had neither the means nor the will to prevent a looming disaster.

"You think *the duchess* is working on a book?"

"Who knows. Perhaps she's penning the much-vaunted sequel to *How to Ruin a Duke*. Perhaps this version will include some of your exploits as well, Cousin. Won't that be delightful?"

LADY EDITH CHARBONNEAU in the throes of ecstasy, even ecstasy occasioned by one of Cook's pear tarts, distracted Thaddeus from the purpose of his call.

Steady on, old boy. "What would you give me in exchange for a liberal supply of pear tarts?" he asked, taking a bite of his own sweet.

"You are teasing me," she replied. "Besides, woman does not live on pear tarts alone."

"Would you like your previous position back?"

She took up the flask and traced the crest embossed on it. "No, thank you. Two years of being Her Grace's companion taxed my patience to its limits. Your mother enjoys ordering other people around, and I abhor being told what to do."

"As do I. If you do not want your former post back, then what could I offer you in exchange for your assistance finding the author of *How to Ruin a Duke*?"

"You needn't offer me anything." She set down the flask without drinking and took up her tart again. "I'm happy to give you what aid I can out of simple decency, though I am at a loss for what insight you expect me to bring to the task. Nonetheless, I re-read portions of the book last night, and some of the incidents recounted cast you in a very unflattering light. My temper is roused on your behalf, Your Grace."

She sniffed her pear tart, then took a bite from the crust.

Thaddeus rose, because if he remained on the loveseat, he'd be tempted to sniff *her*. Surely his dignity had gone begging along with his reputation.

"I cannot impose on your time without offering you compensation of some sort. I could sponsor subscriptions to your book of advice, for example, or find you another post as a companion with somebody more agreeable than my mother." Nearly anybody would be more agreeable than Mama in a fretful mood.

"I haven't written my advice book yet. I completed an outline and drafted several chapters, but whoever agrees to publish it will doubtless have suggestions regarding the final form of the book."

The desire to craft an exchange of consideration wasn't merely fair dealing from a business perspective. Thaddeus needed to know that Lady Edith had some means, that she was safe from desperate measures and desperate men.

"What about your brother, my lady? Shall I buy him a commission? Lord Jeremiah is certainly eager to embrace an officer's life." Thaddeus understood and respected his brother's desire to make his own way, but Mama did not. Then too, Jeremiah was the spare, and a spare's lot was to wait for an heir of the body to appear.

Lady Edith rose. "No officer's commission, please. Foster is all the family I have left, though we aren't even related. He has never expressed any wish to join the military, and I would rather he not perish in the Canadian wilderness."

"My lady—Edith—I cannot avail myself of your time without—"

She put her hand over his mouth. "Have you never had a friend before, Emory? Friends help each other. I will help you if I can. Come sit with me." She took him by the hand and led him back to the loveseat.

The novelty of being told to hush and then given an order scrambled Thaddeus's wits, for he not only obeyed her and resumed his place on the loveseat like a good duke, he also made no pretense of putting distance between his hip and hers.

And neither did she.

"Finish your tart," he said.

She delivered such a look to him as would have made a lesser man back slowly for the door.

"I beg your ladyship's pardon. Perhaps you'd consider finishing your tart before we embark on a tedious discussion. I would not want to distract you from your pleasures." Nor could Thaddeus form a proper thought while watching her consume her sweet. Perhaps the infatuations and flirtations that so violently afflicted Antigone, Jeremiah, and other family members were an inherited trait.

The notion was more encouraging than lowering. Thaddeus stuffed another bite of buttered bread into his mouth and fixed his gaze on the pattern of mock orange boughs on the worn carpet before the hearth.

"Where would you like to start?" her ladyship asked, dusting her hands several long moments later.

"With a list of suspects," Thaddeus replied. "Preferably a short list, full of people I don't like and can easily buy off or intimidate."

"You intimidate nearly all who meet you." She wrapped up the bread and put the lid on the butter crock. "I shudder for the young ladies who stand up with you for their first waltz."

"I am competent on the dance floor." In fact, he enjoyed a vigorous set with an enthusiastic partner.

"You are magnificent but your proportions mean most women struggle to keep up with the sweep and scope of your dancing, especially inexperienced women cowed by your glowers and scowls."

Thaddeus tore another pear tart in half and held out the larger portion to Lady Edith. He was torn as well, between pleasure that she had watched his *magnificent* waltzing, and frustration that he'd never asked her to stand up with him.

"I couldn't possibly eat another bite," she said, wrapping up the basket of pear tarts and the cheese in another square of linen.

"Liar." Thaddeus held the tart up to her mouth.

She nibbled, watching him all the while, and his battle against obvious signs of arousal lost ground.

"We will need pencil and paper," she said, patting her mouth with a table napkin.

I will soon need to stand in the cold rain without my coat. "Excellent idea." He retrieved those items from the desk as Lady Edith finished tidying up their meal.

"I will put the leftovers in the pantry," she said, "and you can start on a list of people who have motive to wish you ill, plus literary ability, and enough proximity to you to paint you in a credibly bad light. I'll be right back."

"No hurry," Thaddeus replied. "I fear the list will be quite long."

And she still hadn't told him what he could offer her by way of compensation.

THE PARLOR BECAME SMALLER than ever with His Grace of Emory on the love seat. When he rose to pace, Edith noticed how low the ceiling was, how worn the carpet, and that the water stain where the walls met was growing. But sharing a parlor picnic with him also gave the room a cozy quality, taking off the chill of a dreary afternoon.

Or the food had done that. Good food that had to have come from the ducal kitchen. She recognized the weave of the table napkins, and the flask was embossed with the family crest. A griffin *segreant,* prepared to do as griffins legendarily did and guard priceless treasures on both land, in the manner of lions, and as the eagles did, from the heavens.

Who guarded Emory's reputation, and who benefitted from tarnishing it?

"Before we make your list," Edith said, resuming her place on the loveseat, "can you tell me a bit more about the famous curricle race?"

"The infamous race. What would you like to know?"

"You are not by nature incautious. What possessed you to bet another peer that you could beat him to Brighton in a vehicle you'd never driven before, much less by moonlight?"

The duke held up the plate with half a pear tart. Edith took a bite because she did not want to seem rude.

"I chose to start at moonrise," he said, "because the roads are less crowded and fewer people would be abroad to witness my folly."

"Why race at all?"

He helped himself to a bite of the tart. "My dear, idiot brother had bet his new curricle that he could travel the distance to Brighton and beat his opponent, if not the Regent's record. He must have been half-seas over to make such an asinine wager. Beating the Regent's time publicly is not the done thing, moreover, Jeremiah had only recently won the curricle in a game of cards. He wasn't experienced enough to handle such an unstable vehicle at speed, much less in a race."

This admission was made grudgingly, though Edith could easily picture Lord Jeremiah making a dangerous boast when among his cronies.

"The book depicts the whole incident much differently." Very differently, with Emory nearly going into the ditch and winning by the slimmest margin. "Did you win?"

"I won the race without besting the Regent's personal record, though it was a near thing. I did not want Jeremiah to lose a prized possession, but neither could I have the Regent taking us into disfavor."

"From whom did Lord Jeremiah win the vehicle?"

Emory took another bite of the tart then passed it to her. "Finish this, please. The curricle had been the property of one of his drinking companions who doubtless goaded him into the wager in hopes of recovering the carriage for himself."

"Do you have a name?"

"Not yet, but I will." He scribbled something on the paper. "Any more questions?"

"What about the drinking wager?"

"I will never touch another drop of gin for so long as I live, that's what about the drinking wager. The very recollection makes my head pound and my gut roil."

"And yet, you won that one too."

His Grace grumbled out an explanation: A friend of Jeremiah's had proposed to drink under the table any man holding his vowels in exchange for a return of the IOU. Losing the bet would ruin the fellow, and yet, he was more of a braggart than a drunkard or a Captain Sharp. Emory had accepted the wager, altering the terms such that if the duke could out-drink the other fellow, the duke came into possession of the debts of honor.

"I am a mastodon," he said, "according to a noted authority, and thus able to hold my liquor. I won the bet and gave the notes of hand to Jeremiah to be collected if and when the fellow could pay."

Again, very different from what the book had portrayed.

"It's almost as if," Edith said, "somebody who had no firsthand knowledge of these incidents colored them all with a fierce resentment for you, and relied on readers also not having any firsthand knowledge to fuel the book's appeal."

Emory ranged an arm along the back of the sofa and crossed his feet at the ankles. "One attempts discretion, especially when indulging in rank folly. Those who were witnesses to the lunacy would be unlikely to gossip beyond the masculine confessional of the gentlemen's club."

And what was said behind the walls of a gentlemen's club was not to be repeated elsewhere.

"So we are likely dealing with a woman," Emory went on. "A woman who hears a lot of male gossip, or can consult with male gossips, but not with the men who were present when I was making such an ass of myself."

Edith liked watching his mind work, she liked that he'd abandon formal manners with her, and she liked very much sitting beside him when he did. She loathed that his basic decency had been miscon-strued by some misanthropic female.

"What woman has cause to be angry with you, besides Miss Antigone?"

The duke's expression was bleakly amused. "My mother, but then, she's easily and often vexed. She fits the criteria though: She's quite literary, she has the ear of half the tattlers in the realm, and she might well think a book of this nature would chivvy me into taking a duchess."

"Has it?" That was none of Edith's business, of course, but she wanted Emory to have at least one reliable ally to call his own. When she'd first joined his household, she'd realized that beneath his posturing and consequence, he was a decent fellow.

Even she hadn't understood how decent.

Emory perused the notes he'd made. "Mama's novel hasn't inspired me in the sense she doubtless intended—if she wrote the blasted thing. Who among the young ladies would have taken me into dislike?"

They discussed disappointed hopefuls, matchmakers who might be out of patience with Emory, and wallflowers given to bitterness. That list was troublingly long, though few of the names on it had as much entrée among the gentlemen as a well connected duchess would have.

"A widow, I suppose," Emory said, rising and stretching. "I have been avoiding them in recent months, not that I was ever much of a gallant in that regard. The hour grows late, but we have made progress. When might I call upon you again?"

Edith arranged her skirts and found a ducal hand extended in her direction. A gentleman typically did assist a lady to rise.

Well. She took his hand, but with the side table still before the loveseat, the confines were cramped. His shaving soap was still evident this close—a subtle blend of woods and spice. The fragrance graced a rainy, chilly day with a note of elegance, and memories of the ease Edith had enjoyed in the ducal household.

When she wasn't being run off her feet by endless silly demands.

"May I ask you something?" Emory said, peering down at her. The afternoon light was waning, and the rain had slowed to desultory dripping from the eaves.

"You may."

"Slap me if I give offense, but earlier, when you thought I offered you a proposition of an objectionable nature..."

"I was peckish and out of sorts. You would never—"

He touched a finger to her lips. "If I had, if I'd intimated that I sought a discreet, intimate liaison on terms acceptable to you, would your objection have been to the nature of the relationship, or personally, to the other party involved?"

His dignity was on display, so was his willingness to be dealt a blow, not as a duke, but as a man. Edith became acutely aware of the attraction she'd denied since first watching him turn down the room with this or that marquess's daughter.

He was a fine specimen, she'd long known that. Now he was revealing himself to be a fine man, one whom Edith might have flirted with, had their situation been different.

"My objection would not have been personal to the other party involved."

His smile was slight as he bowed over her hand. "I see. Good to know. It's time I was on my way. Let's continue to consider the conundrum before us, shall we?"

Which conundrum was that? Edith helped him into his coat, and while he stood, top hat in hand, she kissed his cheek. A reward for bravery, a gesture of encouragement to a man much besieged with injustice.

"We'll solve the riddle, Your Grace. The problem wants only time and determination."

He tapped his hat onto his head and pulled on his gloves. "My thanks for those sentiments, and keep well until next we meet."

CHAPTER FIVE

"No good duke goes unpunished."
From *How to Ruin a Duke*, by Anonymous

For five days and six nights, Thaddeus debated possibilities. Was Mama writing the blasted sequel? She tended to her correspondence incessantly, with volumes of letters both arriving to and departing from the ducal residence. At the theater, Antigone sent Thaddeus brooding glances, and at the formal balls, every matchmaker and wallflower came under his scrutiny.

And through all the sorting and considering, he was haunted by one fleeting kiss from a woman he'd spent two years assiduously ignoring. He'd ignored the musical lilt in Lady Edith's voice, the warmth in her smile. He'd ignored her humor and her patience. He had rigidly forbidden himself to do more than notice her figure—she'd been a woman in his employment, and thus her figure was *entirely* irrelevant—and yet, she had a fine figure.

"Shall you eat that trifle," Elsmore asked, "or stare the raspberries into submission?"

Lady Edith was fond of raspberries. Was she fond of Thaddeus?

"Help yourself." He passed the bowl across the table. "Does your mama pester you to take a duchess?"

"My mother is a duchess, pestering anybody is beneath her. With so many potential heirs to the title already dangling from the family tree, she doubtless considers getting my sisters fired off a higher priority, and thank heavens for that. What has put you off your feed, my friend?"

Elsmore tucked into the dessert, and Thaddeus battled the absurd urge to snatch the sweet away, because doubtless, Lady Edith had not had trifle in months.

"I am pre-occupied," Thaddeus said, studying the bottle of cordial brought out with the dessert. "I am considering the notion that my own mother also considers pestering beneath her, while embarrassing me into wedlock does fit her character. She thrives on intrigues and petty scandals."

Elsmore paused, a spoonful of cream and fruit halfway to his mouth. "That book transcended petty scandal a month ago. I've heard some of your famous lines quoted over cards, and my valet asked if I'd like my hair styled à *la épave de phaéton*."

"The vehicle was a curricle, not a phaeton, and I did not wreck it." Though Thaddeus had doubtless finished the race looking as if he'd survived a wreck. The distinction between a curricle and a phaeton was exactly the sort of altered detail a female author would regard as insignificant.

"I heard about the floral society," Elsmore said quietly. "You don't really take their foolishness seriously?"

The Society for the Floral Improvement of the Metropolis was one of a dozen charitable organizations that boasted the Duke of Emory among its honorary directors. That term was a euphemism for financial sponsorship, which Emory had agreed to at the duchess's request.

"Jeremiah didn't grumble all that much," Thaddeus replied. "For him to be the sponsor of record, when he hasn't a groat to spare, amused him enormously. I won't miss two-hour meetings devoted to the benefits of potted salvia over herbaceous borders, but I don't care to be told to stand in the corner by yet another charity."

"How many does that make?"

"Four." In every case, the suggested solution to having a disgraced duke on the board of directors was to quietly request that Lord Jeremiah "serve the cause" for a time instead. Jeremiah was bearing up good-naturedly; nonetheless, a scolding from the very groups who ought to be trumpeting Thaddeus's generosity was annoying.

"If you'd like to turn one or two charities over to me," Elsmore said, "I can find a cousin or sister to attend most of the meetings in my stead."

"Thank you, but I hope that won't be necessary. Elsmore, would you mind very much if I left you in solitude to finish your dessert? The press of business intrudes on my plans."

Elsmore regarded Thaddeus across the table. "I have never seen you so out of sorts. What could be in that sequel you're so worried about?"

"Lies that reflect poorly not only on me, but also on my brother? Jeremiah is hardly a pattern card of probity, but he is my heir. If both of us are sunk in scandal, where does that leave the succession?"

Elsmore poured a dash of plum cordial over his dessert. "Perhaps that's a fruitful line of inquiry? Have you cousins lurking in the hedges that would like to see you and Lord Jeremiah disgraced past all redemption?"

For a duke and his heir that would take a deal of disgracing. Thaddeus rose, because again, he'd like to have the benefit of Lady Edith's thoughts on this possibility.

"You will excuse me. I apologize for leaving you without a companion, but..." *What to say? I am drawn to the company of a woman who no longer owns even a decent tea service?*

Elsmore took up his spoon. "Away with you. Do you know how rarely I am permitted to enjoy a meal to myself? How unique a pleasure it is for me to be free of the burden of polite conversation when all I want is to partake of my food in peace? You have but the one immediate heir, while I have a dozen first cousins all clamoring for my favor and influence. The aunties and their endless progression of god-daughters line up behind the cousins, until I sometimes feel like a waltzing, bowing, smiling automaton."

For Elsmore, who was at all times gracious, mannerly, and pleasant, that amounted to a tantrum.

"Try a bit of scandal," Thaddeus said. "Clears a man's schedule handily."

"Are you complaining?"

"No, actually." The lunch and dinner invitations had all but stopped, leaving only the courtesy invitations which Thaddeus was free to decline. Jeremiah had been happy to do some of the obligatory socializing, proving that fraternal loyalty was not yet dead in Merry Olde England. "I will wish you the joy of your trifle."

While the day wasn't gorgeous, it was at least dry. Rather than summon his coach, Thaddeus walked the distance to Lady Edith's door, stopping only to procure sustenance at the inn where they'd eaten the previous week.

Will she be home to me?

Did that kiss mean anything to her, and if so, what?

What do I want it to have meant?

Thaddeus's imagination took the answers to that last question to all manner of inappropriate places, such that by the time he arrived at Lady Edith's house, he felt like an adolescent standing up at his first tea dance.

"Your Grace." She curtseyed and stepped back. "Won't you come in?"

Was it progress, that her ladyship wasn't warning him to keep the visit short? If so, progress toward what exactly? And what was wrong with civilization that the daughter of an earl had to answer her own door?

"You will think me presuming in the extreme," he said, passing over his parcel, "but I stopped to enjoy a meal at the establishment down the street, and realized that I need not eat in solitude when excellent company was available not far away." *Forgive me, Elsmore.*

"You are being charitable," she said, gesturing him into her house. "I am just hungry enough to pretend I'm delighted to be the object of your kindness."

"My kindness is being held in low regard these days. I have been sent to Coventry by several of the charities to which I've been a staunch contributor." Lady Edith took his coat and hung it on a peg, then accepted his hat and walking stick. She smoothed the wool of his coat, so the sleeves hung straight, a gesture Thaddeus found... *wifely.*

She turned a curious gaze on him. "Why would any charity...? Oh. They don't want to be tainted by your notoriety?"

"They aren't that honest. The hypocrites want proximity to the ducal purse and the family name, but not to the Flying Demon of the Brighton Road."

"He is a rather colorful fellow," Lady Edith said. "Let's eat on the back terrace, shall we?"

The back terrace was a euphemism for an uneven patch of slates at the rear of the house. Grass intruded between the stones, and the garden walls were encrusted with lichens, but irises apparently found the space congenial. A bed of purple flowers along each side wall was just beginning to bloom. Two venerable maples cast the little yard in dappled shade, which also meant that Lady Edith would have privacy when she sat out here.

The wrought iron chairs were sturdy, if ancient, and Thaddeus had no sooner unwrapped his sandwich than an impertinent pigeon came around begging for crumbs. Lady Edith tossed the bird a crust, so of course three more of the damned beggars appeared, strutting about and making pigeon noises.

"How are you?" Thaddeus asked, when the lady had consumed half a sandwich.

"I am well, and you?"

She was not well. She was quiet and troubled, even more than she'd been the last time he'd imposed his company on her.

"I am vexed past all bearing by this damnable book, and I've had a few ideas I'd like to put before you. First, though, might you kiss me again?"

～

SHORTLY AFTER PUTTING OFF MOURNING, Edith had begun keeping company with a local squire who had owned a patch of property near her aunt's cottage. They'd walked out together, and matters had progressed along the predictable lines of a rural courtship.

Within weeks, she'd developed an understanding with her swain, and her prospective groom had developed the ability to charm his way under her skirts, as often happened with engaged couples. When it became apparent that he'd had a fine time with the vicar's daughter as well, and that the vicar was soon to become a grandpapa, Edith had joined the household of a relative in the next county. She did not want a husband she couldn't trust, no matter how skilled he was in the hay mow.

And the gardener's shed.

And the saddle room.

For several years thereafter, she'd told herself that she'd had a near miss, and in exchange for bruised pride, she'd had a precious and rare education. That education had stood her in good stead when she'd become a duchess's paid companion, and rakes and roués had besieged her even under her employer's roof.

Nothing had prepared her for the Duke of Emory bearing sandwiches though.

Edith took up an orange, one of four the duke had brought along with sandwiches, lemonade, meat pastries, and shortbread. His generosity meant she needn't pawn her earbobs today, but that day would soon arrive. She rolled the orange between her palms, enjoying the texture and scent of fresh citrus, a pleasure she'd too long taken for granted.

From most men, a request for a kiss would have been easily brushed aside, but Emory needn't ask anybody for anything. He was a duke, a wealthy, powerful man who had better things to do than share a porch picnic with an impoverished spinster. And memories of him—lounging on the loveseat, pacing the parlor, standing in the rain on her front stoop—had kept her awake late at night.

"You'd like me to kiss you again?" Edith would enjoy kissing him, of that she had no doubt.

"I would, or I could kiss you. The point is,"—he tossed the last of his sandwich crust to the cooing pigeons—"your kiss has been on my mind."

"You have been on my mind too. You and your situation."

He plucked the orange from her grasp and tore off a patch of the rind. "My damned situation seems to be growing worse by the week. I receive only the courtesy invitations these days, and when Mama drags me to Almack's, I'm the only wallflower ever to sport a ducal title."

Watching him peel an orange ought not to have been an erotic experience, but such was the attraction of Emory's hands—strong, competent, masculine—that Edith let herself gawk.

"Even the patronesses *at Almack's* are turning up their noses at you?"

"Not explicitly, but those women excel at innuendo, and there was that business about singing *God Save the King* on the steps of the assembly rooms."

He popped a bit of orange rind into his mouth and shredded another piece to scatter on the paving stones. The birds leapt upon those offerings, nimble little sparrows joining the pigeons.

"According to the book, you sang after midnight, when the doors were already closed." Edith would have liked to have heard him, and liked to have seen the looks on the faces of his audience when he'd held forth.

"I timed my aria for when the orchestra was blasting away on some waltz or other, so I know I wasn't heard inside, but still... Not well done of me."

"Why did you do it?"

He spread out a table napkin and separated the orange into sections. "One of Jeremiah's more foolish friends dared him to serenade Almack's with a drinking song, at midnight, in full voice. Other fellows joined in the nonsense and soon bets were flying in all directions. Had Jeremiah stepped up to the challenge—and you know how little regard my brother has for rules—he might well have been barred from the dances for the rest of the Season. Mama would have been wroth, a petty war would have begun... but my folly was sure to be overlooked, or so I thought."

"Because you are a duke."

"Because I am a duke, and because, until recently, nobody would have believed me capable of such nonsense. Besides, *God Save the King* is regularly sung in every pub and tavern in the realm, and yet, who could object to that song at any hour in any location?"

"Nobody should object, but placed side by side with a half dozen other incidents, even *God Save the King* becomes suspect." Edith sensed a pattern to the tales told about Emory, a consistency regarding the direction in which each vignette was slanted to show him in disrepute, but she could not focus her thoughts on that puzzle.

Not when Emory held out the table napkin, the glistening pieces of orange offered like a bouquet.

"I want to kiss you," Edith said, taking three succulent sections, "and indulge in rather more than that, but I am not interested in anything tawdry."

Emory chose three pieces for himself and set the rest on the table. "You echo my own sentiments. My esteem for you is genuine, but also the esteem of a man who appreciates a woman's intimate company. I am not in the habit of... that is to say... I respect you, and I flatter myself that you respect me as well, thus creating a foundation for rare and lasting goodwill. Jeopardizing your opinion of me is the opposite of my aim. The *very* opposite, if you take my meaning."

If His Grace had ever kept a mistress, he'd done so discreetly enough that even the duchess, *even Lord Jeremiah*, hadn't remarked it. His lordship would have mentioned such a topic purely for the pleasure of testing Edith's composure.

The rotter. Edith nibbled a section of orange, enjoying everything from the juicy texture, to the sweet, sunny flavor, to the tart burst of citrus on her tongue.

"I am not without experience, Your Grace."

"Neither am I, though my recollections of intimate congress are growing dim."

This amused him, and it pleased Edith. "None of the scandals laid at your feet in *How to Ruin a Duke* relate to women." Was that a coincidence or a clue?

"Another factor that leads me to believe the author is female."

"Possibly." She finished her part of the orange and wiped her fingers on the linen Emory had brought along. If she accepted Emory's overture, she'd be embarking on an affair the duchess would have called a friendly liaison. Nothing legal or lasting, and nothing sordid either. No money changing hands, which in Edith's circumstances was an upside-down comfort.

A year ago, even a month ago, she would have been dismayed to be the object of Emory's intimate interest. A lady was virtuous, a duke was a gentleman. The very society that spelled out in detail what a lady must do to maintain her respectability offered not one useful suggestion about how that lady was to keep body and soul together when cast on her own resources.

Hypocrites, the lot of them, whereas Emory offered companionship, pleasure, comfort, and a respite from all woes. Better still, if Edith found she did not enjoy his attentions, she could simply say so without risking judgment from matchmakers and wallflowers.

Perhaps being a lady was over-rated, at least being a relentlessly proper lady.

"Our discussion adds more urgency to my desire to sort out that ruddy book," Emory said, wrapping up the uneaten food. "One cannot go forward in a public sense—for a duke there is always the public sense to be considered—with such a cloud ever present over one's head. Elsmore has suggested I look to the spares for someone with a motivation to ruin me and Jeremiah."

"Lord Jeremiah is hardly ruined by this book, Emory."

"Might you on occasion—when the moment is comfortable—call me Thaddeus? I have asked you to consider sharing personal intimacies with me, after all, and one hopes the undertaking will be accompanied by a certain informality when private." He wrapped up the orange sections in tidy folds of linen, though Edith had the sense his request was anything but casual.

She did very much enjoy watching his hands. "Yes, when the moment feels comfortable." He'd offered to become her lover, after all. The gift of his name was a privilege he'd granted to very few. That gesture suggested a friendly liaison with Emory could be enjoyable in a more than physical sense.

Edith craved the emotional surcease that intimate pleasures could provide, and quite selfishly, she wanted the fortification Emory's regard gave her. Not a perspective she would have understood a year ago, but then, a year ago, she'd been a paid companion.

A post she'd neither wanted nor enjoyed. "Your spare is a second cousin, as I recall."

"A pleasant enough fellow tending his acres in East Anglia. We have him to dinner when he comes up to Town, and he notifies me when his wife presents him with another child so Mama can send along a basket of comestibles and spirits. His idea of literature is an agricultural pamphlet read of a Sunday evening. I can't see him conceiving of, much less writing, an entire book."

"What of your uncles?"

"My uncles?"

"But for you, wouldn't one of them have inherited the title? I'm looking for a motive, Your Grace, for a reason why somebody would cast you in such an unflattering light." *And I am watching your hands and your mouth, and the way the breeze riffles your hair.* Concentrating on the book was becoming nearly impossible.

Emory leaned closer. "I appreciate your diligence more than you know, but at this very moment, at this very special moment, I am looking for a private place to take you in my arms and indulge in pleasures that make *How to Ruin a Duke* read like an etiquette manual, assuming those pleasures interest you."

His inflection was polite, his tone merely conversational. He rose and the birds fluttered into the boughs, much like Edith's sense of composure had flitted off to who knew where.

She had nothing to lose. He'd be discreet, considerate, and gentlemanly. "I am interested."

"You're certain this is what you want?" Emory asked. "That I am who you want? I haven't gone about the business in the manner you're entitled to expect, but I am very sure of my choice. I make this overture to you in good faith, knowing we still have much to discuss."

He was paying her a compliment—several compliments. Giving her the latitude to change her mind, apologizing for a blunt approach to a topic most people handled delicately, and assuring her of her desirability in his eyes.

"I am certain of my decision too, Your Grace. We have the house to ourselves for the afternoon. Let's go inside." She led the way. Emory gathered up the food and followed.

Edith had never envisioned that she might one day indulge in a friendly tryst with Emory. On the one hand, she was closer to destitution than she'd ever been. On the other, having been entirely forgotten by polite society, she had enormous freedom. She could think of no one with whom she'd rather share that freedom than her almost-ruined duke.

WHOEVER WROTE the dratted book would be furious to know

that its publication had resulted in Thaddeus happening across—for the second time—the woman ideally suited to be his companion in life. Lady Edith had duchess written all over her, in her poise, her dignity, her patience, her sense of humor, her honesty, and her common sense. She even got along with Thaddeus's mother, for heaven's sake.

Thaddeus had kept a distance when Edith had been his mother's companion, but thank benevolent Providence he could make a different choice now.

That he'd embark on an engagement with Lady Edith so precipitously, without the expected folderol, and then consummate the understanding immediately suggested the fictional duke and the real man had a few characteristics in common.

Boldness in the face of a challenge.

A fine appreciation for physical pleasure.

Indifference to convention when convention stood between him and somebody he cared for.

Thaddeus had no sooner set down the parcels of food than Lady Edith stepped near. "My circumstances are humble, Your Grace."

"What do I care for circumstances when I'm about to kiss you?"

This earned him a smack on the lips. "I care. I'd like for this encounter to be the stuff of fairytales and pleasant memories." That admission caused her to blush.

So would I. "Very well, fairytales and memories it shall be. I am duly challenged." Though this was only the first of many encounters, most of which would happen beneath the velvet canopies covering his various ducal beds. "I will be content if you enjoy yourself enough to invite me to another such encounter."

She slipped away and headed for the steps that led from the foyer. "Are you coming? My bedroom is upstairs."

He trundled along after her, up the narrow steps, down a short, dim corridor that nonetheless hadn't a single cobweb.

Her bedroom, like the rest of the house, had seen better days, and yet, she'd made this space her own. The quilt was a bright patchwork of green, lavender, and cream squares. The floor polished enough to reflect the afternoon sunlight onto a tarnished mirror hung over a walnut washstand that, given a good oiling, would have been attractive. A sliver of hard-milled soap sat on a folded flannel, and a bound copy of *How to Ruin a Duke* sat by the lamp on her bedside table.

The rug was thick, though the pattern had faded, and the colors might once have complimented the hues in the quilt. A few dresses hung on the line of pegs along the wall, a worn pair of boots arranged beneath them.

What cheered Thaddeus most was a bouquet of half-bloomed irises in a green glass jar sitting on the windowsill. Lady Edith had gathered into the place where she dreamed what comfort and cheer she could find, and now she was to gather Thaddeus near as well.

"I can hardly believe my good fortune," he said. "I awakened focused on that blasted book, but also knowing I had dreamed of you. Again. Lovely dreams they were too. Shall I undo your hooks?"

She gave the irises a drink from the pitcher on the washstand. "We're to undress?"

"One often does, in the circumstances." Though Thaddeus had nothing against the occasional hasty coupling against a wall. The moment didn't seem appropriate to air that bit of broadmindedness.

"Then yes," Edith said, "I would like you to undo my hooks." She set the pitcher on the washstand. "Please." She turned her back to him, posture as stiff as if she were bracing for a scold.

Thaddeus began by kissing her nape, where a faint scent of roses lingered. She was to be his intimate companion in every sense, and only a fool would rush what should be savored.

"You do that well," she said, when Thaddeus had managed to undo all of three hooks.

"My lady is entitled to fairytales." Three more hooks, and he could brush his lips along the top of her shoulder. Such soft skin she had, and how still she stood, like a cat reposing in a shaft of spring sunshine.

Three more hooks and she turned to face him. "Are you entitled to fairytales too, Emory?" She followed her question with a kiss, this one a lingering press of her lips to the corner of his mouth. The off-center starting point left him wild to taste her, but he made himself wait.

To *be* savored was lovely and precious, and a perfect beginning to all that he hoped would follow.

"Shall I undress you?" she asked, slipping the pin from his cravat.

Her décolletage gapped, revealing the top of her chemise and a hint of cleavage. Thaddeus had to focus his mental faculties to comprehend her question. Something about tearing off his clothes...

"Assistance disrobing would be appreciated."

She smiled the smile of a woman who knew her lover to be more nervous than the Flying Demon of Lady Edith's Boudoir ought to be.

Thaddeus's sexual education had begun the week he'd arrived at university, and he'd applied himself diligently to that course of study. Today the curriculum had shifted, from the pleasurable and fascinating business of erotic skill, to the rare privilege of being Lady Edith's intimate and devoted companion. To excel at that scholarship, Thaddeus needed to learn *her*.

She drew off his cravat and draped it over the washstand. His coat came next, and she hung that over one of her dresses.

"I like that," he said, holding out his wrist for her to remove his sleeve buttons. "My morning coat sharing a peg with your frock. It's... friendly." The first word to come to his mind had been *domestic*, but for his prospective duchess, domesticity would mean greater comfort than these surrounds had to offer.

Edith removed his second sleeve button and set both on the bedside table. "Shall you remove your boots?"

He put his everyday handkerchief on the table beside his sleeve buttons. The only place to sit was on the bed, which took up nearly half the room. Lady Edith's chamber must have been the master bedroom at one time, for in all the house, no other piece of furniture was half so imposing.

He sat on the bed and tugged off the first boot. "Are you nervous, my lady?"

"Yes, also... determined."

"Determined? If you think I'll climb out the window to elude your charms, you are very much mistaken." He set his boots beside her bed and stood before her. "Determined on what, exactly?"

"I'm not sure." She stared hard at his chest. "And I can't seem to get my mind to focus on the question when you're about to remove your shirt."

He bent near. "Actually, I'm about to remove your slippers, if you'll permit me that privilege?"

Determination was an interesting quality to bring to the start of relationship, or the start of a new phase of a relationship.

"I am determined as well," Thaddeus said, going down on one knee. "I am determined that you will enjoy yourself, that you will never have cause to regret joining me in these intimacies."

He untied her slippers, which were so worn at the heel as to barely qualify as shoes. Her stockings were neatly mended, her garters plain. With each article of stitched, faded, and worn clothing, Thaddeus's respect for Edith grew.

She was allowing him to see her reality, to see the evidence of her poverty, and her dignity in the face of adversity. That trust, given to a man whom half of London now regarded as beyond the pale, laid him bare as a lack of clothing never would.

He rested his forehead against her knee. "I want to buy you every frilly garter and silk stocking in London, every..." Everything. The world. Whatever her heart desired. Her trousseau would be the delight of every modiste and milliner in Mayfair.

She ruffled his hair. "You will buy me nothing. I've been hard at work on a new literary project, and I have high hopes for its success. I'd very much like your opinion on the whole undertaking, but we can discuss that *later*."

Thaddeus rose. "Once my breeches come off, you won't get a sensible word out of me."

She undid the first button of his falls. "A duke rendered speechless. How often does that happen?"

More buttons came undone. "My guess is, it will happen frequently when I'm private with you." What a revelation that was. For so long, Thaddeus had regarded his duty to marry as only that— an obligation hovering near the top of his long list of obligations, but never quite ascending to the highest position. He had an heir and a spare, and while marriage might entail some pleasant aspects, as a dinner obligation might include a good selection of wines, he'd never imagined himself in a match that involved passion, much less...

Lady Edith stepped back, having undone the falls of Thaddeus's breeches.

"Your dress next?" he asked.

She nodded and reached for her hem, but Thaddeus stopped her. "Allow me."

He drew the dress up slowly, careful not to catch any hooks or buttons on her hair. Her chemise was worn to a whisper, remnants of white work embroidery still visible about the hem. She'd tied off her stays in front, which made untying them simple.

"That moment when a woman is freed of her corsetry has to count among the most pleasurable of her whole day," Edith said, folding her stays and laying them on the shelf of the washstand. "You mustn't tell anybody I said that."

"Your secret is safe with me. I feel the same way about shedding evening attire." They shared the sort of smile lovers often exchanged, not erotic, but pleased and trusting. "Shall we to bed, my lady?"

He longed to remove her wrinkled shift and behold the naked whole of her, but that decision was hers.

"Bed in the middle of the day seems so decadent," she said, climbing onto the mattress. "But it's not as if we're to indulge in the nap, is it?"

"A nap would be more indulgent than lovemaking?" Thaddeus pulled his shirt over his head and draped it over another one of her dresses.

"In some regards, yes. Napping is the ultimate indulgence. I've been tempted to climb under the covers and not wake up until..." She scooted beneath the quilt. "My brother has a play under considera-tion. The theater told him they'd make a decision last week, but they've put him off again."

Thaddeus wanted to offer her reassurances. His wealth was considerable. He could buy her brother a theater, guarantee her the right to nap all day when she pleased to, and promise her a world where waking up would be, if not a joy, at least not a sorrow.

The lady was all but naked amid the pillows. She did not need fine speeches from him now—more fine speeches.

Instead, he peeled out of his breeches and linen and stood naked beside the bed. "Are we agreed, that if I doze off after our exertions, you will do me the great honor of joining me in slumber?"

Her smile was sweet, naughty, and wistful. "We are agreed. Naps all around in the middle of the afternoon. Won't you please come to bed, Your Grace?"

Thaddeus stroked the erection already at full salute. "Perhaps now would be a good time to abandon proper address?"

She patted the bed. "You may call me Edie. Come to bed, Thaddeus."

He came to bed.

CHAPTER SIX

"Some scandals are infinitely more diverting than others." From *How to Ruin a Duke*, by Anonymous

"Mama, your lap desk has become an appendage of late." Jeremiah took the wing chair facing Her Grace's loveseat. "Don't you collect enough gossip during the Season to sustain you?"

She did not so much as look up from her scribbling. "If you were more attentive to correspondence, you might have a diplomatic post by now. One never knows when an old school chum or his papa might hear of a vacancy."

"Preserve me from a post where I must eavesdrop over cheap wine at some pumpernickel court, or worse, perish of lung fever in St. Petersburg."

The duchess dipped her quill. "And yet you long to perish of malaria in the jungles of India. How like a male to bring not a jot of logic to his own situation. Emory could likely get you a position in France or Belgium. Possibly Italy. Even the Germans have excellent wine, if that's the criteria by which you evaluate an opportunity."

She was in a mood, as only Mama could be in a mood. "Why

hasn't Emory hired you a new companion? It's been what, three months, since Lady Edith quit the field?"

Now Mama looked up, her gaze suggesting Jeremiah had told a ribald joke at a formal dinner party, a transgression he hadn't committed for three dreary, well-behaved years.

"Her ladyship left this household six months ago, sir. She refused to remain even when I offered to increase her salary by half. Perhaps you know why that might be?"

"Haven't a clue. Women are fickle. Witness, nobody was willing to marry the old dear, were they?" He'd stretched the facts a bit with that remark. Lady Edith wasn't old, wasn't even close to old, more's the pity.

"And nobody is clamoring to marry you either, my boy. They aren't even clamoring to marry your brother these days, and that is a problem I had not foreseen."

The afternoon was taking a tedious turn. "Angels defend us, when a duke has to work at winning a woman's favor. He should be able to simply wave his... *hand*, and line up potential duchesses for parade inspection, is that it? A title acquits a man of all faults, from lack of humor to lack of humility and everything in between. Emory doesn't even trouble over his wardrobe overmuch, and yet, you claim he's to have any duchess he pleases at the snap of his fingers."

Mama went back to her writing. "Jealousy is such an unbecoming trait in a man who wants for nothing and never has."

"Spite is no more attractive in a woman who has everything she desires and more. And as for my wants, what would you know of them? You are too busy summoning your coven to choose the next hapless bachelor and giggling demoiselle to consign to wedlock. I want more than dancing slippers and good wine for my lot, Mama. A man can make his fortune in India, he can escape the thankless tedium of perpetual heir-dom. He can live his own life."

"I have given birth to two idiots, though you, as the better looking and more charming of the two give me the greater sorrow. Marry an heiress if you don't care for heir-dom. Stop whining about India, where you can be felled by fever within a week of strutting off the boat. Emory will stand firm against buying you your colors until his own nursery is in hand. If you haven't the patience to serve out that sentence, then do something productive."

Perhaps only an idiot could give birth to idiots. Jeremiah ought not to hold such sentiments toward his only surviving parent, but Mama ought not to be such a shrew.

"I am now responsible for serving in Emory's stead on no less than four charitable boards."

"And you find," Mama said, setting aside her letter, "that what you thought would be great fun—impersonating the duke—is so much tedium. Why do you think I did not offer to serve in his stead?"

Mama was at her most vexing, which was very vexatious indeed, when she was right. "You declined the honor of supporting charitable causes because you're too busy running the realm from your lap desk."

She also hadn't a companion to drag along with her to the meetings, and doubtless, Lady Edith had done any real work associated with those gatherings. A twinge of guilt had Jeremiah on his feet.

"Off to mind the press of business?" Mama asked. "Or the press of Mrs. Bellassai's person to your own?"

"For your information," Jeremiah said, making a decorous progress toward the door, "I haven't frequented her establishment for some weeks. My family is already battling enough scandal that I needn't stir that pot." Besides, the lady had made it plain he wasn't welcome, of all the nerve.

Mama took out another sheet of paper. "Jeremiah, I despair of you. I truly do. It's a wonder you weren't the subject of some scandalous book: *How to Waste Good Tailoring and a Generous Allowance*. Find a decent woman with adequate settlements who'll have you, and perhaps Emory will follow your example. Lord knows you seem unable to follow his."

India was not far enough away from such maternal devotion. The Antipodes were not far enough away.

"Would you have me follow him onto the pages of the tattlers, Mama? Though I do believe his reputation is improved by the mischief recounted in that book."

"You think so because, as noted, you haven't an ounce of sense. That book went too far, Jeremiah, and I'm learning that many of the incidents recounted weren't half so madcap as they've been portrayed."

This appeared to worry the duchess. Well, good. Without a companion to vent her spleen upon, Her Grace was clearly in need of something to occupy her. Fretting over Emory would serve nicely.

"I'm going out," Jeremiah said. "Maybe I'll run into an heiress who has a use for a man who's charming, witty, intelligent, handsome, kind to children and animals, and,"—he opened the door—"patient with the elderly."

He closed the door just as a soft thud sounded against the other side, proving he was not a useless cipher after all. If Mama was back to throwing her slippers—a behavior she'd eschewed under Lady Edith's watch—then Jeremiah had at least cheered up his mother.

Though if she were to hire another pretty, soft-spoken, endlessly agreeable companion, that would cheer Jeremiah up a bit too.

EDITH'S AFTERNOON had taken on the quality of a fairytale. She beheld an entirely naked, very well made lover in a frankly aroused state, and that lover was climbing into bed with her. While the part of her brought up to be a pattern card of feminine decorum admitted to a touch of consternation—His Grace of Emory could rebuke the sovereign with little more than a raised eyebrow—the rest of Edith rejoiced.

Poverty was lonely and uncomfortable. A lady fallen on hard times became invisible to those who could help her, and all too obvious to those who'd mock her. Thaddeus offered a respite, a place and time set apart from life's frustrations, and he offered her the pleasure of his intimate company.

"Come here," he said, settling on his back and raising an arm. "We must deal with the bow and curtsey."

Edith snuggled against his side. "I beg your pardon?"

"The part where I admit I don't know everything about pleasing a lady, though I have, through diligent study, learned that if a woman is asked, she will often tell me when I'm on the right path—and when I'm not. In the latter event, or even in the former, please don't wait to be asked."

If this bow and curtsey was part of intimate protocol, then Edith's education in frolicking had heretofore been neglected. Her previous experiences hadn't included much in the way of such consideration other than, "Hold still," "Hush, for the love of God," and, "Thanks, pet. Hope you don't mind that I nodded off for a bit."

"You are on the right path," she said, tracing the muscles of Emory's chest. "If I'm not batting at your hands, yanking on your hair, or telling you to for pity's sake give me room to breathe, you're on the right path."

He drew a pin from her hair. "Somebody has not acquitted himself according to the standard to which you, or any female, is entitled." More pins followed the first, forming a pile on the bedside table, until Edith's braid came loose. "I have a theory," Emory went on, "that decent women are kept in sexual ignorance so men might wallow in blissful selfishness, but my theory does not comport with available observations."

Such talk, full of long, prosy sentences, and long, lofty words, inspired Edith to wrap her hand around another long, impressive display.

"What observations are those?" she asked.

"A moment, if you please. My speaking powers are overwhelmed by my gratitude. Do that again."

She stroked him with a slow, loose grip. "About your observations?"

"I haven't any, other than to observe that your touch is divine."

"Focus, Emory. You believe a woman's sexual ignorance allows men to be selfish, but something contradicts your theory." What a delight, to talk in bed and tease a lover.

"If all I wanted was to spend," he said, moving his hips in counterpoint to her hand, "I could and do afford myself that pleasure regularly. If what I want is more than simple animal gratification, then pleasing my lover can only... increase.... my own... satisfaction."

In the next instant, Edith was on her back, a naked duke draped over her.

"Allow me to demonstrate." His kisses began softly, a buss to her check, a ticklish nuzzle along her jaw. The Duke of Emory had a playful streak—and so did Edith. She kissed him back, until flirtatious fencing became dueling in earnest.

When he broke the kiss, they were both panting. "Edith, at the risk of being precipitous..."

She wrapped her hand around him again. "Now would be wonderful. Right here,"—she scooted her hips—"and right *this very moment.*"

Silence spread, the quiet all the more profound for the banter and wrestling that had preceded it. Emory moved slowly, his rhythm perfectly designed to shift the mood from lusty to intimately precious.

A thread of sadness wove its way past Edith's growing desire. This interlude was stolen against loneliness, worry, and despair, and Edith would not have traded it for all the creature comforts in the world. Still, she could long for more. Emory spoke of being welcome in her bed again, but Edith could not afford to develop expectations where he was concerned.

"Why the sigh?" he whispered, pausing to kiss her brow.

"I'm happy." Part of the truth.

"Let's see if we can make you happier."

He did, oh, he did. The diabolical wretch inspired such an explosion of pleasure that she cried out, clinging to him and wringing the last drop of satisfaction from him, only to lie spent as he withdrew and finished on her belly.

The bliss of gratification was all encompassing, chasing away every regret and doubt Edith had ever claimed. If she'd kept her post as a companion, she could not have had this moment, Emory drowsing in her arms while she sketched the petals of an iris on his back. If she had remained in his mother's employ, the distance between her and Emory would have been unbridgeable, the swift currents of propriety and differing stations ever separating them.

"Being a well mannered mastodon," Emory said, "I will make use of that handkerchief, if you'll pass it to me."

Edith obliged, resenting the intrusion of practicality even as she appreciated Emory's lack of pretension. He was brisk and thorough about the tidying up, and when she expected him to be just as brisk about donning his clothing, he instead pitched the linen in the direction of his boots and rolled to his side.

"Let's move on to the truly decadent portion of the program," he said, pulling Edith into the curve of his body. "Let's have a nap, shall we?"

He had the knack of cuddling without smothering, of being warm but not hot, of keeping a moment light without shading into frivolity. He was, in short, the fairytale lover of Edith's dreams, and she was going to miss him for the rest of her life.

THADDEUS DRIFTED off on a rose-scented breeze. For the rest of his life, the simple, profound, mysterious delight of making love with Edith Charbonneau, soon to be Edith, Her Grace of Emory, was to be his. That great gift made up for all the slanderous books anybody could ever write about him or his progeny.

Edith was a passionate, inventive, demanding lover, and Thaddeus was honestly, blissfully worn out. Withdrawing had been a habit, and thank God for that. If Edith wanted a lengthy engagement,

Thaddeus would oblige with good grace, provided the engagement wasn't celibate.

His nap was short and deep, as if his soul knew he'd at last found his way into the right bed. Edith, by contrast, slumbered on, allowing him the smug pleasure of concluding he'd loved her to exhaustion.

And, true to mastodon form, he was hungry again. They'd shared one meal on the back porch and another in the parlor. Why not bring his lady a snack in bed?

Thaddeus eased from the covers and donned shirt and breeches in silence. Edith stirred sleepily, a fetching picture amid the pillows. Her braid had come loose, a golden skein curling past her shoulder, and one rosy breast peeking from beneath the quilt.

"Food," he muttered. "Sustenance. Allow the lady to keep up her strength. We aren't all mastodons."

The notion of rearing a herd of little mastodons and mastodonesses with Edith cheered him as he made his way to the kitchen and retrieved a glass of lemonade, an orange, and two pieces of shortbread. He passed Edith's desk, where her work in progress had clearly occupied her prior to his arrival.

He didn't think to peek, though she'd mentioned discussing the project with him. His intent was to leave her a note, a small expression of fondness for her to find after he'd left, though fondness was putting the situation mildly. Thaddeus finally understood all the friends who'd become distracted, smiling, oddly quiet creatures upon the occasion of taking a spouse.

"They are happy, those fellows. I suspect their wives are too." He set the food on the edge of the desk and took the chair. He was so far gone on newfound dreams of connubial joy that he was even pleased to be sitting in the very chair where Edith sat.

"Daft," he said, taking a bite of a shortbread. "But happy. A fair trade."

He reached for a sheet of foolscap, though Edith's manuscript sat just to his left. Her penmanship was all that a lady's should be, graceful, legible, and without a blot or correction.

He didn't mean to peek, truly he didn't, and yet...

Dear reader, if you assume the escapades of the Duke of Amorous were sufficient to fill only one volume, I must respectfully inform you that you are in error. His Grace's peccadillos are more interesting and numerous than you have been led to believe. That revelation astounds the imagination, I know, but read on and be amazed....

The shortbread turned to ashes in Thaddeus's mouth. He absolutely *was* astounded, at his own stupidity. His own gullibility. His own...

"The mastodon became extinct, probably because he was no smarter than I have been."

Thaddeus could not bring himself to read on, and before he could retrieve the rest of his clothes from the bedroom he needed time to marshal his wits. He rose from the chair, feeling unclean, furious, and...

Determined, by God. The word took on new meaning, in fact. Perhaps Lady Edith had been determined to extract the last ounce of revenge upon his family for some slight from Mama, perhaps her ladyship was angry at all of polite society. Not by word or deed would Thaddeus gratify her petty maneuvers with an opportunity to fling her excuses in his face.

He forced himself to breathe slowly and evenly, to set aside hurt feelings and shame. He returned the rest of the food to the kitchen for his appetite had been replaced by nausea. Logic came to his aid, and a plan began to take shape. If Lady Edith thought she could destroy the reputation of a duke, well, she'd tilted at that windmill, and Thaddeus was still standing. She'd failed to account for the fact that, much more easily than a duke could be brought low by undeserved defamation, he could push an impoverished schemer into utter ruin merely by airing the truth.

First, he would depart the premises without disclosing what he'd learned.

Second, he would have a word with Mama, and through her vast network of gossips, he'd put the truth of Lady Edith's perfidy before all of polite society.

Third, he'd offer her ladyship a small sum in exchange for the rights to her scribblings and a promise that she'd quit the metropolis, never to return.

Fourth, he'd get quietly drunk and try to forgive himself for having trusted her.

When he returned to the bedroom, he found the author of his troubles still asleep, the picture of feminine innocence. He tucked the covers up around her, because the sight of her dreaming so peacefully exacerbated his temper.

How dare she? He dressed quickly and quietly, seething all the while. He'd provided her a home and a livelihood for months, and she'd thanked him by turning her back on his family, then penning a pack of misrepresentations and exaggerations. The nerve, the unmitigated hubris, the sheer, unpardonable...

He'd just finished tying his cravat when he realized Edith watched him from the bed.

"Must you go?" she asked, sitting up. "I know better than to ask that. You're a busy man, but I wish you could tarry longer."

So she could snack on the remnants of his dignity? Thaddeus pulled the knot in his linen snug and smiled at her over his shoulder.

"Alas, I must leave, my lady. I wish I had no cause to abandon you, but I am compelled by the duties of my station to quit the premises. You needn't see me out." He didn't want her hands on him, didn't want to see her unclothed, didn't want to acknowledge what a great, pathetic fool he'd been.

She fished her chemise from beneath the covers and slipped it over her head. Thaddeus fiddled with his sleeve buttons rather than gawk at what he should never have seen.

"I'll at least kiss you farewell," she said. "This interlude was an unexpected pleasure. I hope you have no regrets?"

Oh, he had regrets. He regretted not trusting his first instincts where she was concerned, he regretted that she was so much that he could esteem and everything he abhorred. He regretted ever welcoming her into his household.

"Regrets are so tedious," he said, consulting his watch. "If you have regrets, I hope they won't trouble you for long." Three or four eternities should be sufficient, provided they were spent in a purgatory of unrelenting opprobrium.

She left the bed and drew on a dressing gown that had been draped over the footboard. "I have no regrets. None at all."

She snuggled up against him, and he nearly embraced her out of... what? Stupidity? Reflex?

"I really must be going," he said. "Duty calls and all that." He sounded like Jeremiah, sidling away from responsibility while pretending to move briskly toward it, though getting free of Lady Edith's company had become imperative. She wasn't acting guilty, she wasn't acting smug.

She seemed sad to him, but that had to be more of her deceptive nature on display.

"Then be off," she said, smiling up at him. "I have work to do, and I'm sure you have appointments to keep."

He braced himself to endure a kiss on the mouth, but she instead kissed his cheek and lingered near for a moment, then stepped back. His escape was apparently to be successful, no shouting, no accusations, no disclosing his intentions where she was concerned, no... anything.

"Good-bye," she said, gathering the dressing gown around herself.

The bed was rumpled behind her, her feet were bare, and her braid was coming undone. Nonetheless, her bearing was dignified, and that—the quality of her silence, the calm in her gaze—vexed Thaddeus into nearly blurting out what he'd found.

He bowed without taking her hand. "Good-bye." By sheer force of will, he made his way down the steps and out the front door, pausing only to collect his hat, gloves, and walking stick. He kept marching, no looking back, no last glance over his shoulder to see if the lady watched him depart.

He'd been a fool. Women had been making fools of men since the dawn of history. Perhaps somebody should write a book about that, about all the times men had been led astray by...

His steps slowed as he approached the corner. He did steal a glance at the tired, humble dwelling where he'd left a piece of his heart and all of his delusions. Lady Edith stood in the window of the upper story, a pale figure who didn't look to be gloating. She dabbed at her cheek with the edge of a shawl, the quality of the gesture suggesting that Thaddeus had, in fact, left her in tears.

She moved away from the window, and he stepped off the walkway, nearly getting himself run over by a stylish phaeton pulled by matching bays.

"I HAVE THE BEST NEWS, EDIE!" Foster took her by the hand and waltzed with her around the parlor before he'd even removed his top hat. "The very, very best. Behold,"—he stopped mid-twirl and swooped a graceful bow—"the next playwright-in-residence at the Maloney Lane Theater."

Joy made a good effort to push aside Edith's sorrow. "Playwright-in-residence? They will produce your work?"

"My works—plural." Foster doffed his hat and caught it on the handle of his walking stick. "Three plays a year for the next two years. I am to contribute farces and interludes for other major productions, and I have a say on what those productions might be. My duties will be endless. I'm to assist with casting, find sponsors, monitor the directors, consult on the costumes..." He executed a double pirouette and then dipped another bow.

"I have work for you, Edie. Stitching costumes, assisting with stage direction, choosing the props, writing the playbills. I told the committee that my sister is my muse, and I must have your inspiration to call upon. They were shocked, you being a lady and all, but that bunch enjoys shaking things up. Witness,"—more twirling ending in a leap—"they hired me."

He landed in a kneeling positions as lightly as a breeze-borne leaf in the center of the hearthrug. "Say you're pleased, dearest Edie. I know the theater isn't quite proper, and you'd rather I become a famous author, but my heart's with the stage."

He rose and dusted himself off, as Edith must dust herself off.

"I am so pleased, and so proud of you, Foster. I don't know what to say. You have accomplished the impossible with nothing to aid you but determination and providence."

"Not so." He tossed his hat through the doorway, so his millinery came to rest on the sideboard. "I had your faith in me, I had your careful eye reading all of my rough drafts. I had you to cheer me on when the larger houses turned up their noses and told me my work was hopeless. I had the knowledge that you were proud of me simply because I'm too stubborn to give up. All those years of bouncing through the homes of cousins and aunties, you took up for me. You refused to be separated from me and I am gloriously happy to be able to repay a small portion of your loyalty now."

He looked gloriously happy, and well he should. "I knew that if you knocked on the right doors with the right material, your talent would win the day. I am beyond elated for you." Though the prospect of working in a theater... that was another step away from the expectations of a lady.

More like a grand leap in the opposite direction, but not necessarily in the wrong direction. A woman had to eat, though she did not live by bread alone.

"There's more, Edie. I haven't occupied myself entirely with peddling my plays, you know."

If he announced that he was taking a wife, she would... be happy for him, right after she ran back upstairs and indulged in another bout of useless tears.

"Don't keep me in suspense, Foster."

"I've been looking at houses. We can afford to move, Edie. I've found a place I'd like to show you—now, this instant. It's not far, and it's on a little private square. We'll have real grass off the back terrace, nearly three square yards of it, so you can take some irises to plant there if you're of a mind to. Say you'll look at it with me, please?"

Edith didn't want to go anywhere. She wanted to crawl back to bed and contemplate the great folly of having shared that bed with His Grace of Emory. He'd been a tender, considerate, passionate lover, both sweetly affectionate and diabolically skilled.

The moments of drifting off to sleep in his arms had been a greater gift even than the erotic glories. For a short while, Edith had felt cherished and sheltered, all the cares and worries held at bay by a lover's embrace.

She'd woken to find a distracted duke rather than an indulgent lover in her bedroom. Emory had dressed quickly, apparently intent on stealing away without bidding her farewell, and that had been a blow to her heart. No coin had changed hands—Edith would have flung it in his handsome face—but his haste had turned a stolen pleasure into something less. His manner, so brisk and casual, had confirmed that tawdry needn't always involve malicious gossip or monetary arrangements.

She'd lied to him, of course, for when she'd seen him consult his watch in her very bedroom, she did regret yielding to temptation with him. She'd liked him better when she'd known him less intimately, but then, he'd given her exactly what she'd asked for, hadn't he? A stolen moment, a time apart, no expectations on either side.

Foster set his hands on her shoulders. "I've sprung my good news on you all of a sudden, and I haven't once asked about your book. How comes the new project?"

"I made a good start, and I have the sense progress will be swift. I know what story I want to tell."

"Always a plus, when the tale reveals itself at the outset. Will you come see this house with me? It's a lovely day for a walk, and I can't wait to get you away from this dreary little street."

A notion worth supporting. "We must not trade on your expectations, Foster. The theater committee can change their minds."

He took her by the wrist and led her to the front door. "Indeed, they can, in which case, they have to buy out the balance of my contract. I haven't watched you haggle with everybody from the coal man to the fishmonger for no purpose, Edie. They are stuck with me, and I have so many ideas for new productions that tossing three at the Maloney each year will be the work of a few afternoons."

Edith donned her pink cloak, though the garment was on the heavy side for the day's weather.

"You need a new bonnet. Let's start there, shall we?" Foster plunked her hat onto her head. "Let me buy you a new bonnet, at least, to celebrate the great day."

"How about a new cloak instead?" Edith said. "We can stop by the milliners and find some new flowers for this bonnet, but a new cloak would be much appreciated."

"You wear blue quite well, though lavender is also quite pretty on you." He opened the door and bowed her through, the gesture automatic with him.

Edith stopped on the threshold and wrapped him in a hug, and bedamned to any neighbor shocked by such a display of sibling affection. "I do love you, Foster. You are the best of brothers, and I am so proud of you I could take out a notice in the *Times*."

"That tears it," he said, giving her a squeeze. "We look at this new house, buy you a new cloak, and then we stop for ices at Gunter's."

Inspired by his great good spirits, Edith found a smile. "Never let it be said I declined an invitation to Gunter's, much less a new cloak."

They moved down the steps arm in arm, though even the afternoon sunshine was an affront to Edith's mood. Why had Emory turned up so distant on her, and if he ever did come around again—bearing sandwiches and professing to want her opinion on his troubles—would she even open the door to him?

"What color cloak would you like?" Foster asked. "Perhaps we should buy you two, or better still, two cloaks and a new shawl or three."

What a dear, darling brother he was. "One cloak, and any color so long as it isn't pink."

"WHAT THE HELL is wrong with me, that I can miss a woman who'd betray my trust and the trust of my family to such an execrable degree?" Thaddeus asked, while in the square around him, children threw sticks for gamboling puppies and couples flirted on benches.

Why must London in springtime be so dreadfully jolly?

Thaddeus had parted from Lady Edith a week ago, and with each passing day, he told himself to have a blunt discussion with his mother, and then an even more direct conversation with her ladyship. And yet, day followed day, and Thaddeus's mood grew only more bleak as he did exactly nothing about a most bothersome situation.

"Maybe nothing's wrong with you," Elsmore said, tipping his hat to a nursery maid pushing a perambulator. "Maybe your conclusions are what's in error."

Thaddeus had kept to himself the intimate details of his last encounter with Lady Edith, but he'd told Elsmore the rest of the tale: Her ladyship was writing the sequel to *How to Ruin a Duke*, which all but proved she'd written the first volume.

Or did it?

"I know what I saw, Elsmore. I saw yet another manuscript bruiting about the follies and foibles of the Duke of Amorous, and written in her hand. She wrote enough letters and invitations for Mama that I recognized her penmanship."

And heaven help him, that was another fact that weighed in favor of the lady's guilt: Every jot and tittle of gossip that Mama had been privy to by virtue of correspondence had doubtless passed before Lady Edith's eyes.

"You don't want her to be the guilty party," Elsmore said,

touching his hat brim to a pair of giggling shop girls. "You are an eminently logical man. Some evidence must be contradicting your own conclusion."

"Must you flirt with every female and infant you pass, Elsmore?"

"I enjoy the company of females and infants. Right now, I don't much enjoy your company, old man. Here's a suggestion: Knock on Lady Edith's door. Rap, rap." He gestured in the air with a gloved fist. "Put the question to her: Are you writing the next installment of my ruin, or did I misconstrue the situation when I ever-so-rudely read your work without your permission?"

"She left it in plain sight."

"And....?"

"And that is not the behavior of a guilty woman." That conclusion bothered Thaddeus, because it gave him hope. He did not want to have hope, he wanted to have the whole situation behind him.

Mostly. "She also said she wanted to discuss the project with me. She was doubtless dissembling."

"You saw evidence of three other projects in progress? Some poetry scribbled in draft? An epistolary adventure featuring a plucky governess, a leering viscount, and a runaway carriage or two? Maybe she's working on a biography of King George?"

"I saw only the one work, but I didn't exactly rifle her drawers."

Elsmore twirled his walking stick. "Because I am your friend, and because the current arrangement of my features has become dear to my mother and sisters, I will not comment on that statement."

"Lady Edith didn't act guilty, and she didn't display the sort of means that a popular book should have generated."

"Oh dear." Elsmore kicked a ball back to a knot of little boys across the square. "Facts in contradiction to your assumption. Whatever shall you do, Your Grace? Shall you fume and fret for another week? I think so. I think you don't know what to do for once. Somebody should write a book about that. The Duke of Emory has been felled by Cupid's arrow. His legendary sense has deserted him, and I, for one, am delighted."

"You, for one, are obnoxious. What the hell am I do to? I can't trust the woman and I can't seem to find the resolve to threaten her with ruin." Unless Thaddeus wanted to risk writing to her ladyship, threatening her with ruin would mean seeing her again, and that...

He wanted to see her again, wanted her to protest her innocence, and he wanted to dunk his head in the nearest horse trough until his common sense returned. He also wanted to know that Edith was well, that she hadn't been evicted from the drab little house on the tired little street.

"Emory, I have known you since you were a prosy little prig taking firsts in Latin without trying. What are you always telling me when I face a difficult choice?"

Thaddeus answered without thinking. "Good decisions are made based on good information." Which pronouncement was no damned perishing help whatsoever.

"So consult with your Mama, chat up your uncles and aunties, have a word with your cousin Antigone, and a blunt talk with Lord Jeremiah. I find the elders and infantry are often more observant than I am, and they all know Lady Edith. They've all read the book, they all know you. Ask for their perspective, and you might learn something useful."

Elsmore was awash in family, and he seemed to delight in the role of benevolent patriarch. He could kick a ball straight across the square because at family picnics, he doubtless played with his nephews. He made shop girls smile because his legion of lady cousins all relied on him to partner them on their expeditions to the milliner's, and he had perfected the roles of favorite nephew and devoted cousin.

The varlet. "I suppose even your perspective might occasionally bear a passing resemblance to useful."

"Talk to your mother, Emory. Don't lecture her, humor her, or interrupt her. Talk to her."

Must I? But yes, he must. A woman in a pink cloak hurried down the street at the side of the square, and Thaddeus nearly sprinted after her. The shade wasn't quite ugly enough to be Lady Edith's cloak, but London held a plethora of pink cloaks when a man never wanted to see one again.

Or when he dreamed about them every night.

"If you'll excuse me," Thaddeus said, "on the off chance that your suggestion has a scintilla of merit, I must consult with my mother."

He would have parted from Elsmore on that note, but Elsmore's hand on his arm stopped him. "If it's any consolation, my mother and sisters adored Lady Edith. She's either the best confidence trickster in Mayfair, or the instincts that prod you to exonerate her are to be trusted. I liked her, and while I am uniformly pleasant to all in my ambit, I don't permit myself to actually *like* too many of the unattached ladies."

Because a duke's liking was easily misconstrued, and yet, Thaddeus liked Lady Edith too—or had liked her, and then much more than liked her.

"My thanks for your sage advice," Thaddeus said. "Regards to your family."

"Likewise." Elsmore strode off in the direction of the squabbling boys, whom he would all doubtless treat to an ice. The damned man was a curious sort of duke, but he was a more than dear friend.

Thaddeus quit the square at a fast march, before another pink cloak or outlandish bonnet could distract him from his next challenge.

CHAPTER SEVEN

"A titled fool is Cupid's favorite target."
From *How to Ruin a Duke*, by Anonymous

"Mama, might I have a few minutes of your time?"

The duchess slowly put down her book as if a distant strain of music had caught her ear. "A moment, please." She rose from her chaise and went to the window. "I see neither a falling sky nor winged swine, and yet, a miracle has occurred. His Grace of Emory is asking *me* for a moment of *my* time rather than the converse."

She crossed the room to take Thaddeus's hand and place it on her brow. "Am I feverish? Perhaps dementia is to strike me down at a tragically young age. Or maybe my hearing is failing. Tell me the truth, Emory. Did you or did you not just ask for a few minutes of my time?"

"I did, and the matter is of some import."

She returned to her chaise and took up her book. "All of your matters are of some import—to you. If you're thinking of offering for that hopeless Blessington girl, please spare me the discussion. She'll make you miserable, and the only person in this household permitted to dabble in misery is myself."

Thaddeus sat on the end of her couch. "*Are* you miserable?" He'd recently realized that one could be miserable amid abundance or one could be content with little. A few irises in a jar brought just as much joy as the two dozen roses purchased to bloom on Mama's writing desk. The trick was to notice both, to appreciate them.

"No, I am not miserable," Mama replied, smiling faintly. "Emory, are you well? This business with that dreadful book has affected your humors."

"I am in good health, but troubled. Did you write *How to Ruin a Duke*, Mama?"

She turned a page. "I am in good health as well, thank you very much." She kept up the pretense of reading for another half a minute. "No, I did not write that book. As far as I can tell, none of your uncles or aunts did either. Antigone hasn't the self-discipline to write a whole volume, and Cousin Anstruther hasn't the wit."

"You've been trying to discover the author?"

A basilisk stare greeted the inquiry. "No, Thaddeus. I've been trying on bonnets all day while rumors abound that a sequel is to be published. When I tire of admiring my reflection, I ring for confits and tea to restore my strength. Self-absorption can be so taxing, don't you think? You would know, after all."

"I thought perhaps you wrote *How to Ruin a Duke*." She had the self-discipline, the free time, and the acerbic wit.

She set her book aside again. "You think that I...? I don't know whether to be flattered or insulted. The person who *should* have written that book is your late father. He meant well, but his notions of how to bring up his son and heir were sadly lacking. Do you know, I wish at least some of the incidents in that blasted book were true."

"They were all true, up to a point, and then the author took liberties with the facts."

"Doom to any who take liberties with the facts, of course, which suggests the author knew you well enough to know how intolerable you find even everyday falsehoods. Whom do you suspect, Thaddeus?"

She almost never used his given name, but then, they almost never talked. They chatted, they quarreled, they exchanged a few comments over breakfast, and yet clearly, Mama was—in her way —an ally.

Good to know.

"I suspect everybody and nobody in particular, but I have wondered if Lady Edith Charbonneau would have a reason to wish me ill."

Mama drew her feet up and wrapped her arms about her knees. "Lady Edith? I cannot think her capable of such malice. She is a truly kind woman. I should know for I tried her patience to the utmost. If she were to write a book excoriating any member of this family, she would go after Jeremiah."

To Thaddeus's consternation, Mama was in complete earnest. "Jeremiah? He's the only member of the family to claim a surfeit of charm." Thaddeus tried to dredge up any mentions made of Jeremiah in his discussions with Lady Edith, and... nothing of any substance came to mind. They'd talked of Mama, Antigone, Cousin Anstruther, but—significantly—not about Jeremiah except in passing.

"Jeremiah exerts himself to be charming when he wants something, Emory. Have you ever noticed that he offers to take me driving toward the end of the fortnight even when it's not his turn? He uses the public outing to press me for advances on his allowance. He knows I will not quarrel with him in the middle of the carriage parade, just as I know he will never pay me back."

Thaddeus got up to pace. "He could not have borrowed money from Lady Edith. She hasn't any, and her wages weren't that generous." Though if Jeremiah had borrowed money from her and not paid the loan back, would that justify a grudge serious enough to result in a slanderous book?

Mama watched him, her expression putting Thaddeus in mind of a cat about to swipe a paw across the nose of an annoying kitten. "Do you truly believe I have employed three different companions in the past five years because my sour nature alone defeats them?"

Thaddeus had thought that very thing. "Lady Edith, at least, left without having another post to go to. Something or somebody made the situation here intolerable, and thus I've speculated that she has a motive to write a nasty book."

Mama swung her legs over the side of the chaise and slipped her feet into a pair of embroidered house mules. "I wasn't aware that Lady Edith hadn't located another post."

"Not as of last week. She's attempting to make a living writing domestic advice, but I gather she hasn't found a publisher yet."

Mama stared at her slippers. "I have wondered whether you were aware of the problem Jeremiah poses. I am finally ready to let you send him to India, Emory. He should have known better than to bother Edith. She is a true lady, and if she'd condemned him publicly, she would have been believed."

Thaddeus felt again the queasy, disoriented dread he'd experienced in Lady Edith's parlor. "You are saying that Jeremiah—*my brother*—bothered a woman in the family's employ? He pressed his attentions upon her ladyship uninvited?"

"He's not you, Thaddeus, to observe all the courtesies and protocols. I fear the boy takes after me rather too much."

"You would never inveigle a footman into improprieties, Mama. You are sure Jeremiah forgot himself with Lady Edith?" Thaddeus wanted this flight to be one of Mama's attempts at humor, a mistake, anything but the truth. And yet... the facts, the damnable, inescapable facts, supported Mama's conclusion.

"Edith left to avoid Jeremiah's advances." Mama rose. "She did not come right out and say that. She hinted, I ignored her hints. The previous two companions had come to me with similar tales. I thought one or two women misconstruing Jeremiah's friendliness was possible, but when Edith... She didn't want more money, she didn't want to become the object of unkind talk, she didn't want anything but the wages due her and a decent character. I gave her both."

"Three women, Mama? He's behaved abominably with *three* women and I'm only learning of it now? Are the maids safe?"

"The housekeeper knows to assign them in pairs. They are safe. It's as if Jeremiah is jealous of my companions because I have a playmate and he does not. He also thought strutting around in your shoes with those damned charities would be a great lark, but he's learned otherwise. No organization is more inefficient or pompous than an eleemosynary guild devoted to flowers, unless it's the Charitable Committee for the—"

Thaddeus held up a hand. "Please do not attempt to change the subject. I can barely credit that my brother has betrayed the one ironclad rule of gentlemanly deportment and imposed his attentions on women drawing wages under this very roof."

Mama set her book on the mantel. "He's a spoiled brat, Emory. I know because I am too. You have escaped our fate, which makes me wroth that you have been the butt of that awful book. You have given no one cause to treat you thus—and certainly Lady Edith would not have done so—but then, London is full of spoiled brats, isn't it?"

Thaddeus was torn between the compulsion to find Lady Edith and apologize to her on bended knee—on his damned hands and knees if necessary—and the urgent need to beat Jeremiah senseless.

"You're truly willing to let me buy Jeremiah a commission?" Thaddeus asked.

"I had hoped to keep him safe, but when it comes down to it, my companions aren't safe when he's underfoot. He runs with a naughty crowd, his gambling debts have to be considerable, and he's not maturing as he should."

Jeremiah had gambling debts—substantial gambling debts—and proceeds from the sales of a popular book would help pay them off.

Jeremiah ran with a crowd of inebriated idlers who challenged each other with the most ridiculous and dangerous wagers.

"Jeremiah was involved in every embarrassing, inane incident portrayed in *How to Ruin a Duke*, Mama. Most of them I undertook to spare him a lost wager, a dangerous prank, or a stupid duel. I

suspect my own brother is literally the author of my present difficulties."

"Don't kill him," Mama said. "If anybody is to wring his wretched
neck it should be me, but Thaddeus?"

He stopped halfway to the door. "I'll do better, Mama. I will take
you driving when you don't ask it of me, I will inquire after your
health. I will find you another companion who—"

She patted his chest. "Stop. If you turn up doting on me now, I
will disown you. About Lady Edith?"

The Lady Edith who was entirely innocent of wrongdoing?
"Yes?"

"She fancied you. She was discreet about it, she never said a
word, but she knew when you'd come home at night from the way the
front door closed. She learned how you take your tea. She knows you
cannot be trusted around Italian cream cake."

"Neither can she."

"Well there you have it. You'd never want for something to bicker
over if you married her."

"Married her?"

"She's an earl's daughter, you fancied her too, and Jeremiah will
have to remain in the army for at least several years before he can sell
his commission. Now go pummel your brother."

She kissed his cheek and shoved him on the arm.

"Mama, I can for once promise that your wish will be my
command." He stalked from the room, though—drat the damned luck
—the butler reported that Jeremiah was out, and had not said when to
expect him home.

"EDIE, why didn't you tell me you'd gone to the agencies again?"
Foster's question was more hurt than chiding, though he'd waited
until the maid of all work had withdrawn from the breakfast parlor to
pose it.

"Because I've been to the agencies many times. I did not expect a post to become available." Except that this time, Edith had told the sniffy little clerk that she was willing to accept a position anywhere in Britain except London. She'd had three choices within a matter of days.

"You'll come back to see my opening night won't you?" Foster asked, setting the teapot near her elbow.

"I made that a condition of accepting the offer. Manchester isn't so very far away."

"Manchester is more than 200 miles on bad roads, Edie. You couldn't find anything closer?"

Both of the other positions had been closer. "The household in Manchester will suit me. I won't have to face polite society again, and you can't know what a relief that will be."

Every tall man striding along the walk in a top hat and morning attire gave Edith a start, and she'd bid Emory farewell nearly ten days ago.

Foster poured her a third cup of tea—luxury upon luxury—and sat back. "You don't have to face polite society here either. I only mentioned working at the theater because I love being there, and I thought you liked having your own money. You could do more writing, which you seem to delight in, and I wouldn't have to fret that you're perishing of cold and overwork in the north."

"I won't perish." If watching Emory march away, and not hearing from him at all, not even the obligatory anonymous bouquet, hadn't felled her, nothing would.

"You won't flourish either. Anybody who can sit at that writing desk for more than a week straight, scribbling away hour after hour, has a vocation not to be ignored. Your book is quite witty and deserves to be published."

How many times in recent months had Edith longed for even a second cup of tea? She was on her third of the morning, and it did nothing to comfort the hollow ache she'd carried for days.

"If the book has promise, that's because I had months to study my subject." And she'd have the rest of her life to wonder what had sent him out the door in such an odd mood. "Emory is the soul of decency, of that I have no doubt." Perhaps he'd had bad experiences with women before, women who clung and tried to extort promises from him.

No matter. He was gone and he wasn't coming back.

"But you aren't even attempting to find a publisher," Foster said. "The past six months have taken a toll on you. The Edie who all but raised me would be waving that manuscript under the noses of every publisher in Town, and why you won't allow me to make inquiries on your behalf utterly defeats my—"

"Please, Foster. You'll be late for rehearsal." She'd written that manuscript out of a need to exorcise a broken heart, or perhaps to justify her decision to become intimate with Emory. He was a good man, a bit stern, a bit imposing, but good. The way he'd left her, nary a word of explanation, wasn't in keeping with his character.

The other duke, the *How to Ruin a Duke* fellow, *he* would have availed himself of a lady's favors and then dodged off to his clubs to brag of his exploits.

"I'm away then," Foster said, rising. "I wish you'd reconsider leaving London—and me. I will miss you desperately." He kissed her cheek and bustled off to a job that was making him happier by the day.

"You will miss me for about twenty minutes," Edith said to the empty room.

This house was in a much nicer neighborhood than the last, and while it was tiny, it was also sturdy, spotless, and situated on a quiet street. The back garden was half in sun and half in shade, but nobody had thought to plant flowers there.

Edith finished her tea and retrieved her new cloak—dark blue—then went around to the mews in the alley and borrowed a bucket and trowel. As she traveled the several streets to her previous abode, she realized that walking unaccompanied no longer bothered her. To go back to the polite fiction that a lady needed an escort at all times would be like donning a corset that laced too snugly, and she wasn't looking forward to it.

Perhaps Manchester would be different. For a certainty, it was rumored to be dirtier than London, which simply did not seem possible. Edith turned onto her former street and fished in her pocket for a coin. James, the lad who aspired to become a crossing sweeper, was idling as usual beneath a lamp post.

"How fare you today, young James?"

"Miss Edith! I thought you'd piked off."

She dropped the coin into his grimy little mitt. "My brother and I have moved. I'm back to dig up some of the irises so he'll have a few flowers at the new house. When I'm through, you should pick a bouquet to sell to passersby."

The coin disappeared into a pocket. "I can sell your flowers?"

"You'll likely have more luck if you offer them at a spot with plenty of foot traffic. Oxford Road, for example. Pick a bunch and sell them, then pick another bunch tomorrow. Offer them to people dressed well enough to spare a coin for a flower." To devise that scheme would have been beyond her six months ago.

"I like flowers," James said, falling in step beside her. "They smell pretty, like you."

"Flatterer. Bring a few to your mother too. The flowers should not go to waste, and they only bloom for a short time. The new tenant won't move in until the end of the month, and by then the irises will be fading."

James skipped along at her side and chattered about everything from the Mad King to his friend Cora the mudlark. In no time, Edith had a bucketful of muddy roots and green foliage.

"If I sell all of these, I'll be rich!" James said, burying his nose amid his bouquet.

"You will have a few coppers," Edith replied. "Save them for when your mama has nothing to spend at market, and she will thank you for it."

He accompanied her halfway back to her new abode, choosing a busy intersection for his commercial venture.

"Thanks, Miss Edith. Mama will thank you too."

Miss Edith. Being Miss Edith as opposed to Lady Edith wasn't so bad. Lady Edith could not have set this boy on the path to earning money. She would not have carried a muddy bucket down a London street just to ensure her brother had something to remember her by.

And—this thought pounced, like an unseen cat springing from the undergrowth—*Miss Edith* would not have surrendered her post because a philandering numbskull of a courtesy lord had caught her on the backstairs.

James separated a half dozen stems from the armful he'd been carrying. "You should have these, Miss."

"That is very kind of you, James." Edith took two flowers and added them to her bucket. "Good luck with your venture."

"That fancy cove came back around, you know. The tall gent with the fancy walking stick." James had the grace to say this quietly.

"I beg your pardon?"

"The man with the expensive coat." James took a half dozen steps along the walkway at a purposeful march, shoulders angled slightly forward. "All business, that one. He paid a call or two on you before you moved. He came around yesterday and the day before and fair pounded the door down. I told him you'd moved. He gave me tuppence and told me to take a bath. Be he daft?"

"My caller came by again?"

"Twice. He's not friendly. I still have the tuppence and I don't have to take a bath until Saturday."

All manner of emotions welled at James's news. Pleasure, consternation, curiosity, and not a little anger. What sort of lover waits more than a week to stroll by again? Why not send a note? A letter, a bouquet? A little farewell message? *Anything?*

"Thank you for telling me this, James. It matters." Though just how it mattered, Edith did not know.

"If he comes around again, do I give him your direction?"

A young fellow walking a large dog hovered nearby, apparently intent on purchasing flowers.

"No need for that, James. I'm off to Manchester in a few days. I believe your first customer awaits."

She left James transacting business with all the aplomb of London's premier flower nabob, and was soon in her new back yard, tucking iris roots into rich, warm soil. She watered the plants sparingly—irises could rot if overcome with damp—and considered the rest of her day.

She knew now how Emory had felt about discovering the author of *How to Ruin a Duke*. He'd been beyond curious, he'd *had* to know exactly who and what had brought him low. Finding that answer had become a quest for him.

Edith had spent more than a week focusing on memories of her time with the ducal family. She'd gone through the nasty book page by page—thank heavens a friend had been able to borrow the bound version for her from the lending library—she'd considered each incident in detail. She had a very good idea exactly who had penned those lies, and before she left London, she would share her suspicions with Emory.

And then—after conveying to His Perishing Grace a few other sentiments—she would get an explanation from him as to why he'd come back to call on her, and why he'd been least-in-sight for more than a week before he'd done so.

JEREMIAH, with suspiciously convenient timing, had chosen to drop out of sight for a few days just when Thaddeus urgently needed to pummel him. His lordship occasionally did this, sometimes to indulge in a marathon card game, sometimes to make a madcap dash to Brighton with friends.

Thaddeus suspected Jeremiah also disappeared periodically to provoke Mama to worrying and to avoid creditors.

Thaddeus's temper had not cooled in the *slightest* during Jeremiah's absence, but he had put the time to good use nonetheless.

"You will excuse us," Thaddeus said to Jeremiah's valet, as his lordship snored away the morning, naked to the knees amid snowy sheets and satin pillows.

"Of course, Your Grace. Found Himself on the stairs at cockcrow. He's likely to wake with a devil of a head."

And that will be the least of his worries. "Splendid. As of next week, his lordship will no longer need your services. Your wages will continue until we can find you a new post. You will have a glowing character and some severance as well."

The man wrinkled his nose. "You needn't pay me severance, Your Grace. I was preparing to give notice. I know the young gents are full of high spirits, but that one..." The valet shook his head. "I'll not speak ill of my betters. You need not worry on that score." He picked up the muddy boots at the foot of Jeremiah's bed and departed.

Thaddeus's gaze landed on a razor strop hanging on a paneled privacy screen in the corner of the room. He opened the bedroom curtains wide, took up the strop and delivered a glancing blow to his lordship's backside.

"A valet has more honor than my heir."

Jeremiah stirred. "Go away, darling. I'm not in the mood to play anymore."

Thaddeus brought the razor strop down again, not as gently. "Get out of that bed. *Now.*"

Jeremiah rolled over and propped himself on his elbows. "What the devil? Emory, what on earth are you about?"

"Why did you do it, Jeremiah?"

Jeremiah eyed the strop. He sat up and scratched his chest, his hair a greasy mess, his eyes rimmed with shadows. "Had a bit of an orgy as best I recall. If you'll send my valet—"

Thaddeus flung a dressing gown at him. "I asked you a question, and unless you want a private reading of *How to Beat the Hell Out of a Courtesy Lord*, you will answer honestly."

Jeremiah shrugged into the dressing gown and rose to belt it around his middle. "Why'd I dash off that bit of tattle everybody finds so amusing?" His air was defiant, though he was keeping an eye on the length of leather in Thaddeus's hands.

"Why did you try to disgrace a brother who's never been anything but decent to you?"

He yawned and stretched, not a care in the world. "One of the fellows said it couldn't be done. Said nobody could tarnish the reputation of His Grace of Emory, and I took the bet."

"Why?"

"Because I am bloody bored waiting for you to find a duchess? Because I could? Because I didn't want to beg you for more coin or scarper on my debts of honor?"

Thaddeus hung the strop back on its hook, lest he lay into his brother for the sin of sheer stupidity. "Instead you pester Mama for coin, just as you pestered her companions for favors. Not the done thing, Jeremiah."

Jeremiah poured himself a glass of brandy from a decanter on his clothes press. "A little harmless flirtation never hurt anybody. You might know that if you'd ever given it a try."

Thaddeus threw a heeled dancing slipper at him, which caused the brandy to slosh over Jeremiah's chest.

"I well know," Thaddeus said, "the difference between private dealings undertaken by consenting adults, and the unwelcome advances you visited upon those women."

Jeremiah tossed back half of his drink—on an empty stomach at mid-day. "If it's any consolation, the average companion apparently knows how to use her knee to excellent advantage. Lady Edith damned near gave me a shiner to go with my bruised jewels. With respect to the book, you needn't cut up so. I hadn't planned on writing more than the one volume, but needs must when a fellow likes the occasional wager. The second book—"

"Was tossed on the fire in the library two days ago because your arrogant lordship left the manuscript sitting in plain sight on your desk. You face a choice. Slink out the back door of this house with the clothes on your back after you've apologized to Mama, or report to Horse Guards three days from now, which three days you will spend selling your worldly goods to pay any debts you still owe.

"If you choose the military," Thaddeus went on, "you will have a commission as a lieutenant in the infantry, and you will take ship for India or Canada, I care not which. You are unwelcome in this house until you prove you deserve the honor of association with your own family."

Jeremiah set down his drink and scrubbed a hand through this hair. "A lieutenancy? I should be at least a major."

"Keep talking, and you will be a vagrant. What's it to be? The dubious charity of your drinking companions or that life of adventure you always claimed you wanted, no protections, no social conse-quence, nothing between you and misfortune but blind luck and the kindness of strangers. Surely that will make an exciting tale—assuming you survive the living of it."

Jeremiah had gone even paler than he'd been upon climbing from the bed. "Mama won't like this, Emory. You don't want her misery on your conscience. Allow me to spare you that fate. I'll spend the rest of the year at the family seat, no bother to anybody. I can even pen a retraction of the more creative incidents conveyed in *How to Ruin a Duke*. Every peer will commiserate with you, and all will come right. I'll get to work on it straightaway, and you can print my letter of apology in the *Times*."

Jeremiah's smile was the terrified parody offered by a boy who realizes his fate has been sealed.

"Either leave this house within the hour or prepare to take up your commission." Thaddeus had pondered how to set up the choice so it *was* a choice, but not a decision even Jeremiah could bungle. He let a silence build, though Jeremiah looked near to tears.

"The infantry has some lovely uniforms." Jeremiah's hand shook as he picked up his drink. "Three days, you say? Don't suppose a week—?"

"Seventy-two hours, if I have to drag you to Horse Guards myself. You will also write a letter of apology to each of the ladies whom you insulted, starting with Lady Edith."

Jeremiah stared into his drink and nodded. "Not well done of me, I do see that."

Perhaps the remorse was real, perhaps it was for show. Thaddeus didn't particularly care. His next priority was to find Lady Edith Charbonneau and pray she was in a forgiving mood. He was thwarted from pursuing that goal by the footman who informed him a guest was waiting in the blue parlor. The caller sought a brief audience with His Grace if the duke was at home.

The footman held up a silver tray bearing a single card: J. Ventnor, Publisher.

Bloody hell. "I'll see him, but no damned tea tray, if you please. He won't be staying long."

~

EDITH DONNED HER NEW BONNET, took up her blue parasol, left the top button of her new cloak unfastened, and gathered her reticule.

"And His Grace had better be home to me," she muttered. The walk to Emory's doorstep took a quarter hour, and if anybody in his fine neighborhood thought a lady traveling alone on foot was unusual, Edith *did not care*. A woman who could write a first draft of a book—a good book, though not overly long—in less than two weeks need not quibble over niceties.

She rapped the knocker against the door twice and it opened almost immediately.

"Lady Edith! Do come in, my lady." The butler stepped back, his characteristic reserve replaced with a smile. "What a pleasure to see you, ma'am, and on such a fine day. Shall I take your bonnet and cloak and see if Her Grace is at home?"

Edith passed over her hat. "I'm actually here to see His Grace, and my call is not entirely social."

White brows drew up. "Between us, my lady, His Grace's mood of late hasn't been entirely social either. Perhaps you'd like to wait in the blue parlor? That was always your favorite as I recall."

The blue parlor was the everyday guest parlor, not as formal as the gilded wonder where Her Grace received company during her at homes, not as comfy as the family parlor.

"The blue parlor will do. I can see myself down the corridor."

The butler hesitated. "Might I tell the staff you're keeping well? We've missed you and wondered how you're faring."

"I've missed you too. Please thank everybody for their concern. I have a new post, and my brother has become playwright-in-residence at the Maloney."

"Oh, that is excellent news, ma'am. Excellent news." He bustled off, doubtless to spread that excellent news belowstairs.

Edith *had* missed the staff here, but she would eventually make new friends in Manchester. She let herself into the blue parlor expecting to have a few moments of solitude to compose her thoughts.

"Your Grace, Mr. Ventnor. Excuse me. I did not know the room was occupied." Both men were on their feet, suggesting the discussion had been something less than cordial.

Ventnor aimed a puzzled smile at the duke. "I thought you said her ladyship's whereabouts were unknown, Your Grace?"

Emory looked tired and a bit grim, but otherwise hale. "Had I known Lady Edith would do me the very great honor of calling upon me, I would have sent you packing ten minutes ago, Ventnor. My lady, do come in. Please come in, rather. Mr. Ventnor was just leaving."

Ventnor passed Edith a card. "I read your samples. You have quite a gift, my lady. Domestic advice doesn't do justice to your voice, and I would very much like an opportunity to discuss other projects with you."

"On your way, Ventnor," Emory said, jabbing a finger in the direction of the door. "Now."

Ventnor offered Edith an unhurried bow, came up smiling, nodded to the duke, and left.

"The damned man tried to contact you at your previous address," Emory said, closing the door behind the departed publisher. "He recalled that you'd been employed as Mama's companion and stopped by to ask if I knew of your present direction."

"What did you tell him?"

Emory stood before her, his gaze troubled. "I've missed you. I didn't tell him that. I've been an idiot. I didn't mention that either. I've been dreaming of pink cloaks.... How are you?"

What mood was this? "I am well, thank you. And you?"

"Jeremiah wrote that blasted book. I'm buying him a commission and he will be gone from London directly. I owe you an apology."

An encouraging start. A *very* encouraging start. "Shall we be seated, Your Grace? Lord Jeremiah's authorship of *How to Ruin a Duke* doesn't surprise me."

"Figured it out, did you? Well, I hadn't." He took Edith by the hand, then let her go. "Apologies. I did not mean to presume. Jeremiah presumed, didn't he?"

"He tried to," Edith said, taking a place on the sofa. "Just the once, but clearly, I made an enemy of him when I refused to oblige him. Quitting my post was the better part of discretion."

"I made an enemy of him when I expected him to manage on a merely generous allowance. Might I sit with you?"

Where was the harm in that? "You may. I brought you something, a parting gift."

He came down beside her. "Parting, my lady?"

Oh, the scent of him, the sound of his voice... Only a ninny-hammer let trivialities like that pluck at her heartstrings.

"I've accepted a post in the north. My brother has a position with the Maloney Theater, and he doesn't need me hovering about while he embarks on gainful employment."

"I see." Emory studied the carpet for a moment. "I do not see, rather. Not at all. I have a confession."

"I'm not sure I want to hear it." Not if he was about to tell her he was engaged or nearly so to some heiress. That would explain his behavior, though Edith couldn't believe he'd hop into bed with one woman while being in expectation of marriage to another.

Other men would, not Emory.

"This confession does not flatter me," he said. "You had mentioned to me that you were working on another writing project. I happened to see the first few lines when I last called upon you."

"My book," she said, assaying a smile. "I've finished the first draft, and I rather like it."

"Jeremiah had written a complete draft as well, another compendium of half-truths, exaggerations, and complete fictions."

Edith put a hand on Emory's arm. "I'm sorry. That had to have been a blow." Once a rotter, always a rotter. She ought to have suspected Lord Jeremiah much sooner.

The duke took her hand in his. "I thought *you* were penning the sequel. I had convinced myself that you hadn't written the first volume, but then I came across those pages, which promised more of the same drivel. I did not know what to think, and I left without giving you a chance to explain."

Edith had puzzled over the manuscript's opening lines for hours. She'd puzzled over Emory's abrupt departure for days, and she'd never connected the two.

"The first few pages were to lead the reader astray," she said, "to make them think more foolishness and slander would follow. That's not what I did with the story. See what you think."

She withdrew a sheaf of papers from her reticule and untied the string that bound them. "This is my farewell gift. You may do with it as you please, and I will sign all the rights over to you or to the charity of your choice."

He took the papers and began reading, sparing her only one

curious glance. Edith rose to pace, very unladylike of her, but she could not sit still while he was so silent.

A few moments later he made a snort-ish sound. "By God, you have Mama to the life."

"You're at the part about the mouse?"

"The dread, fiendish rodent as you term it. Poor little fellow was terrified."

Emory had caught the mouse in his bare hands and carried it to the garden, while Her Grace had stood on the piano bench bellowing for the footmen to bring her a brace of loaded pistols.

"Mama does not care for mice, but you make me out to be some sort of paragon." He set the papers down. "Is the rest of the book like that?"

"Do you like it?"

"No," he said. "No, I do not like it. I *adore* it. I *love* it. I wish... I am enthralled, and you cannot possibly give this to me when Ventnor was willing to breach the ducal citadel in hopes of convincing you to work for him."

"I cannot work for Mr. Ventnor if I'm moving to Manchester. You truly think my prose is acceptable?"

Emory rose but remained by the sofa. "My lady—Edith—did you hear what I said? I read the opening lines of this masterpiece and jumped to the worst possible conclusion. Then I took my leave of you, convinced you meant me ill. Had I not confronted my mother with my suspicions, I might have started untoward talk about you. Revenge should be beneath every sensible man, but I had a plan, you see. I am mortified to add that becoming inebriated figured prominently in this plan."

"I would have liked to have seen that."

His smile was crooked and dear. "Do you forgive me?"

"For what? You entertained an erroneous theory, Your Grace, but you assembled all the relevant facts before taking action. I admit I was puzzled by your silence, but then, I did not—*I do not*, that is to say—have any expectations where you are concerned." His explanation made sense and allowed Edith to part from him on friendly terms.

So why was she blushing and all but stammering?

"I have expectations of myself," he said, coming near and possessing himself of her hand again. "When I leap into bed with a woman, and she with me, and we are compatible in every detail of our natures, right down to both of us being untrustworthy in the presence of Italian cream cake, then I expect myself to offer for that woman. I would not have risked intimacies with you otherwise, my lady. The consequences are too momentous. Not to put too fine a point on the matter, I will follow you to Manchester and sing maudlin ballads beneath your window—at midnight—if that will win your favor."

Edith forced herself to hold his hand lightly. "You erred in assuming I would write a slanderous book about you. I erred in allowing you to leave without establishing how things stood between us. I told myself I wanted only an interlude, a memory, but I was not honest."

He covered her hand with his. "Is that still all you want?"

What did she want? A month ago, the answer was simple: A decent post for herself, a future for Foster.

Now? She wanted much, much more. "I want to sit beside you in your curricle the next time you race to Brighton, I want *God Save the King* at midnight, I want,"—she kissed him—"more of that, and the pleasures that follow."

"And if I sing *God Save the King* at midnight only for the woman wearing the Emory tiara, are you still interested?"

That question occasioned more kissing. When Edith recalled that the drapes were open, and the parlor was visible to anybody peering over the garden wall, she drew back enough to rest against Emory.

"Yes, Your Grace, I am still interested."

"Yes, you will be my duchess? What about the blandishments of Manchester?"

"Who will rescue me from dread, fiendish rodents in Manchester? Who will arm-wrestle me for the last piece of cream cake in Manchester? Who will help me polish my next book in Manchester?"

Emory tucked an arm around her waist and walked her to the sofa. "Have you a title for that book, the one that paints me in such a flattering light?"

"Not a flattering light, sir. An accurate light. I thought I might call it, *How to Rescue a Duke*."

Rather than assist Edith to take a seat, Emory settled in the corner and pulled her into his lap. "I think we should begin your research on the third volume in the trilogy."

Sitting in his lap was a novel and cozy experience. Edith scooted about until she found a pillow to wedge against the armrest. "A *third* volume? Have you more interesting incidents to regale me with, Your Grace? Whatever would the title of this third volume be?"

Emory waited for her to settle. "The third volume will be for private reading only, and will outshine the other two for its wit, passion, and sheer cleverness. That tome will be titled, *How to Ravish a Duke*. Perhaps you'd like to explore the topic with me now?"

"Such a topic will require much study, Your Grace."

"Then we'd best get started, my love."

And so they did.

TO MY DEAR READERS

To my dear readers,

What fun, to write a story about books and how they can get us into and out of trouble! Lady Caroline Lamb truly did wear her welcome thin in Polite Society with her literary efforts, but then, as we read, she wasn't wildly popular before she took up her pen.

Did you happen to notice Wrexham, Duke of Elsmore, in the role of Thaddeus's sounding board? I noticed him too, back in **My One and Only Duke**, first in my Rogues to Riches series. He trotted onto the page, said a few interesting, charming things, and trotted right back off again. I was left to wonder, "Who *was* that guy and what's *he* doing in this series?"

The answers to that those questions lie in **Forever and a Duke**, the third book in the Rogues to Riches series, which hits the shelves in November. Seems Elsmore is also falling in love (what a surprise!), but with a lady who wants no parts of any titled gentlemen, least of all a duke. Eleanora Hatfield is great with numbers, and Elsmore desperately needs a competent auditor, but she has no patience with charming aristocrats. None, I tell you, so how she and Elsmore end up smoochin' is truly a mystery.

Excerpt below!

If you'd like to stay up to date with my new releases, special deals, and pre-orders, you can do that by simply following me on **Bookbub**. The folks there sound out short emails relating to new titles or deep discounts—only. If you'd like more of the kitten pics and highlights from my illustrious doin's, you can sign up for **my news-letter**. I will never EVER sell, lend, or trade your personal information for any reason.

Keep an eye peeled for a new title on my Coming Soon website page. Emily Larkin and I are planning a novella duet for this fall that has both kitties and smoochin' in it. If Emily is a new-to-you author, please take a peek at the excerpt below from **Primrose and the Dreadful Duke**. You will soon have it on your figurative keeper shelf.

Happy reading!

Grace Burrowes

EXCERPT FROM FOREVER AND A DUKE

Read on for an excerpt from **Forever and a Duke**, book three in the Rogues to Riches series!

WREXHAM, Duke of Elsmore, knows something is amiss with his accounts, and he's turned to bank auditor Eleanora Hatfield to help him untangle the mess. Ellie has no patience with aristocratic men—for reasons—and yet, Elsmore has grown on her and made no secret of his regard for her. He's devoted to family, kind-hearted, and unpretentious. If only he weren't a duke...

"WE HAVE NO PRETENSES BETWEEN US," Elsmore said. "You are honest with me. You don't expect me to bring good cheer and ducal beneficence to every exchange. You skewer me if I toss out too much small talk and I adore you for that. You do me the very great honor of dealing with me as if I am capable of grasping a significant problem and perhaps even solving it. To you, I am more than a prize to be hauled onto the dancefloor." He kissed her temple. "You scold me."

"Somebody should scold the pair of us." Instead, Ellie's arms which had been obediently at her sides, wound around his waist, inside his morning coat where all was warmth and intimacy. He was lean, muscular, and tall enough that Ellie could rest her full weight against him, like a woman overcome with fatigue.

Or loneliness.

"If you scold me," he said, "I will apologize sincerely, and assure you that I won't presume again." He rested his cheek against Ellie's crown, and she stole another moment of forbidden pleasure.

This mutual interest in one another had no future. Not because he was a duke—dukes took mistresses, they had liaisons, they seldom made the most faithful of husbands.

Ellie had no future in any intimate capacity with Elsmore precisely because she was *not* honest with him and never could be.

"If you apologize," Ellie said, stepping back, "then I must do likewise. I am disinclined to apologize for harmless familiarities enjoyed when we are private. Those familiarities, though, are a distraction from my appointed task. We'd best eschew them going forward."

He cradled her jaw against the warmth of his palm. "Mightn't you leaven that damned sensible pronouncement with a bit of reluctance, Eleanora?"

Nobody, nobody ever, had spoken her name before with that combination of tenderness, desire, humor, regret.

I am an idiot. But was she an idiot for declining what he offered or for craving it? She stepped closer, pressed her mouth to his, and took one kiss to save against all the damned sensible pronouncements by which she was doomed to live.

ELEANORA HATFIELD'S kiss wasn't sorting itself into any tidy column. She pressed her mouth to his and her body to his, desire leading the charge. Her hands—those marvelously competent, usually ink-stained hands—wandered his chest, ribs, and back as if she were wrapping arrows of desire around his entire person. Then she sank her fingers into his hair, angled her head, and gentled her kiss from plundering to wandering.

Two minutes ago she'd told him they would focus strictly on business. All Rex could focus on now was *her*.

He kissed her back, accepting her invitation to taste and touch. She was more slender than he'd thought, her clothes bulkier. Petticoats and corsetry frustrated the craving to touch her bare skin. He settled for stroking her hands and face, especially the tender join of her neck and shoulder and the soft flesh of her bare wrist.

She turned her head as if to listen to the caress of his thumb against her palm and he dared to press her closer, lest she mistake the impact she was having on him. Rex had learned years ago to control his urges, lest they control him. There was no controlling his reactions, though, not to her, not this time.

And what a relief that was, what a pleasure and a joy to be simply a man in good health enjoying a kiss with a woman who desired him for his own sake.

Eleanora eased her mouth from his and pressed her forehead to his chest. "The soup will get cold."

So plaintive and paltry, that display of common sense, so dear. "While everything else threatens to go up in flames."

ORDER YOUR COPY of *Forever and a Duke*!

EXCERPT FROM PRIMROSE AND THE DREADFUL DUKE

Read on for an excerpt from **Primrose and the Dreadful Duke**, book one in the Baleful Godmother – Garland Cousins series by Emily Larkin!

OLIVER DASENBY IS the most infuriating man Primrose Garland has ever known. He may be her brother's best friend, but he has an atrocious sense of humor. Eight years in the cavalry hasn't taught him solemnity, nor has the unexpected inheritance of a dukedom. But when Oliver inherited his dukedom, it appears that he also inherited a murderer...

Oliver might be dreadfully annoying, but Primrose doesn't want him dead. She's going to make certain he survives his inheritance—and the only way to do that is to help him catch the murderer!

OLIVER'S next partner was Lady Primrose Garland, the sister of his oldest friend, Rhodes Garland—and the only unmarried young lady in the room whom he knew *didn't* want to marry him.

"Lady Prim," he said, bowing over her hand with a flourish. "You're a jewel that outshines all others."

Primrose was too well-bred to roll her eyes in public, but her eyelids twitched ever so slightly, which told him she wanted to. "Still afflicted by hyperbole, I see."

"You use such long words, Prim," he said admiringly.

"And you use such foolish ones."

Oliver tutted at her. "That's not very polite, Prim."

Primrose ignored this comment. She placed her hand on his sleeve. Together they walked onto the dance floor and took their places.

"Did I ever tell you about my uniform, Prim? The coat was dark blue, and the facing—"

"I don't wish to hear about your uniform."

"Manners, Prim. Manners."

Primrose came very close to smiling. She caught herself just in time. "Shall we discuss books while we dance? Have you read Wolf's *Prolegomena ad Homerum?*"

"Of course I haven't," Oliver said. "Dash it, Prim, I'm not an intellectual."

The musicians played the opening bars. Primrose curtsied, Oliver bowed. "I really *must* tell you about my uniform. The coat was dark blue—"

Primrose ignored him. "Wolf proposes that *The Iliad*—"

"With a red sash at the waist—"

"And *The Odyssey* were in fact—"

"And silver lace at the cuffs—"

"The work of more than one poet."

"And a crested Tarleton helmet," Oliver finished triumphantly.

They eyed each other as they went through the steps of the dance. Oliver could tell from the glint in her eyes and the way her lips were tucked in at the corners that Primrose was trying not to laugh. He was trying not to laugh, too.

"You're a fiddle-faddle fellow," Primrose told him severely.

"Alliteration," Oliver said. "Well done, Prim."

Primrose's lips tucked in even more tightly at the corners. If they'd been anywhere but a ballroom he was certain she'd have stamped her foot, something she'd done frequently when they were children.

"Heaven only knows why I agreed to dance with you," she told him tartly.

"Because it increases your consequence to be seen with me. I *am* a duke, you know." He puffed out his chest and danced the next few steps with a strut.

"Stop that," she hissed under her breath.

"Stop what?" Oliver said innocently, still strutting his steps.

"Honestly, Daisy, you're impossible."

Oliver stopped strutting. "No one's called me that in years."

"Impossible? I find that hard to believe." Her voice was dry.

"Daisy." It had been Primrose's childhood nickname for him, in retaliation for him calling her Lady Prim-and-Proper.

Oliver had been back in England for nearly a month now, and that month had been filled with moments of recognition, some tiny flickers—his brain acknowledging something as familiar and then moving on—others strong visceral reactions. He experienced one of those latter moments now. It took him by the throat and wouldn't let him speak for several seconds.

Because Primrose had called him Daisy.

Oliver cleared his throat. "Tell me about that book, Prim. What's it called? Prolapse ad nauseam?"

"*Prolegomena ad Homerum.*"

Oliver pulled a face. "Sounds very dull. Me, I much prefer a good novel. Especially if there's a ghost in it, or a headless horseman."

And they were off again, arguing amiably about books, the moment of emotion safely in the past. Primrose knew a lot about books. In fact, Oliver suspected that she preferred books to people—which would be why she was still unmarried at twenty-seven. Primrose was a duke's daughter *and* she was pretty—that ash-blonde hair, those cool blue eyes. If she wanted to be married, she would be.

Therefore, he deduced that she didn't want to marry. Which made her unique in a ballroom filled with young ladies on the hunt for husbands.

"Do you know Miss Ogilvie?" he asked her.

"Vaguely. She seems quite nice."

"Nice? She's a dashed harpy, is what she is."

"You can't call her a harpy," Primrose objected. "A siren, perhaps, but harpies have claws and—"

"Miss Ogilvie is a harpy," Oliver said firmly. "Beneath the evening gloves, she has claws."

"Now *that* is hyperbole."

"It's metaphor," Oliver corrected her. "She's a *metaphorical* harpy. She wants to feast on my carcass." And *carcass* was a metaphor, too; it wasn't his body Miss Ogilvie wanted to devour, it was the title and fortune that he'd so unexpectedly inherited.

Primrose uttered a small sound that his ears barely caught.

"Did you just snort, Prim? That's not very ladylike."

"You're the most idiotic person I've ever met," she told him severely.

Oliver opened his eyes wide. "Ever? In your whole life?"

"Ever."

"High praise, Prim. Very high praise. You quite unman me."

This time Primrose *did* roll her eyes, even though they were in the middle of a ballroom.

Oliver grinned at her. He could tell she was struggling not to grin back.

At that moment, the dance ended. Oliver escorted Primrose from the dance floor. He could see Miss Ogilvie out of the corner of his eye: the glossy ringlets, the ripe bosom, the dainty evening gloves that hid her metaphorical claws.

"Marry me, Prim," he joked. "Save me from Miss Ogilvie."

"I'd sooner marry a crossing-sweeper. You're even more of a fribble than that cousin of yours."

"I'm wounded." Oliver placed his hand over his heart, tottered a few steps, and sank down on a gilded chair. "*Mortally* wounded. I may expire here, right in front of your eyes."

"You can't expire now," Primrose told him. "Miss Ogilvie is waiting to dance with you."

Oliver pulled a face. "Maybe I *should* become a crossing-sweeper."

"Addle-pate," Primrose said.

Oliver laughed and climbed to his feet. "Thank you for the dance, Prim."

Primrose demurely curtsied, as all his other partners tonight had done. "It was a pleasure, Your Grace."

"Don't, Prim," Oliver said, and this time his tone was serious.

Primrose's glance at him was swift and shrewd. She didn't ask what he meant; instead, she said, "Away with you, Daisy," and made a brisk shooing gesture. "Miss Ogilvie fancies herself as a duchess."

"Not *my* duchess," Oliver muttered. "Not if I have any say in the matter."

ORDER YOUR COPY of ***Primrose and the Dreadful Duke*** by Emily Larkin!

46527260R00166